Convent

Copyright © 2009 Gerelyn Hollingsworth
All rights reserved.

ISBN: 1-4392-4682-3
ISBN-13: 9781439246825

To order additional copies, please contact us.
BookSurge
www.booksurge.com
1-866-308-6235
orders@booksurge.com

Convent

A Novel

Gerelyn Hollingsworth

2009

To the Mothers and the Sisters

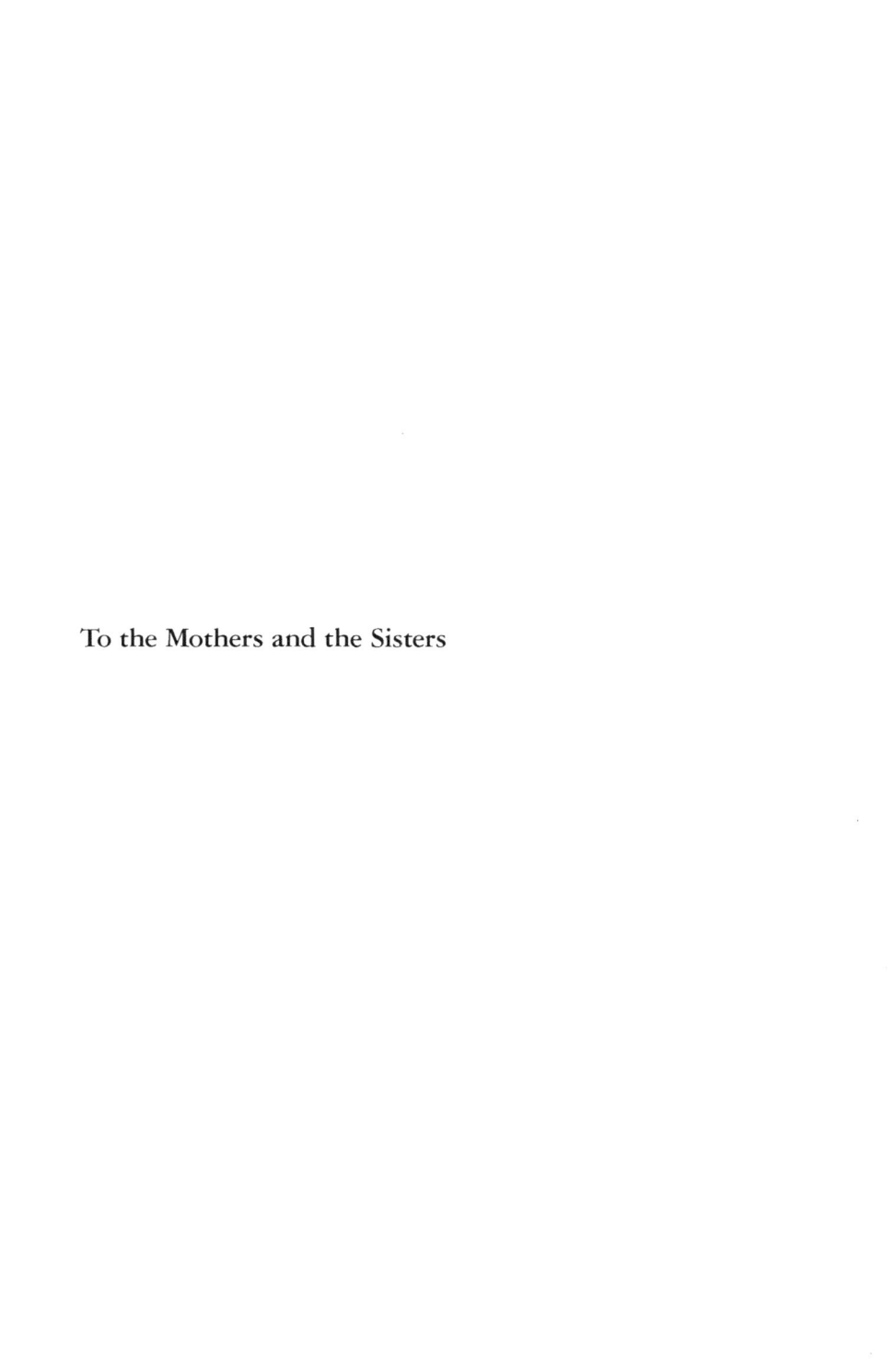

Chapter 1
Postulant

Entrance Day
Thursday, July 28th, 1960

On the day I entered the convent, Sister Marsha met me on the motherhouse steps. "There's something I want to tell you," she said, "while I still have the chance."

We wouldn't be talking for the next two-and-a-half years. Novices and postulants were not allowed to talk to the professed nuns except on Christmas Day and the Feast of the Assumption. I wasn't sure why. Who was likely to corrupt whom?

Sister Marsha already knew everything about me. For four years I lived in her dorm at Rosaline Academy. She was prefect of day boarders, and I was a day boarder – a girl who lived at school during the week but went home for weekends. There were usually about ten day boarders at Rosaline Academy, about eighty full boarders, and about ten day students.

Of the day boarders, four or five were like me, girls from Kansas City whose parents' schedules made boarding school convenient. I lived only a block from Rosaline, but my parents worked nights at their two movie theaters. When I was in grade school, they had only one theater, so my mother stayed home, but as I was about to start high school, they bought a second one. Day boarding at Rosaline Academy was the obvious solution.

Other day boarders, including my roommate Sandy Meade, were Air Force brats, daughters of officers stationed at Whiteman

2

Air Force Base. There was no Catholic high school in Knob Noster, so they boarded at Rosaline.

Day boarders lived with Sister Marsha on the third floor of the Farmhouse, the oldest building on campus. My roommate Sandy Meade and I talked to her about everything.

Sister Marsha was also our journalism teacher. Sandy Meade and I signed up for the school newspaper on our first day at Rosaline Academy. Sister Marsha invited all the freshmen to attend the first meeting of the *Tidings* staff, but Sandy and I were the only ones who went.

The editors, two seniors, assigned us the two beats they considered least desirable – the motherhouse beats. Starting the next day, Sandy and I called on Mother Paula and Mother Aurelia every morning after breakfast. Mother Aurelia was the superior, and Mother Paula was her assistant. In the summer before our sophomore year, they switched jobs; Mother Paula was elected superior, and Mother Aurelia became assistant. We went to their offices on the main floor of the motherhouse, and they gave us news: press releases about their activities, ideas for features about Rosaline history, information about speakers and performers who were coming to the academy, announcements of their forthcoming books, items about the buildings and the campus, old pictures from the archives. We got so many column inches from the material they gave us, that by the end of our sophomore year, my roommate and I had earned the editors' positions. As editors of the *Tidings* during our junior and senior years, we spent hundreds of hours in the journalism room with Sister Marsha. We talked to her about everything.

In addition to her duties at the academy – teaching and prefecting the day boarders, Sister Marsha was the convent printer. The Rosaline nuns had a small sideline to teaching – the publication of devotional booklets, prayer leaflets, and vocation brochures for the pamphlet racks in church vestibules. While Marsha worked on the Rosaline Press side of the room, setting type and printing on the tiny press, and Sandy Meade and I worked on the *Tidings* side, typing our stories, editing the other reporters' stories, laying out pages, drinking coffee, and reading the school newspapers that came to us from high schools all over the country in exchange for ours. We talked about everything.

When I graduated from the academy and went away to a college run by Benedictines, the order I expected to enter, Marsha's letters drew me back to the Rosalines instead. She arranged the meeting at which I asked Mother Paula to accept me as a postulant. After Mother Paula said I could enter the convent at the end of July, Marsha hired me to work as a counselor at Camp Rosaline until entrance day. She was the camp director.

At night, after the campers had gone to bed, while the other counselors swam in the lighted pool and the other camp nuns sat by the pool talking, Marsha and I made pizza or brownies for them, or we took inventory in the storeroom, or we walked around with flashlights checking gates and doors. We talked about everything.

Now she was about to administer her final words of advice. "The novitiate is not the community," she said. "I want you to remember that, no matter what happens."

It was her charitable way of warning me about Sister Wulfram, the novice mistress.

I thought I could make it through Sister Wulfram's novitiate. I intended to avoid attracting her attention.

I thought the way to survive the next two-and-a-half years would be to have a friend. If I had a friend, someone I could talk to freely, I thought I could make it through to Profession. I had observed my teachers, and I knew that the closest friendships between nuns were formed in the novitiate. There was something about being in the crucible together. Sister Marsha's best friend was Sister Francine, the choir mistress.

I already knew a few people in the novitiate. My old roommate Sandy Meade was Sister Alexandra now, a first-year novice — a canonical, as they were called. There were two other former academy girls in the canonical class, as well.

And there was a second-year novice, Sister Valentine, who I thought would be my friend when she got to know me.

And I already knew four of the eight other girls about to enter the convent with me. Two had gone to St. Albert's grade school with me, one a year ahead of me and one two years behind, and two had gone to Rosaline Academy with me, one a year behind me and one two years behind.

With a friend to talk to, I thought I could make it through Wulfram's novitiate.

My parents were coming up the steps. We had driven to the convent even though we lived so close. We had to deliver my trunk to the northeast door. My parents had done that and had parked the car. Sister Marsha greeted them, and we went inside.

Everyone was in the Alumnae Room. It was hot, and there was no air conditioning in the convent, but it was 1960, so the men and boys were in suits and ties, and the women and girls were in dresses and high heels. The French doors to the balcony were open, and some of the men had drifted outside for a breath of air.

There were a few priests in the crowd, including the pastor of our parish, St. Albert's. He was pleased to have three girls from the parish entering the convent. There were parents and brothers and sisters clustered around each prospective postulant.

A few people were sitting in the wicker chairs, but most were standing, talking loudly, and laughing excitedly. There were a few nuns present, but Sister Wulfram, the novice mistress, was not in the room.

The largest and noisiest cluster was the Fitzpatrick family, well-known in St. Albert's parish. When I was in grade school, there seemed to be a Fitzpatrick in every class. Judy, the only girl in the family, was two years behind me at St. Albert's. She waved at me, and the brother who had been in my class made a face at me and folded his hands in mock piety.

At exactly two o'clock, Sister Wulfram came into the room. The noise continued, but everyone was aware of the novice mistress's imposing presence. She was over six feet tall, big-boned, ramrod straight. Her posture was so erect that her black veil hung from the crown of her head to the back of her knees without a break. A perfect column. She moved as if she were on wheels.

She glided around the room from family to family, smiling slightly, nodding regally, shaking hands. Only the raucous Fitzpatricks made her laugh a little. She came to my little group last. She shook hands with my parents.

Sister Wulfram was about forty years old. Her face was long and Prussian. Her lips were thin. Her hooded eyes were emerald green and cold as ice.

She went to the door and made a slight gesture with her hand. We left our mothers and fathers and followed her.

She led us down the southwest hall and across the rotunda to the little elevator in the northeast hall. We crowded into the elevator, and Wulfram closed the brass grille and pushed the button. The elevator groaned and rattled as it rose. I had never been above the first floor of the motherhouse before. No one spoke.

6

I was standing behind the girl from Ireland. I had heard there was to be a girl from Ireland in my class, and this had to be her. She had red hair and freckles, and she was blushing so furiously that her face and neck were several shades of purple. No American could blush like that. It went well with her blue dress.

We got out of the elevator on the third floor. Sister Wulfram spoke to us in a low voice. "You will go into your rooms and change into your postulant clothes. Put on your Sunday blouse and skirt, a petticoat, shoes, and stockings. You need not wear tee-shirts this first day. When you are dressed, come back out here."

She showed us to our rooms. They were real rooms, thank God, not curtained-off areas of an open dormitory. Mine was first, next to the fire escape landing by the elevator. It was about nine by eleven, with a tiny closet, off-white walls, brown linoleum floor, brown-stained woodwork and doors, a transom, a radiator, a single light bulb in the center of the high ceiling, a window with a shade but no curtain. There was a white metal bed with a white cover. There was a chest of drawers with a small mirror above it. There was a crucifix on the wall. There was a tiny desk with one drawer. No desk lamp. A straight chair at the desk.

My trunk was in the room.

I went to the window. Because of the X-shape of the building, my view was not very good. My window overlooked the red tile roof of the chapel. I could see pigeons strutting on the roof.

I took off my high heels. I took off my brown-and-white-checked sailor dress and my half-slip. I took off my nylons.

I opened my trunk. My mother had made three black postulant blouses and skirts, three black petticoats, and four green gingham aprons. We had been given a list of items to bring and the numbers of the patterns to be used. The black petticoats had a deep hem so they could be let down and still worn after we received the habit. I put on a petticoat and the Sunday blouse and skirt. The Sunday set was made of a heavier cotton than the everyday ones. The blouse had long sleeves and no collar. The skirt was A-line, mid-calf length. I put on a pair of heavy black stockings and a pair of nun shoes. I went out into the hall.

When we were all assembled, Sister Wulfram led us out of the northeast wing, through the rotunda, and into the southeast wing. This short hall ended at a closed door. "That is the door to the Novitiate," Wulfram said. "The novices are in there, waiting to meet you."

She had a piece of paper in her hand. "I will line you up according to rank," she said. "In the convent, our place in rank is determined by the date on which we enter. When more than one postulant enters on the same day, the oldest goes first. Your rank determines where you will sit in chapel and in the refectory.

I was hoping I would get to sit by the girl from Ireland, or by the girl with the great suntan, or by Rita, the girl who had been a year ahead of me at St. Albert's grade school.

"You will be known as the Nine Choirs of Angels," Sister Wulfram said, as she arranged us.

I wondered what would happen if someone left. Would we be renamed the Eight Beatitudes? The vocation brochures said leaving the convent was no disgrace, but of course it was. If you left too soon, you looked foolish. I knew a girl who left the Sisters of St. Joseph after a week. If you left after too long, you looked troubled. My cousin married a woman who had been a Sister of Charity for ten years.

"Audrey Thorney is fifth in line," Wulfram said, showing me where to stand. I was the middle Choir. Which Choir was fifth? Thrones? Powers? What were the duties and attributes of those middle Choirs? The girl who had been a year behind me at the academy now turned out to be four days older than I was. She was ahead of me in line. Behind me was Susan with the suntan.

Wulfram demonstrated on the oldest postulant what we were to do when she opened the door to the Novitiate. We were to go to her first and then to each novice in turn. We were to clasp forearms and say, "I humbly beg your sisterly love and holy prayers."

Sister Wulfram opened the door and went in. The white-veiled novices were standing in a row from the door to the far wall. Wulfram took her place at the beginning of the row.

The Novitiate was a large room, maybe forty by fifty, with windows on three sides. On one side of the room, there were student desks and a teacher's desk. On the other side, there were library tables and chairs. There were no upholstered chairs in the room. The only comfortable-looking chair in the room was a Windsor rocker. There were several bookshelves against the walls, and there was an upright piano. There were no curtains on the windows. The floor was covered with the same brown linoleum found throughout the building.

The first four of my companions greeted Wulfram and moved along to the novices. When it was my turn, I said to Wulfram, "I humbly beg your sisterly love and holy prayers."

"They're yours, Sister," she said. It was like medical students being called Doctor from the first day.

I moved to the first novice, oldest in the class of five second-year novices who had entered the convent in February, 1958, the winter of my junior year at the academy. They were now just a month from Profession. I didn't know any of them. Two of them had been in a Latin class with me at the academy when they were postulants, but we had never spoken.

Girls who entered the convent before graduating from high school finished at the academy. There were usually two or three postulants attending academy classes and sometimes one or two second-year novices. First-year novices, canonicals, did not study secular subjects during the one year of novitiate required by Canon Law, so they were not seen in academy classrooms.

A postulant or second-year novice taking a class at the academy would never speak to the girls. She would answer the teacher's questions or take a turn reading aloud, but she was not allowed to speak to the students. If a student greeted her in the hall with "Praised be Jesus Christ," she would answer, "Now and forevermore," but that was all.

I moved along the row. Next to the group of five second-years came a group of ten second-year novices. There had been twelve in this group, originally, the largest class in Rosaline history. They had entered the convent the summer before my senior year at the academy.

My roommate and I spent a lot of time watching them when they were postulants. Sandy Meade had a pair of Air Force binoculars powerful enough to reveal the mountains on the moon. We used them to observe the novices and postulants. Our favorite in the class of twelve was Valentine O'Hara.

Miss Valentine was said to be the daughter of a Tulsa oil millionaire. Sandy Meade found it hard to believe. "Rich people don't hunch over like that," she said. "The bigger they are, the better they like it." Miss Valentine was six-three, and she stooped in an apparent effort to appear shorter.

Sandy Meade and I spied on the novices and postulants from our room in the northeast corner of the third floor of the

Farmhouse, the highest point on campus. We kept the same room all four years. We had unparalleled views of the Lilac Field, where the novices and postulants played softball on warm evenings after supper, and of the South Drive, where they walked with the novice mistress on Sundays after dinner. Miss Valentine walked alone, behind everyone else. She was gangly and awkward in her postulant outfit. The sleeves of her blouse were too short. Her cape was too short. Her bangs, sticking out from her too-short postulant veil, were growing out of a bad bleach job.

"Rich people don't have protruding teeth," Sandy said. "She looks like Bugs Bunny."

"She reminds me of Jo in Little Women," I said.

"Katharine Hepburn or June Allyson?"

"Neither. The way she was in the book."

In February of our senior year, Sandy and I watched Miss Valentine and her eleven companions receive the habit. Many of the full boarders and nearly all of the day boarders went home for Reception weekend so guests from out of town could use their rooms, but my roommate and I stayed at school to see the ceremony. Sister Marsha asked us to look after some friends of Miss Valentine's who were coming up from Tulsa for Reception. There were three of them. We picked them up at Union Station in my mother's car.

We took them to Winstead's for hamburgers. We walked around the Plaza. We tried on clothes in Chasnoff's and Harzfeld's. We stopped for popcorn at Topsy's. We had a bowl of chili at Margarita's. We stopped by my mother's movie theater to give her back her car. More popcorn. We walked up the hill to school. In the dorm, Sandy and I served the girls from Tulsa a midnight feast — sardines, tequila, banana bread, and Stover's chocolates. Through all of it, we pumped them about Valentine O'Hara.

She was the richest girl in their class, the girls said, and at their school, everyone was rich. She was the most popular girl in their class. She didn't date, but at their school, the girls said, you didn't have to be popular with boys to be popular. She smoked like a chimney and drank like a fish. She was the smartest girl in the class. She read Latin for pleasure. She had Winnie the Pooh in Latin. Winnie ille Pooh. When she told everyone she was entering the convent, no one could believe it. With one exception. Valentine's best friend, Anna Marie Bauer, said she would enter the convent with her.

Anna Marie was also the exception to the rule that everyone at their school was rich. She attended their school on a scholarship. She was one of the few in their class who didn't have a car. Valentine O'Hara's parents paid for Valentine and Anna Marie to go on a last fling before they entered the convent. They went to Hollywood and stayed at the Beverly Hills Hotel. Then they went to New York for another last fling and stayed at the Waldorf.

Valentine O'Hara was going to keep her own name in religion, the girls said. At Reception she would become Sister Mary Valentine. Lots of Rosaline nuns kept their baptismal names, so it would not be unusual, but just to make sure, Valentine's mother had given a huge donation to Mother Paula.

The girls from Tulsa got a little drunk and cried about Buddy Holly. My roommate and I continued to question them about Valentine.

"Rich people don't enter the Rosalines," Sandy Meade said. "They go to the Madames of the Sacred Heart."

Now, as a new postulant, I stood in front of Sister Valentine, a second-year novice. "I humbly beg your sisterly love and holy prayers," I said.

She was even taller up close. She loomed over me. Instead of looking at me, clasping my arms firmly, and responding to my greeting audibly, as Sister Wulfram had done, and as the first thirteen novices in the long row had done, Valentine kept her eyes cast down, barely extended her arms, and mumbled her response. She was very thin. Her habit was faded almost to gray. Her bony shoulders seemed about to jut through the worn cotton. I wondered if we would be friends. We would be in the novitiate together for only six months. Then Sister Valentine would make vows and get her black veil and leave the novitiate.

Once, when I was a senior at the academy and she was a postulant, I almost spoke to her. The academy was on retreat, and I was ditching a conference. I took a blanket and my portable radio and my cigarettes and went down to the Grotto to enjoy the autumn leaves. I spread my blanket by the moat and sat down on it. I lit a cigarette and turned on the radio.

News flash. Pope Pius XII was dead. The long vigil was over. They had tapped him on the forehead with a silver hammer and called out, "Eugenio! Eugenio!!" No answer. Dead. I tried to feel the way people said they felt when Roosevelt died. He was the only pope I ever knew.

Someone was coming. The iron gate clanked open. I put out my cigarette and turned off the radio. Who was coming? The academy girls were all in the chapel, listening to the retreat master's conference. The nuns wouldn't be down here at this time of day. It was a postulant. Miss Valentine. She had something in her hand. A small box. She went over to the little bridge. The giant goldfish recognized her and rushed to her. She opened the box. The fish climbed on each other's backs to get at the food. Hosts. She tossed Communion hosts at the gaping gold and white mouths.

She looked over at me. I was sitting under a maple tree. The sun blazed through the red leaves. I wanted to say, "The pope is dead. We are the only ones who know." The students weren't allowed to listen to the radio during retreat, and the nuns wouldn't be listening to the radio at all. But I said nothing. Miss Valentine might be scrupulous. She might think she was committing a sin if I spoke to her. She dropped the remaining stacks of hosts onto the frenzy of fish and left. She slammed the iron gate on her way out.

After a few minutes, the convent bell began to toll. They knew.

I went back up to the Farmhouse. The radios were on, and everyone was talking. My roommate said, "He ended retreat early so we could listen to the news."

"How was the sex talk?"

"He said if a boy takes you home from a date and then gets killed in a wreck on his way home, if he burns in hell for all eternity, it's your fault."

Naturally.

I moved from Sister Valentine to the youngest second-year novice. I greeted her and moved to the first canonical novice. There were seven canonicals. There had been eight in this group, originally. My old roommate Sandy Meade, now Sister Alexandra, was the youngest. When I got to her, instead of extending her arms and waiting for my request for her sisterly love and holy prayers, she grabbed me, hugged me, pounded me on the back, swung me around, and yelled, "Welcome, Audrey! Welcome! I knew you'd be back! I have prayed for this every day!" Everyone started laughing, even Wulfram.

Next to Sister Alexandra were two postulants who had entered the convent five months earlier. They were a month from receiving the habit. One was a tiny woman in her thirties, a late vocation. She was about four feet eight inches tall. I greeted them.

When all the greetings were finished, Wulfram told the nine of us new postulants to sit down in chairs that had been arranged in a semi-circle. Nine novices brought our postulant capes and veils to us and put them on us. Sister Alexandra put mine on me. After she snapped the collar of my cape behind my neck, she patted me on the back. After she tied my veil behind my hair, she patted me on the head.

I was happy to see her, too. It was wonderful to see her beautiful face again. I hadn't seen her since we graduated from the academy. I had begged her to go to college with me and enter the Benedictines with me, but she was determined to stay at Rosaline. Before boarding school, Sandy Meade had never lived in one place more than a few months. She entered the convent two months after graduation.

Sister Wulfram led the nine of us postulants out of the Novitiate and down the ramps to the first floor. We would not use the elevator again, she said. Only the professed nuns used the elevator. Novices and postulants used the ramps, the east ramps only. The X-shaped building had ramps on both sides of the rotunda. The novitiate used the east ramps and the community used the west ramps.

Wulfram took us to Mother Paula's office. Mother Paula welcomed us to the convent and gave us her blessing.

Wulfram took us into the chapel and showed us our places. We would sit in the front pews until school started and the academy girls came back. As we genuflected to go into the pews, I noticed that the oldest member of our group did not know how to genuflect. She went down awkwardly on the wrong knee and nearly tumbled over.

Wulfram took us to the Alumnae Room to show our parents how we looked in our postulant outfits. We went outside and walked around the campus for awhile with our parents. My dad noticed that my veil restricted the movement of my head. I thought it would become more comfortable in time.

By four, everyone was gone.

Wulfram took us back upstairs. She showed us the bathroom we would use. There were big mirrors, several windows, six sinks beneath the windows, four stalls with toilets, and four stalls with bathtubs. One toilet stall and one bathtub stall were for Wulfram's use. The other three were for us. There were large old-fashioned shower heads above the bathtubs, but there were no shower curtains.

Wulfram told us to go into our rooms and unpack our trunks. She spoke to us in a low voice, demonstrating the importance of silence in the halls. She told us we were never to talk in the bathroom, in the corridors, in the refectory, or on the ramps. Those were places of silence. And a sister never entered another sister's room. If we were ever assigned to share a room, which we would not be as postulants, that room was a place of silence. We were never to speak during a time of silence or in a place of silence, and in addition to not speaking, we were to move quietly, to close doors quietly, to do everything with attention to silence. We were to walk quietly and keep our hands under our capes, not swinging at our sides.

We went into our rooms and closed the doors quietly.

The clothes I had worn to the convent were gone. Where were they? Had they been placed in my parents' car? Had they been put away somewhere for me to wear home in case I left the convent? Maybe they had been placed in the academy costume room, labeled Midwestern College Girl, Summer, 1960.

I hung up the everyday postulant blouses and skirts in the closet. I put the four pairs of white pajamas, the four white bras, the six white pants, the black petticoats, the swimsuit, the six white tee-shirts, the four green gingham aprons, the twelve men's handkerchiefs, and the five pairs of black stockings in the lower drawers. I put the toiletries in the top drawer. I put the towels and washcloths and the second pair of nun shoes in the closet. There was a black bathrobe hanging in the closet already. We had been told not to bring bathrobes. Our summer and winter robes and slippers and our shoulderettes were purchased from a convent supply company in Chicago.

I put my bible and my missal and my two copies of *The Imitation of Christ* on the little desk. The English edition was Sister Marsha's gift to me. The German edition, *Das Buch von der Nachfolge Christi,* was a gift from the Benedictine who had been my German teacher at college. She felt it would help me keep up with my German. She had sewn a black cloth cover on it with long cross-stitches. Under this cover I had hidden my boyfriend's picture and the ticket stubs from our last date, July 18th. We watched Kansas City beat Baltimore five to one. We sat in Sec. 9, Box 17M, Seats 3 and 4. My boyfriend wrote on my ticket stub with his scoring pencil, "When this you see, say one for me." He asked me to put it in my prayer book and take it to the convent with me.

My other piece of contraband was an eyebrow pencil. This I had hidden in the binding of a book of music. We had been instructed to bring any musical instruments we played and our music. I had left my piano at home, but there were many pianos at Rosaline, including the upright I had noticed in the Novitiate.

I had taken piano lessons since first grade. I hoped I would now be taught to play the pipe organ. I left the music in my trunk.

I left my sewing box in my trunk. My mother and I bought the box and its contents in the notions department at Emery Byrd's.

I put my pearl rosary under the pillow on the bed. My aunt gave it to me when I graduated from Rosaline Academy. It was from Jaccard's.

I left my place setting of silver and my napkin ring in the trunk. These were from my mother's silverware.

At five, the bell rang. Wulfram had instructed us to meet her in the rotunda at that time. We stood by the railing. We watched the novices go down the ramp. Over the railing, we could see the two floors below. Black-veiled professed nuns and white-veiled novices were going to the chapel for Vespers.

"You will not be attending Vespers or meditation this first evening," Wulfram said to us. "Instead, I will take you down to the refectory and show you what we do at supper."

She led us down the ramps to the ground floor. There, beneath the chapel, was the refectory. It was the same size as the chapel. There were windows along the east and west walls. A large crucifix hung on the north wall. At that end of the room was the head table with five places for Mother Paula and the council. There were long tables placed at right angles to the superior's table, and the area between those tables was open. There were additional tables at two sides of the room. These were temporary, Wulfram explained, used only at this time of year when nearly all the nuns were home at the motherhouse, finished with summer school, waiting for retreat.

At each place, there was a white tin plate turned upside down over a napkin in which the silverware was rolled. There was also a glass, a cup and saucer, and two small bowls, one for cereal, one for fruit. At each place, there was a booklet containing the prayers sung before and after meals. Wulfram showed us where we would be sitting. Our places were at the table farthest from the head table.

We would use stainless flatware from the academy students' dining room until after retreat, Wulfram said, instead of the silver place settings we had brought from home. She showed us how to unroll the white napkin. One end of it went on the table and the other end on the lap. The white tin plate went on top of the napkin. We would not get a clean napkin every day, only every week. After each meal, the napkin would be rolled up with the silver in it and placed in the napkin ring. Wulfram showed us how that was done.

I sat between Miss Eileen, the girl from Ireland, and Miss Rita, the girl who had been a year ahead of me at St. Albert's grade school. The first, third, fifth, seventh, and ninth postulants sat on the east side of the table. The second, fourth, sixth, and eighth postulants faced us from the west side. For these first few nights, the nine of us would be at one table, Wulfram said. She would sit at the head of our table to show us how to pass the food, and what to do during grace, and how to wash our dishes at the table at the end of the meal.

Meals were taken in silence, ordinarily, Wulfram said, but these two weeks between summer school and retreat were a time of relaxation for the nuns, so Mother Paula usually permitted recreation at table. That meant we would be allowed to talk.

At five-thirty some of the novices came into the refectory. They would be serving the meal, Wulfram said. Sister Valentine was one of them. The servers went to a table near the door to the kitchen and stood behind the chairs. Sister Columba, the convent portress, one of the oldest nuns in the community, came into the refectory and went to the same table. Those who were on duty during a meal, the servers and the portress and the table reader, ate a half-hour before the community – half-table, it was called. Since there would be recreation at supper, no table reader would be eating at half-table.

Wulfram took us out of the refectory and into the ground floor rotunda. She showed us which areas on this floor were off-limits to us: the southwest corridor, which led to the academy girls' dining room, and the northeast corridor, which led to Nazareth, a guest suite. The kitchen, in the northwest corridor, where food for both academy and convent was prepared, was not off limits, but we were not to go in there unless we had a reason to be there. We could go into the kitchen at mid-morning or mid-afternoon to get a snack from the meat block, a place where the kitchen sisters put out bread and jam. The only hall we could use on the ground floor was the northeast one. Even there, we were not to go into any room other than the linen room. Wulfram showed us this room and told us we would sort laundry here on laundry days. She then showed us the trunk room, which was across the rotunda from the refectory. The trunks lined up on the floor belonged to the professed nuns, Wulfram said. Novices and postulants kept their trunks in their rooms. There were meat lockers at the far end of the trunk room. In an open space between the lockers and the rows of trunks, there was a low round table where we would cut grapefruit, Wulfram said.

At six, we could hear the Angelus bell ringing in the dome on top of the motherhouse. Wulfram took us back into the refectory. We stood behind our chairs. She led us in the Angelus. After a few minutes, the other two postulants, those who were five months ahead of us, came into the refectory, leading the procession from the chapel. The novices and the professed nuns followed them. Mother Paula came in last. Each sister stood behind her chair, facing the crucifix, with her grace book in hand. I had never seen so many nuns in one room before. There were about a hundred fifty professed nuns. They were beautiful in their black habits and black veils.

They sang the long grace, the two sides of the room alternating verses, and then they sat down, moving their chairs quietly. A novice, one of the group closest to profession, stepped up onto the reader's stand and sat down. Mother Paula tapped her bell, and the novice began to read aloud. The nuns at the tables turned over their tin plates and unrolled their napkins. The door to the kitchen opened, and the servers wheeled a large cart into the refectory.

Valentine and the other servers had pinned the big outer sleeves of their habits tightly around their arms, and they were wearing starched white aprons. They took the platters and bowls from the cart and served them to the nuns at the head of each table, including ours. Wulfram took a platter with slices of baloney on it. She took a slice and passed the platter to the postulant at her left.

In addition to baloney, there was vegetable soup, sliced tomato and cucumber, hard-boiled eggs, bread and butter, crackers, and canned peaches. I felt embarrassed by the food. I wanted to explain to Miss Eileen from Ireland that this was not the best food she would get at Rosaline. This was supper. Dinner at Rosaline was at noon. There would be meat and potatoes and vegetables and gravy and cake. I couldn't say anything. The novice on the reader's stand was reading. The nuns were eating. It was very quiet.

After a few minutes, Mother Paula tapped her bell. The reader stopped reading and said, "Let us bless the Lord." All the nuns said, "Thanks be to God." Then they burst into conversation.

Wulfram nodded to us. "You may talk," she said.

I could see my teachers from the academy sitting at various tables, talking and laughing with other nuns. I wished I could sit with them instead of with Wulfram. She had not smiled at us. There had not been a touch of warmth in her voice. There had been no friendly word.

Miss Rita, at my right, turned to me and grinned. Miss Eileen, at my left, was blushing and staring at the slice of baloney on her tin plate.

The servers had emptied the cart of its platters and bowls and removed it from the refectory. Now they were walking around with pots of coffee, black or white, pots of hot tea, pitchers of iced tea, pitchers of milk, and pitchers of buttermilk. Wulfram told us how to tell which was which by the shapes of the pots and the pitchers. Sister Valentine came to our table with a pot of tea. She poured tea for Sister Wulfram and then stood before Eileen. "Spot of tay, Miss Eileen?" she asked.

"Please, Sister," Miss Eileen said. She turned her cup over. "Thank you, Sister." It sounded like, Tank you.

"Sure, and me fayther goes to the auld sod every year," Valentine said, pouring Eileen's tea.

"Does he, Sister?" Eileen asked. She was blushing crimson and purple.

"Sure, and begorrah."

At the end of the meal, little pans and rubber spatulas were passed down the table. Each person scraped whatever was left on her dishes into the pan. Then, dishpans with steaming soapy water and steaming rinse water were passed. Each sister washed her own dishes with a little mop in the dishpan, while the sister to her right rinsed her dishes and dried them with a dish towel. When everyone was finished, Mother Paula tapped her bell again, and everyone stood and sang the grace after meals.

Wulfram took us outside to the Lilac Field. Evening recreation was from seven till eight. I had hoped to use this first recreation period to get acquainted with Sister Valentine and to catch up with Sister Alexandra, but we played softball. There was no chance to talk.

At eight, the bell rang for night prayer. We went into the chapel. There was a Rosaline Prayer Manual at each of our places and a Little Office of the Blessed Virgin Mary. I sat between Miss Eileen and Miss Rita, just as I had at table. When night prayers were over, Wulfram signaled to us to follow her. We went up the ramps. It was now a time of even deeper silence than during the day. Wulfram whispered to us that we could take our baths and go to bed. We were not to get up when we heard the 5:30 rising bell, she said, but were to wait for her to wake us at 6:00.

I went into my room. I stood by the window. I could hear the traffic on 47th Street.

I knew I would be in this place for a time, but I knew I would not die here.

❖ ❖ ❖

The Next Day
Friday, July 29th, 1960

Wulfram woke us at six. We were not allowed to take baths in the morning or showers at any time. We were to wash and dress and be in the rotunda at 6:30.

Before taking us down to the chapel, Wulfram told us morning prayer and morning Office were over, so we would be walking into the chapel in the middle of meditation. We were to go silently up the side aisles to our places. Mass would begin at seven.

Postulants were last to go to Communion but were first to go downstairs to the refectory after Mass. Wulfram explained to the two youngest postulants how to lead the procession through the side chapel, through the sacristy, down the back steps, and into the refectory.

The singing at Mass was beautiful. I was wondering if Miss Eileen was enjoying the music. It was a Low Mass, so we sang four hymns in English. Sister Francine, the choir mistress, directed the singing from the steps in front of the Communion rail. It was thrilling to hear her soprano again. "My soul is thirsting for the Lord. When shall I see Him face to face?"

After Mass, we went down to breakfast. There was no recreation at this meal. Sister Valentine was the table reader. She read throughout the meal. First, a passage from the Rule of St. Augustine. Next, a passage from the Constitutions of the Congregation of St. Rosalia. Then, the day's entry from the Roman Martyrology. Next, the day's selection from Pius Parsch. It was all very interesting. I wondered how long it would be before I was appointed table reader.

For breakfast, there was hot or cold cereal, toast, soft-boiled eggs, oranges, milk, coffee or tea.

When everyone was finished, Mother Paula tapped her bell to signal the end of the reading. Valentine said, "Let us bless the Lord." Everyone said, "Thanks be to God." Everyone stood to sing the grace after meals.

Valentine knelt and kissed the floor by the reader's stand. That was to make amends for any mistakes she may have made, Wulfram explained to us after everyone else had gone. There was no procession out of the refectory at the end of meals. The professed nuns and the novices left by various doors to go to their morning duties.

For the novitiate, it was the time for cleaning.

Two novices who had gone into a little service room off the refectory came out with gingham aprons on. They had taken off their guimpes and their undersleeves. They had pinned their big sleeves up to their shoulders. One began removing the dishpans and the scrap pans from the tables. The other pulled all the chairs back from the tables to prepare to dust mop the floor.

Wulfram led my eight companions and me out of the refectory and up the ramp to the first floor. There, various novices were dusting, dust mopping, vacuuming. All wore gingham aprons over their habits, but they had not removed their guimpes or sleeves. This was in case a secular passed, Wulfram explained. I understood what she meant. This was the time of day Sandy Meade and I used to call on the Mothers for news for the *Tidings*. We always gawked at the novices at work dusting and vacuuming. If we passed a novice we knew, a former academy girl, we would snicker.

Sister Wulfram said postulants were never to go down the southwest corridor where the parlors and the Alumnae Room were. We were never to go down the northwest corridor where the priests' serving room and the priests' dining room were. We were never to go down the southeast corridor where the business office and Mother Paula's office were. We were never to go down the northeast corridor where the bishop's department and Mother Aurelia's office were. The bishop's department was a two-room suite used by the bishop when he visited and by retreat masters when they came to preach retreats.

Unless we had a cleaning duty, the only place we had permission to be on the first floor was in the chapel.

Wulfram led us up the ramp to the second floor. We were not allowed to be anywhere on this floor, and no one in the novitiate had cleaning duties here. This was where the professed nuns' rooms were.

Wulfram led us up the ramp to the third floor. As we emerged from the ramp into the rotunda, we saw Sister Alexandra by the railing. My old roommate had her big sleeves pinned up to her shoulders. She had taken her guimpe and her undersleeves off. She had a gingham apron on. She was dust mopping the floor around the railing. She turned and smiled her beautiful smile at us.

Wulfram stopped and glared at her. "Sister Alexandra," she said in a loud angry voice, "is this the example you intend to set for these new sisters? Are you going to stand there leaning on that mop all day?"

Sister Alexandra lowered her eyes. "Thank you, Sister," she said. "May God reward you."

I sensed that Wulfram's brutal correction of my friend was for my benefit. I had attracted the novice mistress's attention already. She was demonstrating her power to me and getting back at Alexandra for greeting me with such exuberance the day before.

Alexandra had not been leaning on her mop. She had been dusting the floor with diligence and grace, the way she did everything. My old friend's attention to detail had caused us to win a national journalism award for the *Tidings* our senior year. Wulfram's correction was unwarranted and untruthful.

Wulfram told us we were not to go down either of the west corridors. The novices' rooms were in the southwest corridor, and the rooms in the northwest corridor were used by professed nuns who came to the motherhouse for a short time. At the present time all those rooms were occupied, because so many nuns were home for retreat. Those nuns for whom there were no empty rooms in the motherhouse were staying in the academy dorms, empty of students for the summer.

Wulfram showed us the closet in our hall where the mops and rags were kept. She told us to go to our rooms and make our beds. We were to dust our rooms and dust mop the floors. We were to meet in the postulant room at nine o'clock. Bring notebooks and pens.

There were three rooms on the south side of the rotunda, each about twelve by twelve. The middle one was Wulfram's office. The east one was the postulant room. The west one had no name, but had two library tables and several chairs in it like the postulant room. At nine o'clock, my companions and I were sitting in the postulant room in silence.

Wulfram came in. We stood. She told us how to greet her when she entered a room. We were to say, "Praised by Jesus Christ." She would respond, "Now and forevermore." She led us in a prayer and told us to sit down. She sat down at her desk. She handed each of us a booklet. "Silence" was its title. By a Rosaline Sister. No name given. Published by the Rosaline Press, Kansas City, Missouri, 1948. Imprimatur and nihil obstat. I wondered if the author's name was unmentioned in case she left the convent.

Wulfram said the virtue of silence was to be the subject of our first particular examen. She explained that the particular examen was like the more comprehensive examination of conscience, but it was done at noon instead of at night, and it focused on one virtue rather than on all our faults. We were to read this booklet and use the lists of questions in it to help us examine our consciences and count our offenses against the virtue of silence.

Wulfram left us to study the booklet. She went to the Novitiate. It was time for the Hour, the class she held with the novices every morning beginning at nine.

We sat in silence, reading about silence for an hour.

At ten, Wulfram returned to the hot little room. She told us we would be taking a course in logic. Our teacher would be Sister Thomas, one of several nuns qualified by a local Catholic women's college to teach extension courses to the Rosaline novices and postulants. Wulfram said we would start our regular classes in September, but until then, we would be spending our afternoons with Sister Thomas in her academy classroom studying logic.

Wulfram also assigned us our cleaning duties. These would begin the following morning. She told us the proper way to receive an assignment or a correction from a superior: "Thank you, Sister, may God reward you." I was assigned to help a canonical novice clean the Novitiate.

We would begin rising at five thirty the following morning. We would attend morning prayer, morning Office, meditation, and Mass. We were to follow along in the chanting of the Little Office of the Blessed Virgin Mary as well as we could. We would not be instructed in the recitation of the Little Office, because the community was considering changing to a different Office, one in English. We would be instructed in the chanting of that one when the time came.

Wulfram told us that we would be taking music from Sister Francine, the choir mistress, every morning at 10:30. We would attend that class starting immediately.

We went into the Novitiate. The novices were sitting in the classroom chairs. They rose when Wulfram entered the room. "Praised be Jesus Christ," they said. "Now and forevermore," she responded. She told us where to sit. She left the room.

After a few minutes, Sister Francine arrived. She strode into the room with a big smile on her face. We stood to greet her.

"Stay standing, Sisters," she said. "We'll start with the Reception book."

The five second-year novices who would be professing vows in August and the two postulants who would be receiving the habit would be singing the "Suscipe" in the sanctuary. The rest of us, with the community, would be singing the ordinary and proper parts of the Mass and the hymns for Profession and Reception. Sister Francine intoned the Te Deum.

I was glad that Miss Eileen was seeing that not all Rosalines were as cold as Wulfram. Sister Francine's beautiful voice, her smile, her dimples, her humorous manner, and her expertise with Gregorian chant made her class a pleasant relief from the tension that Wulfram induced.

Sister Francine was pleased with my companions and me and told us so. The three of us who had attended Rosaline Academy were familiar with Francine's teaching methods and with Gregorian chant. The three of us who had attended St. Albert's grade school had learned Gregorian chant from our Benedictine teachers. The three of our companions who went to Albertine High School had learned music from the Rosalines who taught there. Our oldest companion, new to Rosaline and new to Kansas City, had majored in music at her college in California. Our second-oldest companion, new to Rosaline and new to Kansas City and new to Gregorian chant, had a beautiful singing voice and caught on immediately. Miss Eileen was too shy to sing, but Sister Francine smiled at her and encouraged her to try.

At 11:30, the servers left to go to half-table. Francine continued working with the rest of us until the bell rang for dinner.

We went to the chapel. Mother Paula led the Angelus. We said some prayers from the Rosaline Manual. We then made our particular examen in silence. How many times had I broken silence? Not once, so far.

At the end of the brief period of prayer we went down the back steps to the refectory for our first dinner in the convent.

The table reader read for a minute or two, and then Mother Paula tapped her bell for recreation. We could talk. The table reader kissed the floor and then went to her place at table. Again I looked at the professed nuns at their tables and wished I could join their animated conversations.

I talked to Miss Eileen and Miss Rita and Miss Mary Kay. Eileen told us about the day, two weeks earlier, when she stepped off the plane from Ireland. She had started to push open the door to Idlewild Airport when it opened automatically. She was astonished. A miracle. Welcome to America, the doors seemed to be saying to her as they swung open on their own.

She told us about seeing a "black" for the first time. Rita and Mary Kay and I laughed at the word. She might as well have said "blackamoor." We teased her about it, and she laughed with us.

After dinner, the nine of us postulants went out the northeast door. We were on our way to logic. Those of us who were former academy girls knew the longest route to the building where Sister Thomas's classroom was.

Wulfram had not said we could not talk outside, so we talked as we walked slowly across the campus. We started getting acquainted.

The oldest of us, Miss Carol, was twenty-two, a college graduate, a music major. She had brought her flute to the convent. She did not know anyone at Rosaline. A priest in California had told her about the Rosalines of Kansas City and had arranged for her to enter.

The second postulant, Miss Teresa, was twenty-one. She had completed two years of college, majoring in art. She had attended public schools in her small town in Oklahoma. There were no Catholic schools in the town, but Rosaline nuns came to teach religion on Saturdays and for two weeks every summer, and she loved them.

Miss Rita, from St. Albert's parish and Albertine High School, was third. She was nineteen. She had completed one year of college at Mizzou. We had not been friends in grade school, but we were on the same wavelength.

Miss Mary Helen from Rosaline Academy was next. She was four days older than I was, even though she had been a year behind me in school. She was from a small town in Kansas. She had just graduated from the academy in May.

I was next. Audrey Frances Catherine Thorney of 48th and Holly, in St. Albert's parish, in Westport, in Kansas City, in Jackson County, in Missouri, in the United States, in North America, in the Western Hemisphere, on the planet Earth. All my life I had wanted to be a nun, and now I was Miss Audrey, a postulant, one of nine asking to be admitted to the Rosaline Order. I was six months from being clothed in the habit of religion, thirty months from professing first vows. I was eighteen years old.

The sixth postulant was Miss Susan. She was tan from two months of lifeguarding at a country club, and she was friendly and bubbly and cute. She had just graduated from Albertine High School, where she had been head cheerleader. She was not from St. Albert's parish. Albertine was a diocesan high school, and kids from other parishes could attend. Susan was eighteen.

Next was Eileen Moore of Loughmoe, County Tipperary, Ireland. She had just graduated from a girls' boarding school in Thurles. She was seventeen. Her uncle was a priest who was a friend of Mother Paula's. He brought Eileen to America to enter the convent.

Judy Fitzpatrick was next. She was sixteen. She had not yet graduated from high school. She had gone to Albertine High School for three years. Her brothers had been football stars at Albertine, and one was now a novice in the Albertine Order. She was loud and funny, and now, as we walked across the campus, she dared to make a comment about how Wulfram wasn't very friendly.

The youngest postulant was Miss Mary Kay. She had just finished her sophomore year at Rosaline Academy. She was fifteen.

We walked into Sister Thomas's classroom.

Sister Thomas was eighty. She had been one of the first postulants to enter the Rosalines of Kansas City. She had taught at the academy for sixty years. She gave us our logic textbooks. They were relics. The gray binding, the antique typeface, the heavy paper, the deep printing, the names used in the examples – all were from an earlier age. They went well with the old teacher and the old classroom. After a few minutes, Sister Thomas told us to read the first chapter to ourselves. She leaned back in her swivel chair and fell asleep. It was very hot.

We read the chapter and watched the clock. At two-thirty, Sister Thomas woke up. She said we needed a little break. We would walk over to the kitchen and get a bite to eat from the meat block. She would go with us. We went the short way, around the Sacred Heart shrine, across the Lilac Field, and into the motherhouse by the students' door. Sister Thomas took us down the hall and into the kitchen. We slathered strawberry preserves on thick slices of convent bread. One of the kitchen sisters got a pitcher of milk out of the refrigerator for us.

We went back to Sr. Thomas's classroom. She told us to work on the exercises at the end of the chapter. She leaned back in her chair and nodded off. All men are mortal. Clarence is a man. Therefore Clarence is mortal.

❖ ❖ ❖

The First Saturday
July 30th, 1960

On Saturdays, at breakfast, in addition to readings from the Rule and the Constitutions, there was a reading from the Book of Regulations, written by Mother Aurelia, who held the office of superior from 1944 until 1956. The regulations were very detailed. Sister Valentine read a passage about the way a Rosaline sister should raise and lower Venetian blinds.

On Saturdays, instead of cleaning from 8:00 until 9:00 in the morning, we cleaned from 8:00 until 12:00. There were no classes on Saturday. After breakfast, Wulfram told us to take off our capes and put on our aprons. We reported to our first cleaning duties.

The canonical novice in charge of cleaning the Novitiate was so scrupulous about keeping silence, that instead of telling me what to do, she pantomimed it. I was to crawl around the perimeter of the room with a rag she gave me, dusting the floor under the bookshelves. The rag was oiled, but I was not given gloves to wear.

I crawled. The lowest shelves were only a couple of inches from the floor, so it was hard to reach into the farthest corners.

The novice, Sister John Vianney, had the hem of her habit turned up and pinned behind her waist. That way, only her petticoat got dirty when she crawled. She had her sneakers on and an apron, and she had taken off her guimpe and undersleeves. After dusting the floor for a while with a big flannel rag under a big mop, she pantomimed to me that she was going downstairs and outside to sweep the rag. She had turned it over and inside out until every surface was dirty.

While she was gone, I sat on the floor and looked at some of the books. All the books on the shelves I had dusted beneath so far were spiritual. There were cards in the backs with the names of the novices and postulants who had checked them out. I recognized the names of some novices and postulants who had left the convent. They were never to be mentioned. We had learned that already. At supper the night before, Miss Rita had made the mistake of asking Sister Wulfram about a novice who had left. Wulfram's cold hard stare made it clear that the subject was off limits.

I stood up and looked out the window. I could see Sister John Vianney in the driveway below, sweeping the rags.

I sat on the floor by the only bookshelf on the northeast wall. Here, shelved apart from the heavy theology and spirituality on the other side of the room, was an odd assortment of books: a four-volume encyclopedia of wapiti, a few popular Catholic novels like *Don Camillo* and *The Cardinal*, and a few books about St.

Therese of Lisieux. Why was my favorite saint isolated in this farthest corner of the room? I looked in the backs of a few of the books. They had cards, but they had never been checked out.

When Sister John Vianney reappeared, she was sweating from her efforts, and her face was red. Old sweat had dried on the yoke of her habit, leaving traces of white salt. She went into another of her elaborate pantomimes to demonstrate how I was to pick up the last few crumbs of dirt from the floor, those that resisted being brushed into the dustpan. She licked her finger to pick them up, indicating I was to do the same. I was not humble enough for that.

After dinner, Wulfram took the nine of us postulants into the trunk room. We were to learn to cut grapefruit. Wulfram said when we were finished, we were to go upstairs to the postulant room. We were to have a meeting and decide on a symbol, a virtue, and a motto for our group. The virtue was to be one we would strive for together, one that would be a mark of our group. She suggested charity. She said she would be busy all afternoon, practicing for Profession and Reception with the five novices about to make vows and the two postulants about to receive the habit. She left the trunk room.

We sat around the low table which was covered with newspaper. A second-year novice, the oldest in Valentine's group and maybe in the world, showed us how to cut grapefruit.

This novice, Sister Digna, was a widow from Germany, a woman in her late sixties. She was bent and toilworn and bossy. She showed us how to cut around each segment of the grapefruit halves. She was not happy with the way I was doing it. She grabbed the knife away from me and did my first grapefruit over again. Then she watched me like a hawk to make sure I did it her way. My companions and I started talking, but Sister Digna gave us a fierce correction and then led us in the rosary. I felt sorry for her. She was destined to spend the remainder of her life in the kitchen, like the lay sisters of old.

I thought of an evening nearly two years earlier, when I was a senior at the academy. My roommate Sandy Meade and I were ditching evening study hall to watch the novices and postulants play softball on the Lilac Field. It was the first week of school, still light enough for the novitiate to take their recreation outside.

Miss Valentine was the only one who was any good, but the others jumped up and down a lot and shouted. My roommate and I assumed their enthusiasm was for the novice mistress's benefit.

Wulfram didn't play but watched the game from a glider, the kind with two seats facing across a little wooden platform. The old postulant, the widow from Germany, was supposed to be playing deep left field, but no novice was able to hit Valentine's pitches, so no ball ever went out there. At the bottom of the third inning, instead of hustling out to her position, she shuffled over to the glider, apparently intending to join Sister Wulfram. She got close enough to the glider to lift her foot to put it on the platform. At that point, Wulfram, who had been ignoring her approach, turned and gave her a look that sent her bobbing backwards, tugging at her grizzled forelock.

When the inning was over, Valentine, who had not seen what had happened, came off the mound and loped over to the glider. She plopped herself down in the seat facing Wulfram and started rocking the glider back and forth with her big feet as hard as she could. Instead of getting mad at her, Wulfram threw her head back and laughed out loud.

"Wulfram plays favorites," Sandy said.

When the grapefruit halves were all cut, my companions and I went upstairs. We went into the postulant room and had our meeting. Wulfram had made it clear that she wanted us to choose charity as our virtue, but we chose simplicity instead.

It may have been at my suggestion. I had noticed that a few people in the novitiate were slow to the point of being simple, to use my parents' term. I didn't say this out loud or name names, but my companions had noticed the obvious, too. One of the simple ones was in our group – Miss Mary Helen.

She became quite enthusiastic about simplicity as our group's special virtue. She was at ease with her simplicity and seemed eager to ignore Wulfram's suggestion. So were the others. So was I. Simplicity seemed to be a virtue worth striving for, and how could Wulfram criticize us for wanting to be simple? No one said it out loud, but we all knew what we were doing.

For our motto, we chose, "Do whatever he tells you," the words of Mary to the wine steward at the marriage feast at Cana. Our two artistic companions, Mary Kay and Teresa, began sketching tall wine jars. When they had one we liked, that became our symbol.

Wulfram came upstairs at 4:30. She saw the symbol and heard the motto and the virtue. She had no word of approval or encouragement for us.

❖ ❖ ❖

The First Sunday
July 31st, 1960

The rising bell rang an hour later on Sundays. We got up at 6:30. Morning prayer and morning Office were at 7:00. Meditation was at 7:30. Mass was at 8:00, a High Mass with a sermon by the chaplain. Breakfast was at 9:00, with Sunday bread, bacon, and the grapefruit we had prepared the day before. Cleaning was at 9:30. At ten, all the novices and all the postulants attended the Sunday Hour in the Novitiate.

We stood by the classroom chairs arranged in semi-circular rows facing Wulfram's desk. Wulfram handed out mimeographed sheets. On the sheet was a poem: "Just For Today," by Samuel Wilberforce.

Wulfram struck a few keys on the piano to give the pitch. The twenty-two novices and the two older postulants began to sing in four-part harmony. It was a horrible song. We had only the words, not the music. There was no accompaniment.

I was on the right side of the semi-circle. Valentine was on the left. Our eyes met. We shared the recognition that the song was hideous.

"You may be seated, Sisters," Wulfram said at the end of the song. She had two books with her. She placed one sideways on the desk in front of her. She opened the other and propped it on the first. She read a paragraph from the open book and then began to expound on it. Her discourse was long and rambling and full of senseless analogies. She said, "The word 'postulant' comes from the Latin word for 'post'. As a postulant, your job is to stand as straight and silent as a fence post. Your superiors will string the fence around you."

I looked at Sister Valentine. We knew Wulfram was pretending to know Latin.

❖ ❖ ❖

August, 1960

On Monday, August 1st, Wulfram announced that my companions and I would be taking two classes in addition to music and logic – vocabulary and graphoanalysis. Like our logic class with Sister Thomas, these classes were to be short-term.

Sister Mary Charles, Sister Thomas's sister, would be teaching us vocabulary each morning from 9:00 until 10:00. Postulant class would be from 10:00 until 10:30, music from 10:30 until noon, dinner at noon, logic from 1:00 until 4:00, graphoanalysis from 4:00 until 5:00, Office from 5:00 until 5:30, meditation from 5:30 until 6:00, supper at 6:00, recreation from 7:00 until 8:00, night prayer at 8:00. From 8:30 until 10:00, we were to take our baths, get into our pajamas and robes, and then study and do our spiritual reading in the Novitiate. Lights out at 10:00 for postulants. Novices could study until 10:30.

Wulfram told us we were never to take a book from a shelf without her permission. She would assign us the books that would be our spiritual reading for a half-hour each night. We were to continue using our bibles for morning and afternoon meditation. She would assign us meditation books after retreat. The next nine days would be busy for her, preparing the five novices for Profession and the two other postulants for Reception.

Sister Mary Charles came to the postulant room each morning for vocabulary. She was even older than Sister Thomas. They had entered the convent together in 1896. They were boarders at the academy from the time they were minims – pre-schoolers. I had seen pictures of them in their minim uniforms and big hair bows. By the time they were in high school, they knew they wanted to be nuns. One morning after Mass, instead of following the other girls out of the chapel, they followed the nuns to the refectory. Mother Juliet asked them what they were doing. "We've come to stay," they said.

Sister Mary Charles gave my companions and me mimeographed sheets with lists of words on them. She defined the words for us, one by one, and used them in sentences. Abattoir. Abeyance.

After dinner, my companions and I walked across the campus to the academy for logic. We took our time. We talked about our families and our schools. We looked forward to receiving the habit and talked about the names we would get. We looked forward to the Feast of the Assumption when the professed nuns would come upstairs to talk to us. We talked about our favorite nuns from high school, the teachers whose friendship and example had drawn us to the convent. We looked forward to the upcoming Reception and Profession ceremony, scheduled for the Saturday after the Feast of the Assumption. The five would make vows and exchange their white veils for black veils. They would leave the novitiate and go out to teach or go off to college.

We didn't talk about Sister Wulfram. We were learning to fear her.

After our three hours of logic, we attended Mother Aurelia's graphoanalysis class in the Alumnae Room: "Eight Easy Steps."

Mother Aurelia was a handwriting expert who gave lectures on graphoanalysis and analyzed handwriting for lawyers and for private clients. Now she was teaching the basics of her art to the community and the novitiate. All the second-year novices and all the postulants attended. All the temporary professed and many older sisters attended. Wulfram did not attend.

At the first class, Mother Aurelia asked us to write a few paragraphs, so she could analyze our handwriting. She collected the samples to look at later. She taught us the first lesson: "My t's tell tall tales."

Retreat began on August 10th. The retreat lasted five days. Absolute silence. Four conferences a day by the retreat master, an Albertine priest. There was Benediction every evening. The entire community was in residence.

During the five days, there were professed nuns and novices and postulants all over the campus. Some walked slowly down the meandering South Drive with rosary beads in hand. Some sat on the benches reading. Some meditated or dozed in the bentwood chairs under the Pergola. Some knelt before the statues in the Grotto and the various shrines. Some made the Stations of the Cross in the Old Graveyard.

Wulfram told us we were allowed to rest on our beds between dinner and the afternoon conference, and that's what I did. I would take off my postulant outfit and put on my robe over my tee-shirt and petticoat. I would lie on my bed and read my spiritual reading book or look at a book of music or study my German *Imitation of Christ*. I would eat an orange that I had brought up from the table.

I was worried about August 15th. I had the notion that all the professed nuns had a vote on whether or not to allow a postulant to receive the habit. There was a nun who disliked me, I thought. She might blackball me. I would use the Feast of the Assumption to win her over.

The High Mass that morning was beautiful, and there was recreation at the breakfast table. After five days of silence, the conversations and laughter burst out at every table. There were tablecloths on the tables, curtains on the windows, and place cards that the novices had made.

Almost immediately after breakfast, the professed nuns started making their way up to the third floor. They came up the east ramps, ordinarily used only by the novitiate. They were talking and laughing as they came into the Novitiate, and soon there were excited groups in every area of the room.

I was hoping to talk to Sister Marsha, but she was immediately surrounded by other postulants and novices, former academy girls. I would have liked to talk to Sister Francine, but she headed straight for Miss Eileen and started talking to her about Ireland.

I watched Sister Alexandra lead one of the oldest nuns to a chair and sit down with her to talk, even though the old nun was nearly deaf. Alexandra held the old nun's hand and shouted into her ear.

I watched Valentine join a group of junior professed and start laughing and talking with them as freely as if she were already wearing a black veil herself.

The nun I was worried about, Sister Anne Clare, came into the Novitiate. She stood inside the door and looked around the room. No novice or postulant rushed to greet her. I went over to her and wished her a happy feastday. She followed me into the crowded room, and we stood in a corner by the closets.

Sister Anne Clare had been my Latin teacher for four years at the academy. Sandy Meade and I took Latin year after year, because there were always a couple of postulants and a novice or two in Sister Anne Clare's classes. Now Anne Clare asked me how I had liked the Benedictine college I had attended for a year. She had graduated from that college before entering the convent. She majored in Latin. I told her I liked it very much. Sister Anne Clare was very nice to me, and I stopped worrying that she would vote against me. She had caught me with various ponies over the years, translations of Caesar and Cicero that I checked out of the public library, but apparently she had forgiven and forgotten.

The next two days, August 16th and 17th, the motherhouse emptied out, as most of the nuns left for their missions. Rosaline missions were not in the wilds of Africa, but in the cities, suburbs, and small towns of Missouri, Kansas, and Oklahoma.

Life on the missions was freer and more fun than life at the motherhouse. I knew this from observing my grade school teachers. Most Rosalines taught grade school. Thirty or so taught high school, fifteen at Rosaline Academy, and fifteen at Albertine High School.

Even though it was just a few blocks from the motherhouse, the nuns who taught at Albertine High School had their own convent — an ante-bellum brick structure on Westport Road, the old Santa Fe Trail. It had been a hotel once, the site of the famous poker game in 1863 at which Mother Juliet Sly's father won the sixteen acres that would become the Rosaline campus.

My companions and I returned to our schedule of logic and music and vocabulary. The graphoanalysis lessons were over.

Reception and Profession took place on Saturday, August 20th. The five second-years made vows, and the two postulants received the habit. A few days later, the five newly professed juniors left for the missions they had been assigned to. Now there were ten second-year novices, nine canonicals, and nine postulants in the novitiate.

Now the additional tables were removed from the refectory, and everyone sat at the long tables, the professed at the two tables nearest the head table, and the novices and postulants at the lower tables. Wulfram no longer sat with us. She sat at her place in rank with the other professed nuns. There was recreation every day at dinner, and Miss Eileen and Miss Rita and I were becoming friends, thanks to our daily conversations at table.

We had our final exams in vocabulary and logic on August 31st.

❖ ❖ ❖

September, 1960

The novices and postulants spent the first five days of September at Camp Rosaline, a twenty-acre property the nuns owned near 103rd and Holmes, still rural then. Each summer, little girls first and then high school girls and then deaf girls attended three-week sessions, supervised by nuns and college-age counselors. At the end of the summer, the camp had to be cleaned and locked down for winter, and the novitiate did that each year.

We swam at camp. My companions and I had been told to bring swimsuits to the convent, and this was the first time we used them. One afternoon, as I climbed out of the pool, I noticed that Wulfram was watching me. She said, "I like your bathing suit. It's very modest."

It was the first time she had spoken to me other than to tell me to do something or to correct me for something. I was surprised that she would comment on my bathing suit, and it made me uncomfortable.

We slept in the bunkhouse, the novices at one end and the postulants at the other. Wulfram slept in the camp nuns' quarters behind the office. We ate outside at tables on the pavilion. Three of the second-year novices, including old Sister Digna, did the cooking. In the morning, there was Mass on the pavilion, celebrated by an old priest who lived near the camp. During the day we could swim, climb up to the hayloft in the barn, fish in the pond and in the creek, and hike down to the Blue River.

The horses had been moved to their winter stables, but their fragrance lingered in the barn. Bud and Sugar and Maude and Queenie. They paid for their winter lodging by appearing in the American Royal parade every year.

Wulfram arranged things at camp so there was little interaction between the novices and postulants. While the novices were at work, scrubbing the bathrooms and cleaning the kitchen storeroom, the postulants could swim. While the novices swam, the postulants hiked. On our way down to the river, we passed a grass-covered mound that covered a house that had been burned by Quantrill. The chimney still stood, a headstone at the grave of a house.

On Labor Day, late in the afternoon, we returned to the motherhouse. One of the canonical novices, Sister Jean Edward, Wulfram's favorite, drove the old school bus back from camp. She drove in on Holmes, cutting over to Wornall at 75th Street, cutting over to Ward Parkway at Meyer Boulevard. The cicadas were roaring, and the fountains were playing, and Kansas City was at its best. Miss Eileen was impressed by the mansions on Ward Parkway, and I was proud of my beautiful city. Sister Jean Edward crossed Brush Creek and drove up to the convent.

The academy girls had returned to school that day. They were walking around the campus, and they looked at us as Jean Edward double-clutched the old bus up the South Drive.

In chapel that evening, we moved our prayer books and hymnals to our new places, several pews back. The academy girls would occupy the pews in front of us now.

In the morning, they processed into chapel at the end of meditation with their blazers on and their long net chapel veils. I wondered if the girls who remembered me would look at me in my postulant outfit and speculate about my chances of staying in the convent. Sandy Meade and I always watched the novices and postulants returning from Communion. If a novice was unusually thin, and her cincture was hanging low on her hip like a gun belt, we would think she might be leaving.

That day, my companions and I started our regular classes. The two who had not graduated from high school took classes with the academy girls. Those of us who were high school graduates took American history, a college extension course, from Sister Sidonia at 9:00 every morning but Tuesdays.

We had postulant class with Wulfram at 10:00. At 10:30 all the novices and all the postulants took a theology class from Father Andrew, the chaplain. At 11:30, the postulants had a study period.

After dinner, all the novices and all the postulants took music from Sister Francine. At 2:00, the two youngest postulants went back to the academy for more classes, and some of the postulants and some of the second-year novices took an English composition class from Mother Paula. I was assigned to take qualitative analysis with a second-year novice, Sister Regina. Our teacher was Sister Stephen.

From 2:00 until 5:00 every afternoon, Sister Regina and I worked in the academy chemistry lab, analyzing the mysterious bits of metal Sister Stephen gave us. It was pleasant to be in the old room with the big windows open to the campus. I liked the smell of the reagents in the glass-stoppered bottles with the handwritten labels scorched by the bottles' contents. I liked the crumbling mats of asbestos beneath the Bunsen burners. I liked the beakers, the flasks, the glass tubing, the hand-cranked centrifuge. I liked causing the reactions, eliminating the usual suspects, solving the mysteries. Most of all, I liked being away from Wulfram and the novitiate for a few hours. It was like being a real college student again.

Tuesdays were laundry days. The novices rose at 4:00 instead of 5:30 and went over to the laundry, a building across the driveway from the convent's northeast door. They worked through morning prayer and morning Office and most of morning meditation. They came into the chapel at the end of meditation to attend Mass. By that time, the laundry was finished, except for sorting and bundling. The postulants did that from 9:00 until 10:00. We worked at a long table in the linen room. The clean pressed clothes came to us in stacks. We had to sort the individual items onto the numbered spaces on the shelves. Coifs, night caps, skull caps, handkerchiefs, tee-shirts, towels, wash cloths, pajamas, the weird underwear the oldest nuns wore. Each nun's items were stacked, wrapped in one of her towels, and placed on her number on the linen room shelves.

Only the nuns in the community had numbers. Rosaline nuns were not considered to be officially in the community until a year after making final vows. Professed nuns with temporary vows and those with final vows for under a year were called juniors. Juniors, like novices and postulants, had their surnames on their clothes instead of numbers. Our bundles were carried upstairs and lined up on the railings by the ramp.

By the middle of September, it began to get dark too early to play softball, and we began staying inside for recreation.

Everyone sewed except Sister Valentine. Instead of having a sewing box like everyone else, Valentine had a tin candy box full of Speedball pens and bottles of ink. She had a Speedball textbook. She lettered the verses and quotations on the place cards the novices made for feastdays.

Everyone wanted to sit at Valentine's table. She told stories about her father, the Tulsa oil millionaire. He drove a Bentley that had been modified to accommodate his height. He wore a St. Christopher medal that said on the back, "I am a very important Catholic. In case of an accident, please call a bishop."

I was unwilling to jockey for a place at Valentine's table, so we rarely spoke.

I had not yet had a real conversation with Alexandra, either. She and her companions were perfect, as canonical novices were supposed to be. They were observant of silence, careful not to talk about worldly matters at recreation, diligent about their duties. They stuck close to Wulfram at recreation.

I was becoming friendly with most of my companions. There was reading at breakfast and supper, but there was recreation every day at dinner, the longest meal, and since Wulfram was now sitting with the professed, she couldn't hear us. We talked about history.

My companions and I were passionate about our history class with Sister Sidonia. She was an entertaining lecturer, particularly knowledgeable about the Jacksonian period. At dinner, my companions and I discussed her lectures and other historical matters. Miss Eileen knew lots of details about the sinking of the Titanic and lots of Irish history. I knew a little Kansas City history and a little Rosaline history. There was always something to talk about.

If it wasn't history, it was music. We loved Sister Francine's music classes.

My companions and I had learned to fear Wulfram, and the tension was unremitting. She never smiled at us. She never made a personal comment. She never uttered a word of praise, approval, or appreciation. She hadn't screamed at us yet, but we knew she screamed at the novices. In the morning, during our history class in the postulant room, we could hear Wulfram screaming at the novices in the Hour. The door to the Novitiate would be closed, but we could hear her berating them in her loud angry voice.

If the screaming reached an unusually high level, Sister Sidonia would pause in her lecture and look nervous. Sometimes she would end class a little early and hurry down the ramp, apparently anxious not to meet Wulfram in the hall. At the end of the Hour, we would see the novices walk past our door, miserable, downcast. Wulfram would come into the postulant room. For half an hour she would talk about religious life and the importance of silence and the importance of avoiding conversations about worldly matters. It was a relief when the class ended.

Sister Francine, the choir mistress, was delighted with my companions and me. Some of the second-year novices were good singers but not all of them. Valentine barely moved her lips, and no sound came out. The canonical novices were terrible singers, and the intricacies of plainsong escaped them. My companions and I, on the other hand, were good singers, and we became intensely interested in Gregorian chant.

Sister Francine had studied at famous schools of chant, and every summer she attended workshops and seminars on chant. She imparted the lessons she had learned to us. We became neum experts, able to sing quilismas and distrophas and bivirgas with the precision and confidence of our patrons, the Nine Choirs of Angels.

We didn't like Father Andrew's theology classes. The ancient priest, who was the convent chaplain, was an Albertine. He lived with the priests at St. Albert's rectory across the street, but he took his meals at Rosaline, sitting alone in the priests' dining room. A novice served him from the priests' serving room. He was very shaky, so there were always food stains on his elaborate habit. He was retired from decades of teaching theology at his order's seminary, and now the Rosaline novices and postulants were his only students.

Two novices brought him up to the third floor on the elevator. He sat at Wulfram's desk in the Novitiate. The novices and postulants sat in the semi-circles of classroom chairs. He read to us from a sheaf of notes dark with age. We wrote down what he read. There were no questions asked or answered. There was no discussion. His class that fall was about heresies: Albigensianism and Waldensianism and several others. It was hard to stay awake. To make myself stay awake, I practiced writing fast. I wrote down every word Father Andrew said. I did not take shorthand, I just wrote very fast.

One Monday afternoon, late in September, Wulfram told us we would be going downstairs that evening to Nazareth, the guest suite on the ground floor, to watch television with Mother Paula. Kennedy and Nixon would be debating. Mother Paula had decided that it was an event of such historical importance, that we should see it. The novices and postulants who were over twenty-one would vote in November, and this would be a helpful preparation. Only the second-year novices and the postulants were going. First-year novices were not allowed to let any secular matter, even a presidential debate, interfere with the seclusion of the canonical year. Wulfram would go to the community room to watch with the other professed nuns.

When it was time for the debate, we went down the ramps. Mother Paula was waiting for us in a guest bedroom where there was a television set. She was sitting in an armchair. There were no other chairs. Valentine flopped down on the bed. Everyone else had to sit on the window sills or on the floor. We were a few minutes early, and Mother Paula began talking to the novices who were sitting on the floor by her chair. The rest of us talked to each other. I was perched on the window sill by the bed.

Valentine looked up at me and said, "My father says Richard Nixon is the best thing that could happen to this country."

I made a face at her. Why would a person named O'Hara prefer Nixon to Kennedy? And why would Valentine say something like that in front of Mother Paula Rooney who loved anything and everything Irish and had written a book about her Irish ancestors?

Maybe Valentine and I would not be friends after all. I understood that she had been hidden away in the novitiate for over two years. She hadn't seen a newspaper in all that time. She hadn't seen t.v. or listened to the radio. She knew nothing about Kennedy or lunch counter sit-ins or Castro. She knew nothing about anything that had happened since August 28th, 1958.

But I had loathed Richard Nixon since sixth grade. "Nixon lies," I said.

"Tell me one thing he's ever lied about, Miss Audrey," Valentine said.

I said, "For one thing, he lies about his wife's birthday. He always says she was born on St. Patrick's Day. She wasn't."

Valentine said, "Is the precise date of Richard Nixon's wife's birthday important to you, Miss Audrey?"

"People who lie about little things lie about big things," I said.

Mother Paula shushed us with her hand. The debate was about to begin.

❖ ❖ ❖

October, 1960

On the seventeenth of October, a Monday, Sister Francine was unable to come up to the Novitiate for our music class. Wulfram decided we would use the time to work outside. We had been spending Saturday afternoons cleaning up the flower beds and collecting seeds. There was still work to be done.

Wulfram sent the second-years to the Grotto and the canonicals to the Old Graveyard. She kept the postulants with her at the Four-o'Clock bed by the laundry. Here, from the middle of the patch, she could direct our work and hear our conversations. We collected seeds from the Four-o'Clocks. They looked like tiny hand grenades. We pretended to bite out the pins and lob them at one another.

After an hour or so, Wulfram told me to go down to the Grotto and get her trowel from the second-years. I ran down the hill. Valentine and another novice were on their knees just inside the gate, digging up bulbs. The maple trees blazed in the sun.

I climbed up on the iron gate and swung back and forth a few times.

Valentine looked up at me. "Well?"

"Today is my birthday," I said. "I was born October seventeenth, nineteen-forty-one. The day the Kearney was torpedoed in the North Atlantic, and Tojo took over in Japan."

Valentine stood up. I looked down at her from my position on the gate. She said, "I was born February fourteenth, nineteen-forty-one. My mother made a novena that I'd be born on Valentine's Day."

I said, "Remember the day I saw you down here? The day the pope died? When you were distributing Communion to the fish?"

The other novice looked shocked. "Those hosts are not consecrated, Miss Audrey. They're old. Stale."

Valentine said, "You were smoking. The whole place reeked of smoke."

"Gauloise," I said. "Your old brand."

The other second-year said, "Did you want something, Miss Audrey?"

"Sister's trowel."

Valentine gave it to me, and I ran back up the drive. The seed gathering had stopped, and Wulfram was sitting on a bench with my companions standing around her. When I approached, they sang Happy Birthday to me. I was nineteen.

Birthdays were not observed in the convent, but Wulfram handed me a little present wrapped in tissue. A nightcap. The kind the oldest nuns wore to bed. Everyone laughed.

It was a rare break in the constant tension. I wasn't sure why I was singled out for a rare joke by Wulfram.

On Hallowe'en, there was another example of Wulfram's humor. She told us at postulant class to go over to the academy costume room and select costumes to wear to supper that night. It was the tradition for the novices and postulants to dress up as saints on the Eve of All Saints Day.

My companions and I went to the costume room and searched among the racks of clothes.

On the way to the chemistry lab that afternoon, I asked Sister Regina what she and the other second-years would be wearing. She said she was going as Mother Barbara von Gotthier, the first Rosaline to come to America. She told me what a few of her companions would be wearing. She said no one knew what Valentine would be wearing. Sister Wulfram was doing Valentine's costume herself. It would be a surprise.

After Vespers, the novices and postulants went upstairs to put on costumes. We were to wait in the rotunda outside the refectory until the professed nuns were in their seats for supper.

I dressed as St. Scholastica. She had been my invisible friend since childhood, and I hoped to take her name in religion. I had found a very good Benedictine habit in the costume room with a scapular and wimple and veil. I wore a jeweled pectoral cross and carried a stuffed dove in one hand and a staff in the other.

We gathered in the ground floor rotunda. Three floors above us, the Angelus bell was ringing. I was trying to see what everyone was wearing. Valentine was not present. We waited. We could hear the nuns singing grace in the refectory. We heard Mother Paula tap her bell to grant recreation. We heard the nuns talking and laughing. One of the second-years opened the double doors to the refectory, and we went in. We walked up to the tables where the professed nuns sat. We paraded around, giving the nuns a look at our costumes.

"Look at the darky!" one of the oldest nuns kept saying about a canonical novice dressed and made up and wigged as Blessed Martin de Porres.

A second-year novice had starched a pillow case into a Daughter of Charity's cornette; she was St. Catherine Laboure. Miss Eileen was St. Patrick; she was wearing an alb, a green chasuble, and a miter on her red hair. She was carrying a grander crook than mine. Miss Rita was St. Rosalia, Charlemagne's granddaughter, the semi-legendary foundress of our order; she wore a Frankish princess's brocade robes and a diadem on her head.

Valentine was not present.

"Look at the Little Flower!" the nuns exclaimed when they saw Sister Alexandra dressed as a Carmelite, holding a bouquet of roses. She was barefoot.

When our parade was almost over, and we were about to take our seats at the lower tables, the doors from the rotunda banged open, and a man burst into the refectory. A bum. He was holding a whiskey bottle in his hand.

Valentine.

She lurched back and forth in the wide space between the tables. She swayed from side to side and then righted herself. She zig-zagged her way up to the head table, pausing frequently to slurp from the whiskey bottle and wipe her mouth on her tattered sleeve. She had on torn brown slacks, men's shoes gaping open, a rusty old tweed jacket, a crumpled shirt, suspenders, a long wool scarf around her neck, and a workman's tweed cap covering her hair.

The nuns were staring at her. She swept an intoxicated bow to the head table and then turned and staggered back to the doors. She left the room, banging the doors closed behind her.

There was dead silence in the refectory.

"Was that a saint?" Mother Paula finally asked.

Wulfram spoke up. "That was Matt Talbot, Mother." A reformed Irish alcoholic, a leader of the temperance movement.

"Is Matt Talbot a saint?" Mother Paula asked.

Wulfram said, "I believe he's a venerable, Mother."

Mother Paula smiled, and the council smiled, and the professed nuns started to laugh, and pretty soon everyone was laughing.

The servers that evening were junior professed nuns, substituting for the novices on this occasion. They wheeled the cart into the refectory. Valentine did not reappear.

❖ ❖ ❖

November, 1960

The next day was All Saints Day, a holyday of obligation. We didn't have classes, except for an Hour with Wulfram like the Sunday Hour, a class that always began with singing Samuel Wilberforce's "Just For Today." As she usually did, Wulfram made us sing it over and over. "Clip it!" she would shout, and we would attempt to sing it in a way that suited her. No one accompanied the song on the piano. No one ever played the piano except Sister Francine in music class. Wulfram merely struck notes to give the pitch. I wondered if I would still be able to play the piano when I got out of the novitiate.

That afternoon, Wulfram took the novices and postulants down to the Old Graveyard to decorate the graves for All Souls Day. We tied branches of evergreen to the crosses that marked the graves of the founders and of the other nuns who had died before 1945. At that time, the community bought a plot in Calvary Cemetery, and the nuns who had died since then were buried there.

Wulfram told Valentine to tie branches to the tops of the Stations of the Cross. She told me to help her.

As we made our way around the perimeter of the graveyard, decorating the Stations, Valentine told me about her last flings in Hollywood and New York, the penultimate and the ultimate. "Our room at the Waldorf overlooked a private school," she said. "Anglican. The kids had recess on the roof. We could see the kids and the nuns on the roof. Anglican nuns. I love Anglican nuns."

I loved Anglican nuns, too. "I know where there's a stained-glass window of an Anglican nun," I said.

"Where?" Valentine asked.

"In an old Anglican church downtown. St. Mary's."

"Will you show me?"

"Yes." When we both are professed. When we are free.

Wulfram was decorating the founders' graves. Valentine and I walked over to the mound after finishing the Stations. Wulfram adjusted the branches on Mother Juliet's gravestone and those on Mother Augusta's gravestone.

Juliet Sly and Augusta Proff were two friends who attended Rosaline Academy in St. Louis in the 1870s and entered the convent together in 1880. By 1890, they were fed up with teaching in German and praying in German and conversing in German and being criticized in German by the old nuns from Germany for their poor German. They left the St. Louis community with five other nuns and a novice and made a new English-speaking foundation in Kansas City.

One of my companions asked Wulfram to tell us about Mother Juliet and Mother Augusta.

Wulfram said, "They passed the office of superior back and forth for fifty years."

We went inside.

That evening at recreation, a couple of novices asked Wulfram if we could polka. Wulfram went over to the record player. There were only four or five records in the Novitiate, and none of them had been played since my companions and I entered. Wulfram put on the polka album. The novices jumped up as if they were ready to dance, but Wulfram said, "Tonight we'll have two dancers only. Sister Valentine and Sister Terence."

Sister Terence was the 35-year-old canonical who was well under five feet tall. She was the simplest of the simple people in the novitiate. Her movements were awkward, almost dwarf-like. When she sat on the classroom chairs, her feet did not touch the floor. Now she slipped down from her chair, ready to obey.

The novices moved the tables and chairs, and Wulfram started the record. Valentine and Terence began dancing violently around the room. The contrast in their heights and the swooping movements Valentine led her tiny partner through made Wulfram laugh out loud.

I hated her for making clowns of them.

When the record was over, Wulfram turned off the record player. She said, "We'll have a little refreshment now. Miss Audrey's father brought us some apple cider on her birthday, and tonight we'll drink it."

I hadn't known about this. My dad and I loved cider and always bought it for our October birthdays. But it was fresh cider from Unity Farm, meant to be drunk immediately. Surely Wulfram, rumored to be from a farm in Kansas, would know this. The cider would not have held up in the food room, an unused bedroom in the southwest wing, for two weeks. There was no refrigerator in there. The food sat on a shelf.

The cider my dad had brought me was spoiled. Undrinkable. The novices and postulants took sips from their plastic cups but were unable to drink the foamy vinegar. Wulfram gave us permission to pour the cider down a sink.

She had caused the cider to be wasted. She had turned my father's gift into a weapon against me. My companions and the novices must have wondered why my dad brought bad cider. Wulfram didn't look at me to see how I was reacting.

Recreation was inside every night now. It was a time for sewing. We darned our heavy stockings on darning eggs and mended our underwear. When the plain sewing was done, we did fancywork.

Some of my companions, the ones Wulfram considered least dexterous, worked on huck towels. The rest of us embroidered. The finished needlework was to be presented to Mother

Paula for her feastday. She would use the items as gifts for the convent's benefactors.

I was working on a pair of pillowcases stamped with a pattern of flowers. I knew only three embroidery stitches that my grandmother had taught me years before: back-stitch, cross-stitch, and French knots. Wulfram did not teach us to embroider, but just ordered us to do it.

I had hoped to learn to embroider in the convent. Once, when I was in the academy, Mother Paula showed my roommate and me some of the needlework the founders did; we wrote an article for the *Tidings* on how they survived the early months in Kansas City by selling their needlework. Mother Augusta and Mother Juliet made altar linens, vestments, and brides' trousseaus.

On Friday nights, Wulfram did not come to recreation. She and a few other professed nuns went over to Kansas City, Kansas, to visit a chiropractor. They missed Vespers, meditation, supper, and recreation. They returned in time for night prayers. Without the novice mistress present, recreation on Friday evenings was more relaxed. I usually sat with my companions, but in November, Valentine began to bring her pens and ink over to a chair by mine. We were becoming friends.

In our postulant class with Wulfram, my companions and I heard a lot about particular friendship. Wulfram constantly warned us about the dangers of becoming attached to any one sister. She told us about the time she came upon "two novices on the ramp, locked in each other's arms." She said a good religious spent recreation talking to the sisters she liked least.

In the Sunday Hours, Wulfram was analyzing our characters with tests from a booklet on the medieval humours. When she first started reading from it, I thought she was trying to be humorous. It quickly became evident that she was serious. It was painful to listen to her exhortations about bile and phlegm.

Wulfram was uneducated. Before becoming novice mistress in 1956, she taught grade school. Like many of the grade school teachers, she had no degree. The nuns attended summer school year after year, working slowly towards a bachelor's degree, but Wulfram had not completed a degree. She did not tell us that. I had heard that before I entered. I began to think her dislike for my companions and me had something to do with our delight in studying history and chant.

My companions and I had visiting day once a month. Our parents brought picnics, and we ate outside with them. By November, it was too cold to eat outside, so we ate our picnics at tables in the students' dining room. My parents brought fried chicken from Stroud's and cheeseburgers from Winstead's in an insulated bag. They brought popcorn and candy from their theaters.

The first-year novices had only one visiting day during the canonical year. It had already taken place before my class entered. The second-year novices had visiting days every three months. On the day in November when her companions' parents came, Valentine had no visitors. She told me her parents preferred to come separately, on days when no one else was visiting. They did not bring a picnic. When they flew up from Tulsa to visit, they were served a meal in the priests' dining room, the only parents so treated. They brought caviar and avocados for Sister Wulfram when they came, and boxes of Hershey bars for Valentine.

Valentine loved Hershey bars and the color purple and the furry lap robe from her father's Bentley. At night, after night prayer, when the novices and postulants studied silently in the

Novitiate in their pajamas and robes, Valentine wore the furry lap robe around her shoulders.

One evening in November, after supper, my companions and I knelt in the refectory before Mother Paula's table and asked to be received as novices. A few days later, we learned that we all were to be received. We started sewing for Reception.

We had to make coifs and skull caps and night caps and undersleeves. Our habits were being made for us by the old nun who made habits for everyone. Our headbands were being made for us by Sister Francine, the choir mistress, who made headbands for everyone. Our guimpes and collars were being made for us by a nun who specialized in those items. We were measured for our veils and leather cinctures.

Wulfram criticized our sewing and made us rip out seams and start over. My companions and I were drawing closer together through dread of Wulfram. Eileen and I were beginning to take steps toward talking freely and openly.

There was still recreation at dinner every day, but there was reading at breakfast and supper. The supper reading was the important one, the one I wanted to do when I became a novice. Valentine was usually the supper reader. The books read at supper were lighter than the breakfast fare, when we heard of martyrs being grilled and boiled. The supper book in November was a biography of Nano Nagle, an Irish nun. I felt that Mother Paula had selected it to make Eileen happy.

On the Friday after Thanksgiving, Wulfram left with some other professed nuns after dinner. She granted an afternoon of recreation to the novices and postulants. That meant we could talk while we sat and sewed in the Novitiate. It was cold and foggy outside. Inside, the radiators were clanking and the lights were on. It was pleasant to be warm and free of Wulfram for a few hours. Everyone was talking and laughing. Everyone was sewing or, in Valentine's case, lettering.

At four, Valentine stood up. "Who wants to go down to the Grotto with me?" She had to feed the fish.

No one said anything. Valentine gave me a poke on the shoulder. "Come on."

We went down to the linen room and put on choir mantles. The Rosalines no longer wore mantles in chapel; these were old ones that hung on a coat rack to be used by anyone needing a wrap to go outside.

Valentine and I went out the northeast door. It had stopped raining. Brown leaves were stuck to the pavement. We walked slowly down the South Drive, our capes wrapped around us against the cold and the fog.

Valentine told me she was worried about the test we would be taking the next week, the Minnesota Multiphasic Personality Inventory. She said, "If I flunk, they won't let me make vows."

"You couldn't flunk if you tried," I said. "You'd have to be a moron."

I told her that psychological testing of novices had become the fad in the two years since she entered the convent. All the orders were doing it. The nuns were testing their students as well as their novices and postulants. I had taken the MMPI during my freshman year at college. "They say stuff like, I think someone is following me. Some of the time. Most of the time. All of the time."

Valentine wasn't convinced. She asked me how I had come out on the humours test Wulfram had given us.

"A combination of choleric and phlegmatic," I said. "The worst."

"They're all bad," Valentine said.

"They're all meaningless," I said.

"I'm melancholy," she said. "The highest type of melancholy."

"Alexandra is sanguine," I said.

"If I flunk, they won't let me make vows."

"You're not going to flunk. What did your handwriting say?" We had gotten our handwriting analyses back from Mother Aurelia; she had typed them on newsprint. I kept mine in my bible at my place in chapel. I had memorized it.

Valentine said, "I have problems telling myself the truth. I think that comes from the left loops in my o's. I tell the truth to other people, but not to myself. I've got literary ability. And I'm a big showoff. But one with a sense of responsibility."

We were taking the longest possible route to the Grotto, following every twist and turn of the South Drive.

The South Drive had been carved in the hillside by oxen. Mother Paula told my roommate and me about the South Drive when we were sophomores. It was our feature article on the South Drive that put us over the top to be editors of the *Tidings*. Fifty column inches. Before Mother Juliet Sly's father won the sixteen acres at the poker game in 1863, the hillside was a holding pen for mules and oxen waiting to be hitched to the wagons they would pull to Santa Fe. The oxen made their way down the hill to drink from Brush Creek by meandering back and forth, choosing the least steep pathway. When Mother Juliet established her convent on the site, she planted elm trees along the ox path, and later it was paved. By 1960, the elms were gone, replaced by maples. I missed the elm trees that arched above Kansas City's streets when I was a child, making green tunnels. The kids on my block would tear elm leaves into sergeant's stripes and hold them on their sleeves. Hut, two, three, four.

"What did Mother Aurelia say about you?" Valentine asked as she opened the gate to the Grotto.

The fish roused themselves from their torpor and went into a modified feeding frenzy beneath the bridge. Valentine dropped stacks of stale hosts on them. I ate a few hosts.

I said, "Emotionally balanced, but deep feelings. Sharp, analytical thinking, increased by concentration. Concentration intensifies deep feelings and all other traits. Some temper and impatience. Generous, friendly with all, but clannish in friendship, wanting few close friends. Narrow in regard to the views of others. Independent in thought and action. Good organizational ability with sense of responsibility. Strong will. Optimistic."

"You'll be a principal," Valentine said. The hosts were gone, but the fish mouths were still open.

I didn't want to be a principal. That would mean grade school. I wanted to be a high school teacher. History. Valentine wanted to teach English in high school. I hoped we would be assigned to Albertine High School or to the academy. Those were the plum assignments. Especially Albertine. Teaching high school boys required strong nuns.

We started back up the Drive. As we walked up the hill, a car came through the 49th Street gate and up the Drive. Its headlights were on, diffused by the fog. Valentine and I stepped to the side. Sister Wulfram and three other nuns were in the car. They drove past us.

❖ ❖ ❖

December, 1960

After that, Valentine stopped talking to me. I knew Wulfram had told her to stay away from me.

In Sister Francine's music class, we were preparing for Christmas. Latin propers for Midnight Mass. English and German hymns for Christmas morning.

In our postulant class, Wulfram continued to talk about silence and about particular friendship. Sometimes she talked about the three stages of prayer: purgative, illuminative, and unitive. We were still in the purgative stage, still purging ourselves of sin. Wulfram intimated that she was in the unitive stage.

In chemistry, Sister Regina and I were wrapping up the analyses of the old keys and other metal objects in the box Sister Stephen had given us. We were preparing for our final exam.

In history, we were up to the 1930s, another period Sister Sidonia excelled at. My companions and I discussed Roosevelt and Pendergast and the depression at dinner.

At recreation, we were sewing for Reception. Valentine and the other second-years were sewing for Profession.

One morning in postulant class, Wulfram passed out little pieces of paper to us and told us to write on them our three choices for our names in religion. Mother Paula would choose which of the names we would get or assign us a different one. We would learn our names when the bishop called them out at Reception.

Many Rosalines kept their baptismal names, but there was already a Sister Audrey. I wanted to be Sister Scholastica. I was about to write it on the paper when Wulfram said, "I think Miss Audrey should be Sister Emmanuel."

Emmanuel. God with us. People would think I was a megalomaniac. It was a man's name. It didn't go well with Thorney at all. When would my feastday be? I couldn't make good capital E's.

But what was I doing in the convent, if I couldn't obey? God spoke to us through our superiors. St. Therese would not have hesitated for a moment. I wrote down Emmanuel first, Scholastica second, and Nicholas third.

A few days before Christmas, Wulfram took my companions and me down to the chapel. It was time to put up the crib. We were to help her. She was at her fiercest. She gave us brown paper grocery bags and told us to crush them. They would be rocks, the backdrop behind the crib. We crushed them, but not enough. They still looked like bags, not rocks. Then we crushed them too much. They were too soft. Wulfram told us to shade the crushed bags with colored chalk. Too much color. Not enough color. Too smeared. We were holding the chalk wrong. Wulfram stood on a ladder in front of a side altar. She snarled at us while she covered the altar with the crushed bags.

When the rock wall was finished, we were to hand her cedar branches from boxes the workmen had left in the side aisles. These went on the various levels of the altar. Wulfram rejected most of the branches we held up to her. They were too short or too long or too skimpy or too bushy. We had no gloves, and our hands were covered with chalk and resin.

Finally, Wulfram was ready to set up the stable. We were to break straw into the lengths she specified for the manger. Too long. Too short. Too uniform. Finally, the statues. Wulfram lifted each one from its box and placed it on the paper bag hillside. One of my companions, Miss Judy, made the mistake of removing a shepherd from the box herself, instead of handing the box to Wulfram. Wulfram hissed at her about how these treasures were never to be touched by someone with filthy, sticky hands. Only Wulfram was allowed to touch them.

We stood and waited while she arranged the shepherds and the angels and Mary and Joseph and the animals. The Baby Jesus would stay in His box until Midnight Mass. The Three Kings would stay in their boxes until Epiphany. We missed our morning classes.

That afternoon, while Sister Regina and I walked across the campus to the chemistry lab, she told me that the second-years had learned they would all be going to St. Louis after Profession to attend Marillac College, a school for nuns conducted by the Daughters of Charity. I had heard about this before I entered. For the first time, a class of newly professed junior sisters would be sent to college instead of into classrooms.

Sister Regina said she thought she would be told to major in chemistry at Marillac. She had already completed three years of college, two before she entered the convent and a third with the extension courses she had taken in the novitiate. She would probably be a chemistry teacher at Rosaline Academy or at Albertine High School.

On Christmas Eve, Wulfram told the second-years they could wear their serge habits to Midnight Mass. They hadn't seen these habits since their Reception. In the spirit of poverty, novices wore cotton habits on weekdays and habits made of a synthetic serge on Sundays.

After Midnight Mass, the community and the novitiate went to the students' dining room for soup and bread and hot chocolate. The second-year novices, resplendent in their serge habits, seemed like they were professed already. Valentine leaned back in her chair and stretched her legs out in front of her and crossed her feet. Wulfram didn't correct her.

There were two more Masses on Christmas morning, Low Masses with English and German hymns. Ihr Kinderlein, kommet, O kommet doch all. Sister Francine's descants soared above our harmony. My companions and I sang the Huron Carol without accompaniment. After the Masses, we went downstairs to breakfast.

The junior nuns had decorated the refectory. The novices and postulants had not seen it until now. The long tables, usually bare, had starched white tablecloths on them. Instead of our rough everyday napkins, there were linen napkins at each place. There was a can of candy at each place, a one-pound coffee can, covered with Christmas wrap and filled with chocolates. The curtains were on the windows, and there was recreation at breakfast. We ate scrambled eggs and Polish sausage and stollen.

Miss Eileen told me about Christmas morning in Ireland, how the women and children went "crib crawling" after Mass, visiting other churches to see the cribs. The men headed for the pubs while this was going on.

Miss Rita and I told Eileen about Christmas at St. Albert's. The best singer in the grade school sang Stille Nacht in the darkened church just before Midnight Mass. No organ. Just a child's voice singing the old song. Then the lights went on, and another child carried the Baby Jesus up to the crib. The adult choir sang at Midnight Mass, but the entire congregation sang Adeste Fideles during Communion. After Mass, everyone in the church went up to look at the crib. It was illuminated by a light shining through a celluloid color wheel. On the steps outside, everyone wished everyone a Merry Christmas.

Upstairs, after breakfast, Wulfram told the novices and postulants to go into the Novitiate. There, in stacks around the room, were our Christmas presents from our parents. They had been told what to buy. Toiletries. The second-years, about to be professed and go off to college, got suitcases and desk lamps. School supplies. The canonicals and postulants got spiritual reading books and meditation books.

We had turkey and dressing for dinner, and there was recreation at table.

The professed nuns came up to the Novitiate after dinner. I talked to several of my former teachers. I talked to Sister Nora, the academy infirmarian and convent laundress.

Valentine walked past us. "Merry Christmas, Sisters," she said. The first words she had spoken to me in a month.

❖ ❖ ❖

January, 1961

On January 2nd, we began practicing for Reception and Profession. We had learned the music in August, and we had reviewed it with Sister Francine in December. Now in our music classes, we focused almost entirely on the music for the ceremony. In addition to music class, we now spent an hour or two a day in chapel with Wulfram, practicing the moves. She criticized every step we took and every word we sang or spoke. The fear and tension made these sessions terrible.

We were to enter the chapel dressed as brides. I would be wearing a dress one of my cousins had worn at her wedding a year earlier. Two professed nuns were altering the various bridal gowns for us, some borrowed from friends and relatives, some that had emerged from a storeroom in the southwest hall. One by one we were called to the postulant room to be fitted. We stood on a table in the shoes we would wear, white high heels, and the two nuns pinned and tucked.

One day when I was standing on the table, the two nuns who had been pinning the hem of my dress and trying to figure out how to make it more modest decided to go downstairs to look for some white satin to line the lace sleeves. "Do not move," they told me. "We'll be right back."

The day was dark with impending snow, and the lights were on in the postulant room. I could see my reflection in the windows. I saw a bride standing on a newspaper on a table. The bride was wearing a dress she would not have chosen for a wedding to an earthly bridegroom. And she would not have chosen the 1920s-style veil.

I saw the reflection of someone crossing the rotunda. Valentine.

She saw me standing on the table. She came to the door. I turned to face her. "You look beautiful," she said.

I said, "At practice, when you say your vows, you say your name like O'Hera. Very Tulsa. You should say O'Hara. Say it like Gerald O'Hara says it in Gone With the Wind. Katy Scarlett O'Harrrra."

Chapter 2
Canonical Novice

Reception Day
January 28th, 1961

We dressed in our postulant clothes for the last time. We attended morning prayer, morning Office, meditation, and the community Mass. There was silence at breakfast. After breakfast we went upstairs to change into our brides' dresses. The two seamstresses went around to our rooms to button and zip.

At 9:45 we were ready to go downstairs, nine brides in satin and lace and ten novices in serge. We stood in the third floor rotunda in silence. The noise from the first floor came up to us. I looked over the railing at the crowd of guests below. The women were in fur coats. Their fragrances wafted up: cigarettes and perfume.

At five till ten, the guests and the nuns were in the chapel, and Sister Lucy, the great convent organist, was playing a prelude. We went down the ramp and lined up in the hall by Mother Paula's office. Wulfram was still criticizing us. Our candles were not straight. We were walking clumsily in high heels after six months in nun shoes.

At precisely ten o'clock, we heard the sacristy bell ring as the bishop entered the sanctuary to begin the ceremony. Wulfram lit our candles. She gave us no smile or word of encouragement. We heard the crowd of people stand up. We heard Sister Lucy give the bishop the pitch for the Veni Creator. He intoned it, and the nuns in the chapel sang it with us as we followed the cross bearer and the candle bearers and the flower girls up the center aisle.

We went to the front pews and took our places. The Mass began. At the Communion, the second-year novices went up into the sanctuary and knelt on the altar step. The bishop stood before each one in turn as she made her vows. When it was Valentine's turn, she said, "In the name of our Lord Jesus Christ, and in honor of His Blessed Mother, in the presence of His Excellency, Bishop William Harrigan, and of our Reverend Superior, Mother Mary Paula Rooney, I, Valentine O'Hara, in religion, Sister Mary Valentine, do vow and promise to God for three years, poverty, chastity, and obedience."

She had pronounced her name the way I told her to. At the most important moment of her life, she was thinking of me. She signed her vows and received Communion.

When the vows were finished, my companions and I went up to the Communion railing and knelt to receive the Sacrament. We were followed by the nuns and the guests.

At the end of the Mass, my companions and I went into the sanctuary and knelt before the bishop. He asked, "My daughters, what do you demand?" We answered, "The mercy of God and the holy habit of religion." When the questions and responses were over, we went back to the Communion railing. There, Mother Paula, assisted by Sister Wulfram, gave us our habits. Holding our folded habits on our arms, we left the chapel.

We went into one of the main parlors. Nine professed nuns stood by nine chairs. They had our petticoats, headgear, stockings and shoes, arranged for us. They helped us out of our brides' dresses and into our habits. Sister Marsha dressed me. She pinned my hair back, so it wouldn't stick out of my headdress. She put a skull cap on me and a coif. She slipped the heavy serge habit over my head. She put a cord around my waist to take the place of the cincture I had not yet received. She put my headdress on me; it had a temporary white net veiling pinned to it to take the place of the veil I had not yet received. She put my guimpe on me and handed me my undersleeves to put on.

When we were dressed in our habits, we went back into the chapel. The people stood up and turned to look at us in our habits. We went back up into the sanctuary. Again we knelt at the inside of the Communion railing where Mother Paula, assisted by Sister Wulfram, pinned our white veils to our headdresses and removed the temporary veiling. We stood, and Mother Paula girded us with the cincture of obedience. Our cinctures were long black leather belts that looped over the buckle and hung down to the hem of the habit on the right side. A side rosary hung from the buckle. When we were veiled and girded, the newly professed religious came into the sanctuary, and Mother Paula and Sister Wulfram replaced their white veils with black veils.

It was time for the Suscipe. The ten newly professed religious and the nine new novices sang it three times, each time on a higher pitch. We held up our arms as we offered ourselves to the Lord.

At the end of the Suscipe, we knelt on the sanctuary floor and then lay prostrate. Flower girls covered us with black palls. We were dead to the world. The bishop intoned the Te Deum. The other novices and the community chanted while the flower girls threw petals on the palls. Under the palls, we prayed. There was a tradition that you got whatever you prayed for under the pall. On her Reception Day, Therese of Lisieux prayed that purgatory be emptied.

At the end of the Te Deum, the flower girls lifted the palls, and we stood up. The newly professed nuns left the sanctuary and went to their pew. My companions and I stood before the bishop. He gave us our names. When it was my turn, he said, "Miss Audrey Thorney will be known in religion as Sister Mary Emmanuel."

I bowed profoundly.

When we all were named, Sister Lucy played the introduction to Ubi Caritas on the organ. The nuns in the pews began singing. They sang as they processed out of chapel to wait for us in the rotunda. The guests remained in their pews. We left the chapel, singing Ubi Caritas. In the rotunda, the nuns stood in a circle, waiting to greet us. We went to Mother Paula first. "I humbly beg your motherly love and your holy prayers," I said, when it was my turn.

"They're yours, Sister Emmanuel," Mother Paula said, the first to call me by my new name. I went around the circle, from the oldest nuns to the youngest novice.

We ate dinner in the students' dining room. Each newly professed sister and each new novice ate with her relatives. My parents and a few aunts and uncles were there. Our friends were served at additional tables in the ground floor rotunda. After dinner, each of us had a parlor, or an area of a parlor, or, in my case, the landing under the stairway in Nazareth, in which to receive guests.

Wulfram had given me the worst spot. My three best friends came running down the steps to congratulate me. "It took us forever to find you," they said. "Why are you down here in this . . . stairwell?" They asked me if I wanted to forget the whole thing, walk out the door, and go with them over to Sammie's where they would be spending the afternoon. Sammie's was a bar on the Kansas side, a Strawberry Hill place where kids from our college hung out when they were in Kansas City. You could get served at eighteen on the Kansas side.

Two of my grade school teachers from St. Albert's came down the steps to my makeshift parlor. They had already been to Judy's area in the Alumnae Room and to Rita's corner in the first parlor. "Why are you down here in the basement?" one of them asked me.

A couple of nuns from my college had driven down to attend my Reception. One of them handed me a letter she had written to me in German. She was sad that I had not become a Benedictine but happy that I had become a Rosaline. She gave me an enameled St. Benedict's medal. We were allowed to attach two medals to our side rosaries. One would be the Charlemagne and Rosalia medal that all Rosalines wore. This St. Benedict's medal would be the other one on my rosary.

The next day was another day of grace before our canonical year officially began. We were allowed visits from our parents in the afternoon. That afternoon, Sister Valentine and her companions left for St. Louis. Now there were eleven canonical novices and eight second-years in the novitiate.

❖ ❖ ❖

February, 1961

Now we were beginning the year that would separate us from the world. We would be allowed one visiting day only, in late July. Before Mother Paula became superior in 1956, canonical novices had no visiting day at all.

Now we wore the habits we had longed for. We had two everyday habits made of cotton and one Sunday habit made of a lightweight synthetic serge. We also had two white veils, an everyday veil on an everyday bonnet, as the headdress was called, and a Sunday veil on a Sunday bonnet. We would not see our serge habits again until Profession. Or maybe, as second-years, we would get to wear them to Midnight Mass, as Valentine and her companions had done.

Now we attended the Hour every day, Wulfram's class for novices. At our first Hour, Wulfram assigned jobs. She gave the best job, that of sacristan, to her favorite novice, Sister Jean Edward.

Jean Edward had held this important position throughout her canonical year, and now, as a second-year novice, she would retain it. This was unexpected. The sacristan was ordinarily a canonical. It took a lot of time to care for the altar, the candles, the flowers, the vestments, the two sacristies, the altar linens. As a second-year, Jean Edward would be taking college classes, requiring study time. Wulfram did not explain why a second-year novice was appointed sacristan, but the message was clear. No one in the new canonical class was worthy of the honor.

The second most important job, that of refectorian, did go to a canonical, to Judy Fitzpatrick, now Sister David. She was Sister Jean Edward's cousin. During our postulancy, when the Fitzpatricks came to see Miss Judy on visiting days, Sister Jean Edward's parents, the Sheas, came with them, even though Jean Edward, as a canonical, could not see her family. Wulfram always ate with the Sheas and the Fitzpatricks on visiting day. And she always had Eileen eat with them. I had hoped that Eileen would be allowed to take turns eating with the rest of us, but that did not happen.

Wulfram gave me my job. "Sister Emmanuel will be the ground floor cleaner." Not all of it. Just the rotunda, the northeast corridor, the workmen's dining room, the linen room, the men's bathroom, and the part of the southeast wing that ended at the door to Nazareth.

I kept my poker face and my neutral tone. "Thank you, Sister. May God reward you." Wulfram had given me what she considered the third-worst job. The worst was cleaning the novitiate bathrooms. My oldest companion, Sister Carol, got that one again. She had done that job as a postulant, and now Wulfram assigned her to do it again. Sister Carol was not allowed to use scouring powder to clean the tubs, but had to scrape the sides with a single-edged razor blade.

The second-worst job was cleaning the ramps. This went to a second-year, Sister Alexandra.

After assigning the cleaning duties, Wulfram assigned some additional jobs. Sister Eileen would serve the chaplain's supper each evening. Sister Carol was to be the breakfast reader. A second-year was appointed to do the brief reading at dinner. Then Wulfram said, "Sister Emmanuel will read at supper, starting tonight."

"Thank you, Sister. May God reward you." Same blank face. Same flat tone. I never showed enthusiasm or any other emotion to Wulfram.

Wulfram said I was to call on Mother Paula each day after dinner to get the material to read at supper.

Sister Carol immediately raised her hand to ask if she and the dinner reader should also call on Mother Paula each day. Carol had not learned to keep her hand down and her mouth shut.

Wulfram reminded her in a sarcastic tone that the breakfast reading was always the same: passages from the Rule, the Constitutions, the Martyrology, Pius Parsch. On Saturdays, the Regulations instead of Parsch. The two- or three-minute dinner reading was always the same, too: the principal saints of the day from Butler's Lives. "There is no need for the breakfast and dinner readers to bother Mother."

I knew the table reading assignments had come from Mother Paula. After my hundreds of visits to Mother Paula's office when I was working on the *Tidings*, I knew her well enough to know that she and no one else would select the novices who read aloud in the refectory. I knew Wulfram would not have appointed me to this best of jobs if the decision had been hers to make.

Reading at table would help me make it through the next two years, I thought. Of all the deprivations in the novitiate, being denied books and magazines and newspapers was the hardest. I was longing to read something. I was starving for news. The spiritual reading books Wulfram assigned were tortuous. As a postulant, I finished the first one she gave me in a few days and went back for another one. She told me I could not possibly have digested everything in it so quickly. She said I was to start over. I didn't go back again. I devoured the history text we used in our class with Sister Sidonia, footnotes, front and back matter, index, captions. I read every page in the fat Liber Usualis and every page in my thin blue qualitative analysis text. When Sister John Vianney went outside to sweep rags, I read the wapiti encyclopedia in the Novitiate. Now, as the supper reader, I would have better things to read.

That afternoon after dinner, I went to Mother Paula's office. I stood at the door and waited for her to look up, just as Sandy Meade and I had done every morning when we were working on the school paper. Mother Paula looked up and smiled. "Come in, Sister," she said.

She motioned for me to come over to her desk. She handed me a copy of *Time* magazine, a copy of the morning paper, and a copy of her newest book, *Stars For Eternity*.

The magazine had paper clips on several pages. Mother Paula told me to read the articles for the first fifteen minutes. Then I was to read the editorial she had marked in the *Kansas City Times*. Then I was to begin reading her book. She told me she knew I'd do a good job as supper reader. "Enunciate. Project. Those are the important things. And look up as much as possible. Don't mumble down into the book. Look up from the page. That sends the voice out better than any microphone ever can." Mother Paula said I was to go to the refectory each day before Vespers to prepare the reading. "Look it over. Look up any unfamiliar words. Practice."

I walked out of Mother Paula's office carrying the magazine and the newspaper and the book. I went downstairs to the refectory. I stood by the reader's stand. It was one o'clock. At four I would come back to practice. I flipped through Mother Paula's book. I realized that Mother Paula had saved her new book for me to read. At supper for the past several nights, the table reading had consisted entirely of magazine articles. No new book had been started after the Nano Nagel biography. Mother Paula had held *Stars For Eternity* until I became a novice and could read at table.

Mother Paula was working on this history of the Rosalines of Kansas City when I was an academy student. She sometimes showed Sandy and me old pictures or old documents that she was writing about.

I closed the book and put it on the reader's stand with the magazine and the newspaper. I went upstairs to music class.

Sister Francine congratulated my companions and me on our beautiful singing at Reception. Wulfram had said nothing about it. We opened our Libers and began learning the propers for the coming Sunday.

After music, Father Andrew came upstairs for Christology. At three, we had Sacred Scripture with Sister Lucy. As Francine had done, Sister Lucy congratulated us on our beautiful singing at the ceremony. She then lectured to us for an hour on Genesis. It was fascinating, and for an hour I felt like I was back in college.

At four, Sister Lucy left, and my companions and the second-years sat down to study. I went down the ramps to the ground floor. I went into the empty refectory. I stepped up onto the reader's stand. I sat down. I turned on the microphone and adjusted it. Testing, one, two, three, four. I turned on the gooseneck lamp and adjusted it. I read the first article aloud, an account of President Kennedy's inauguration. I read the rest of the magazine to myself.

At four-thirty, I went upstairs to the chapel to meditate early with the table servers. At five, the community and the novitiate came into the chapel for Vespers.

At five-thirty, I went back down to the refectory and ate at half-table with the servers and Sister Columba, the portress. At five-forty-five, the servers went into the kitchen to prepare to serve, and I went to the reader's stand and arranged the reading in the order Mother Paula had specified. At six, I could hear the Angelus bell ringing above. A few minutes later, the novitiate and the community came into the refectory. They sang grace and sat down. Mother Paula tapped her bell, and I began reading.

At the end of the meal, Mother Paula tapped her bell, and I said, "Let us bless the Lord." Everyone responded, "Thanks be to God." I stepped down from the reader's stand and stood while the nuns sang the grace after meals. At the end of grace, I knelt and kissed the floor.

    The next morning was my first day as the ground floor cleaner. The second-year novice whose job this had been until this morning showed me the makeshift janitor's closet behind the men's bathroom. This little triangular area was at the bottom of the air shaft around which the ramps angled. It was lit from a skylight above. Windows to the air shaft provided dim light to the ramps. Someone had thrown a candy wrapper through one of those windows. It lay on the floor, here at the bottom. The second-year picked it up and showed me the mop bucket and the mop, the cleaning supplies and rags, and the stack of old newspapers to be used to protect freshly scrubbed floors. She left me and went to report to her new cleaning duty. I turned up my habit and pinned the skirt behind my back. I took off my guimpe and undersleeves. I pinned up my big sleeves. I put on my apron. There were no rubber gloves in the box of supplies.

    I mopped the northeast hall with the string mop. Swabbing the deck. The bucket had wheels and a wringer. I mopped the floor in the linen room. I mopped the floor in the men's dining room. I cleaned the men's bathroom. Still a few minutes until nine. I went back into the little triangular closet and read a few old newspapers.

    In the Hour that morning, Sister Wulfram gave my companions and me our copies of the Catechism of the Vows. During our two years as novices, we would memorize the contents of the book, she said. We would be assigned several questions and answers every day. She gave us spiral notebooks. We were to take notes during the Hour. Rosalines kept their Hour notes with them throughout their lives, Wulfram said. They referred to them constantly, treasuring the lessons they had learned in the novitiate. Taking good notes in the Hour was important. Wulfram went on for an hour about the importance of taking good Hour notes. I wrote down every word she said.

After the Hour, the second-years had secular classes, and my companions and I had metaphysics from Father Andrew.

As February went on, some of us got haircuts from Sister Loretta. Loretta was a second-year novice who had been a year behind me at the academy. She was a farm girl from Kansas, adept at various things, including cutting hair.

We were not required to get our hair cut. There was no regulation about hair. Each Rosaline made her own decision about her hair. When Wulfram told us we could make appointments with Sister Loretta, she mentioned that her roommate at St. Mary's Hospital, the last time she went in, was a nun from Mexico. This nun had a long braid that reached to her waist. Mexican nuns, since the days of the Revolution when nuns were hung from lampposts, did not cut their hair, in case they had to disband and go into secular clothing.

Some novices, we learned from the second-years, kept their hair cut very short, so if they were tempted to leave the convent, they would have to wait at least a few months till their hair grew back, and maybe in that time they would change their minds and stay. My hair was long, so I had Sister Loretta cut it short. Long enough to leave, if necessary, but short enough to be comfortable under my headgear.

As novices, we now attended the Chapter of Faults on Friday nights after night prayer. We knelt on the floor in the Novitiate, facing the crucifix on the southeast wall. Wulfram sat behind us. One by one, starting with the youngest, we said, "Before our mistress and the sisters here present, I humbly accuse myself of my faults against the holy Rule." We then mentioned a fault or two, something not serious enough to be matter for confession, but perhaps an offense against poverty, something like allowing the hem of the habit to drag on the ramps.

Those who were feeling particularly humble could ask for spiritual alms instead of accusing themselves of faults. This meant that other novices would write suggestions for improvement on little pieces of paper and slip them under the door of the one asking for alms. Giving spiritual alms was a form of fraternal charity. Another form of fraternal charity was reporting the failings of others to the mistress of novices. I was unable to do these things.

Now that we were novices, we rose at four on laundry days. The novice responsible for waking us opened our doors slightly and whispered, "Praised be Jesus Christ."

Getting up at four was difficult. I was always tired. We were supposed to get dressed and then go into the Novitiate for a glass of milk before going over to the laundry. The skim milk, which had sat on a table in a gallon jar all night, was warm and blue. I could not drink it.

In spite of being tired, I liked going outside at 4:30 on winter mornings. We left our guimpes and sleeves in the linen room and then hurried across the driveway to the laundry.

There was a huge mangle for the sheets, pillow cases, coifs, handkerchiefs, night caps, skull caps, aprons, table cloths, napkins, dish towels. Sister Jean Edward and I folded the sheets as they emerged from the mangle. All was done in silence.

Occasionally Robert, the man who kept the laundry machines and the boiler running, would play his banjo and sing while we worked. "Blue Moon of Kentucky, keep on shinin'." Robert was not bound by the rule of silence. He was not even

Catholic. Once when I was a counselor at Camp Rosaline, Robert and his wife came out to sing for the campers. Bluegrass.

Sister Nora was in charge of the laundry. She lifted the wet clothes from the washing machines and put them in the extractor. From the extractor to the driers. From the driers to the mangle. I liked being around Nora, even though we couldn't talk, and I liked folding sheets with Jean Edward. She had gone to the same college I had gone to, a year before me. She had finished her freshman year, just as I had done, before entering the convent. We knew many of the same people, although we hadn't known each other before.

Jean Edward had taken ballet at college, just as I had done. She had gone to Albertine High School. She was the only girl in Albertine history to be prom queen and homecoming queen in the same year. I knew the boy she left behind, and she knew the boy I left behind. We folded sheets in silence, a ballet of folding. Twice the long way, then twice the wide way. Fast, so the manglers did not get ahead of us.

Sometimes Sister Nora would send someone outside to hang rags on the clothesline. Rags did not merit time in the extractor or the driers. I liked doing this, too. I liked being outside alone in the dark. I hung the heavy wet rags on the line and secured them with clothespins. I propped up the sagging clotheslines with the notched poles. I wore a clothespin apron. I looked up at the stars. I thought of my parents, just down the street, still asleep, not yet ready to begin the day, not yet ready to make coffee, or bring in the paper, or discuss the receipts from the night before.

At 6:45, we left the laundry, put on our guimpes and our sleeves, and went upstairs to the chapel to attend Mass. After

Mass, since there were no postulants, we sorted the laundry in the linen room.

Every day at the dinner table my companions and I talked about Gregorian. We discussed the importance of the rhythmic ictus and the rules of chironomy. Wulfram would look at us from her place up the table and give us her cold stare.

At supper there was reading nearly every night. I called on Mother Paula every day, and she gave me magazine articles and newspaper articles to read. She would tell me which section of her book to read next.

Sometimes, instead of telling me what to read, Mother Paula would tell me there would be recreation at supper. This happened if it was someone's feastday. Then, I would read for only three or four minutes before Mother Paula tapped her bell. On those nights, I did not eat at half-table. When the bell rang, I would kiss the floor and go to my place to eat. Sister Eileen would not be in her usual place at my left. Since she served the chaplain in the priests' dining room, she always ate supper at half-table and then went up to the priests' serving room.

Occasionally, Mother Paula would tell me what to read at supper but then decide at the last minute to grant recreation. I would eat at half-table, expecting to read throughout supper, but Mother Paula would tap her bell, ending the reading. These were the nights I liked best. I was free to go upstairs. Since Wulfram was at table, there was no danger of running into her. I would have a precious half-hour to myself.

Before going up to the third floor, I would stop by the priests' serving room on the first floor to chat with Sister Eileen. I would sit at the table in the little kitchen and cross my legs. Eileen would laugh at me for being so bold.

After a few minutes with Eileen, I would go upstairs. The third floor would be nearly dark, the corridors illuminated only by dim bulbs in the high ceilings. I would go into the Novitiate and read a few entries from the wapiti encyclopedia, or I would go into the ironing room and iron my habit.

The ironing room was a bedroom that was not used as such. There were a few bedrooms used for other purposes. One was the food room where Wulfram stored the boxes of candy and other treats our parents sent. Sometimes, before recreation, Wulfram would go into the food room and get a box of chocolates. She would pass it around at recreation. Sometimes she would put a box of chocolates on a little table by the rotunda railing. She would pin a note to the string that hung from a light bulb above the table: "Only one." I disliked the various notes Wulfram pinned to the string, and I disliked being told how to eat or how much to eat, so I took none.

The ironing room was next to the food room. There were two irons and two ironing boards. We were supposed to wear one of our cotton habits for a week. During that week, we were to wash the other one by hand in the bathroom sink, hang it to dry on a hanger in our closet, and then iron it. Sometimes I washed my habits oftener than that. I disliked wearing one for more than two or three days. I enjoyed ironing. Wulfram never came into the ironing room. It was one of the few places on the third floor safe from Wulfram. Sometimes if Eileen and I were ironing at the same time, we would whisper about Wulfram and about the situation we were in. We talked about Wulfram's endless anger.

Wulfram berated the novices about everything, but the most dangerous duty was serving at table. Four novices served each meal. We went into the kitchen, where the kitchen sisters filled the bowls and platters from the pots and pans on the stove.

They handed us the food, which we placed on the serving cart. We wheeled the cart into the refectory and served the nuns from the cart. We poured the drinks after serving the food. We removed the empty bowls and platters from the tables and took them back to the kitchen. We passed the garbage pans and the dishpans at the end of the meal. It was not that difficult, but Wulfram made it the most stressful thing we did. Most mornings, the Hour was an hour of her yelling at us about serving.

I wrote down every word she said.

❖ ❖ ❖

March, 1961

It was Lent, and there was reading at table nearly every evening. I was still reading Mother Paula's history of the order at supper. The first Rosalines came to America from Bavaria in 1852 and settled in St. Louis. Some of them were worked to death by the priests they served. Although their German rule forbade it, they were required by the priests to sing at the parish High Mass and at the numerous evening devotions popular in 19th-century parishes. The nuns were required to teach boys, which Rosalines had never done in Bavaria. This, in spite of assurances by the priest who brought them to America that they would not be required to teach boys.

The nuns slept in basements and lived on cornbread and molasses, in spite of assurances made to their superiors in Bavaria that they would have "salubrious" breezes blowing around their "substantial" house and plenty of good food. The priest who brought the first Rosalines to America made many promises which he did not keep. He wanted the four thousand thalers that

King Ludwig granted each religious order that set up an establishment to help Bavarian immigrants in America. Mother Barbara von Gotthier, a baron's daughter, made a success of her American foundation, in spite of a priest who denounced her from the pulpit and tried to expel her from her order. She succumbed to tuberculosis, the killer of young nuns, just before the priest could turn her out of the convent she founded in St. Louis.

I looked at Mother Barbara's picture in Mother Paula's book. I looked at her beautiful face with its sweet expression. The picture was taken one day in St. Louis when Mother Barbara and Sister Anna, her constant companion, sought shelter from a thunderstorm while they were downtown. They ducked into a daguerreotype studio. The daguerreotypist, a Catholic whose daughter attended their select school, made portraits of them. Mother Barbara died soon after the picture was taken.

The nuns lived in the basement underneath the rectory where the pastor and his mother lived. The door from the basement to the kitchen was nailed shut, ostensibly to guard the reputations of all concerned, but actually to prevent the nuns from sneaking into the kitchen at night and taking the priest's food.

On the night I read Mother Paula's account of Mother Barbara's death, the nuns stopped eating and looked up as they listened. Mother Paula was watching me closely.

Mother Barbara von Gotthier died without Extreme Unction or Viaticum. The priest refused to administer the Last Sacraments to her, and he refused to allow the nuns to go for another priest. He said her condition was not serious, that she would live through the night.

Shortly before midnight, Mother Barbara died in Sister Anna's arms. Before she died, she asked Anna and the others to forgive her for her many failings. She asked them to take care of Miss Wilma, a postulant who would be entering the convent the next day. Sister Anna held her crucifix to Mother Barbara's lips for a last kiss. She collected Mother Barbara's last tears on a linen cloth. By morning, when the priest and his mother came downstairs to the damp cold basement, the nuns had washed Mother Barbara's body and prepared it for burial.

Some of the nuns in the refectory looked like they were about to cry. As they left the refectory after supper, Mother Paula came over to the reader's stand. "You read that very well, Sister Emmanuel," she said.

"Thank you, Mother," I said. I wanted to say, "You wrote it very well," but that would have been presumptuous.

I liked reading aloud. I was learning a new trick. I could look at a paragraph and instantly memorize it. Instead of glancing up from the page occasionally, I could recite several lines without looking down. Sometimes the younger professed nuns would look up at me and see me apparently reciting rather than reading. I would stare at them and keep reciting without looking down. Sometimes I could crack them up with that. There was one young professed nun, Sister Rose Anselm, whom I could make laugh nearly every time with this.

Wulfram did not like it that I was supper reader. At one point, she told Sister Carol and me to switch; Carol would read at supper, and I would read at breakfast. Carol read that night, and I read the next morning, but during the Hour that morning, Wulfram switched us back again. I knew Mother Paula told her to do that. I read at supper that evening.

St. Patrick's Day fell on a Friday. I went to Mother Paula's office as usual after dinner. I thought there might be recreation at supper that night, but Mother Paula said nothing about it. She simply told me to continue reading the chapter in her book that I had begun the night before. I ate at half-table and started to read at supper, but almost immediately Mother Paula tapped her bell, giving recreation. I kissed the floor and left the refectory.

I went up to the priests' serving room to see Sister Eileen. She had served Father Andrew, and he was eating his supper at the head of the ornately carved table in the priests' dining room. Eileen was feeling a little homesick, and while I sat at the little table in the serving room, she danced a jig for me. She held up her skirts and executed a few steps while humming softly. She poured a cup of tea for me and sat down at the little white table. The dumbwaiter was open, and Father Andrew's dessert, a piece of sheet cake with green icing was on the tray. Father Andrew never ate dessert, but the kitchen sisters sent it up every night anyway. Eileen would offer it to him, and he would refuse. Abstemious.

Eileen and I drank tea and talked about Wulfram. After a while, Eileen went into the dining room to clear the chaplain's dishes away and offer him the cake. He refused it, thanked her, and left the dining room. Eileen came back into the serving room and sent the dishes, the tea pot, and the uneaten cake back down to the kitchen in the dumbwaiter.

Sister Wulfram sometimes teased Sister Loretta, the second-year novice who cut hair, about the dumbwaiter. When Loretta was a postulant, she thought the little elevator in the priests' serving room was called the "dungolator".

Wulfram's feastday was the following Monday. The second-years told us to wrap our needlework, whether it was finished or not, as our gifts to Wulfram. This was the custom. Wulfram kept the finished pieces to give to Mother Paula on her feastday. Mother Paula would present them to benefactors. Wulfram gave back the unfinished pieces to the novices who were working on them. She expressed no words of gratitude for these gifts and no words of praise for the artistry and craftsmanship and hours of work that went into making them. Sister Loretta, the best embroiderer in the novitiate, gave Wulfram a large tablecloth, covered with red cross-stitching, a magnificent piece that she had worked on since entering the convent. Wulfram put it to one side without unfolding it.

On Palm Sunday, in the Sunday Hour, after making us sing "Just For Today" several times, Wulfram told us to weave the palms we had received at Mass into fancy shapes. She did not show us how to do this, but simply ordered us to do it. Two or three of the second-years knew how to weave palms, but they were not told to demonstrate. I tried to watch them and imitate their technique, but I was unable to catch on to it. Wulfram yelled at me and at the other novices who were unable to catch on. "Typical," she said to me, as she looked at my unsuccessful effort.

Wulfram did not weave her own palm, but cut it into many short pieces and twisted them into loops. She pinned those loops to a big heart-shaped pincushion someone had given her for her feastday. She pasted a picture of the Sacred Heart at the center of the loops of palm.

Sister Jean Edward, the sacristan, held up her hand. "Shouldn't that be in the sacristy, Sister?" she asked. Wulfram handed it to her. Jean Edward had it up on the sacristy wall by the time we walked through on our way down to dinner.

On Holy Thursday, the main meal was supper. Mother Paula served at table. She wore a starched white apron and starched white cuffs over her tightly pinned sleeves. She handed the platters and bowls to the nuns.

While Mother Paula and four novices served the feast, a professed nun read the account of the Last Supper from St. John's Gospel. We had chicken-fried steak and grape juice and lemon meringue pie.

The next day was Good Friday.

There was no breakfast. At dinner, eaten at eleven that day, there was vegetable soup and stewed fruit. We sat or knelt on the floor to eat the penitential meal, while a professed nun read the Passion. Some of the nuns went up to kneel before the crucifix and pray with their arms outstretched. Mother Paula did this.

At twelve, the liturgical celebration of the Passion began in chapel. We had practiced long and hard for this in music class. Sister Francine had entrusted my companions and me with the Agios o Theos. Between the Reproaches, sung by the community, each of us sang alone. Three of us got to sing twice. Agios o Theos; Sanctus Deus. Agios ischyros; Sanctus fortis. Agios athanatos, eleison imas; Sanctus immortalis, miserere nobis.

It was the first time I sang alone in chapel.

❖ ❖ ❖

April, 1961

There was an Easter Vigil, and afterwards we ate soup and drank hot chocolate in the girls' dining room. I sat with Sister Alexandra at the table where we always sat when we were day boarders. We didn't mention the hundreds of meals we had eaten at the day boarders' table by the glass doors. Alexandra and her companions were still perfect, even though they were second-years now. They wore pen and pencil holsters on their cinctures, and they studied secular subjects, but they were still as perfect as they had been as canonicals. They did not talk about worldly matters or reminisce about school days. I would have liked to talk to my old friend about Wulfram, but it was not possible.

Mass on Easter morning began with the Vidi Aquam. My companions and I chanted the Sequence: Victimae Paschali Laudes. Francine's soprano soared above the choir in the Regina Caeli. Resurrexit, sicut dixit. Alleluia.

The junior nuns had decorated the refectory for Easter. The tablecloths and the linen napkins were on the tables. The tin plates had been replaced with white china plates. Between every two places, there was a Paschal lamb cake, with white icing and coconut wool. Its eyes were raisins. It had a bow around its neck and a little banner.

The next day, Easter Monday, Wulfram announced that in keeping with the morning's gospel about the walk to Emmaus, the town "sixty furlongs" from Jerusalem, we would go out to Camp Rosaline for the day. Camp was sixty furlongs south of the motherhouse. We would not walk, as the two disciples of Jesus did, but we would go on the camp bus. Sister Jean Edward would drive. Wulfram would not be riding with us. She would ride out in the camp car with five junior nuns.

At camp, we got off the bus. We weren't sure what to do. Wulfram was standing by the pond with the five young black-veils. They were laughing and talking. We stood on the pavilion. With the exception of the office, the camp buildings were still locked.

We watched Wulfram and the five. This was the group that had made vows a month after I entered the convent. They had been Wulfram's first class of postulants. Wulfram was appointed novice mistress in 1956 by Mother Paula, the newly elected superior, and these five entered the convent a week later, just before the beginning of my sophomore year at the academy.

They were the first class to have a six month postulancy. Before Mother Paula took office, the postulancy lasted a year.

After a while, Wulfram looked over at us. She told us to eat our lunch.

The kitchen sisters had packed a picnic lunch for us, but the camp tables and chairs were locked in the bunkhouse. We ate the mystery meat sandwiches and drank the iced tea standing up.

Wulfram was still joking around with the five juniors. Two of them grabbed her by the arms and pulled her closer to the edge of the pond. They tried to push her in. She jerked away from them and ran up to the pavilion. She took one of the empty gallon jars the iced tea had been in. The five were chasing her, but she ducked away from them and ran back to the pond. She dipped the jar in the water and filled it. She ran over to one of the five and poured the water on her head. Before the junior could get the jar away from her, Wulfram dodged away and filled it again and drenched another one of the five. I had never seen her move so quickly before. For such a large woman, she was nimble. She ducked and dodged and kept filling the jar with water and throwing it on the juniors. One of the juniors finally got the jar away from Wulfram. She filled it with water and poured it on Wulfram's head. They were all drenched, then. Their veils and habits were dripping with water. They were doubled over with laughter.

The other novices and I watched them. We didn't laugh. We had not been invited to take part in the fun.

I felt that the whole thing was a show for our benefit, that Wulfram was saying to us, See, you will be my friends one day like these juniors are. One day I will laugh and have fun with you as I do with them.

I didn't believe it. I knew she would never be my friend. My friend Eileen was standing next to me. Wulfram treated Eileen abominably. She criticized her round Celtic handwriting. She criticized the way she held her knife and fork. One of the first candid conversations I had with Eileen was about that. In the Hour one morning, Wulfram criticized Eileen for eating with her fork in her left hand. She ordered her to hold her fork in her right hand. Later in the ironing room, I said to Eileen, "I guess Wulfram hasn't heard of the continental method."

Wulfram and the five juniors, still dripping, piled into the old camp car, a '49 Ford. The junior driving the car honked the horn and waved her hand at us as she sped down the dirt road, raising a cloud of dust.

The other novices and I stood around on the pavilion for a while. Then we hiked down to the railroad track. We crossed the track. We threw rocks in the Blue River. We went back to camp. The caretaker was still sitting in the office watching television. A Perry Mason rerun. We got on the bus and drove back to the convent in time for Vespers.

The next day we resumed our regular schedule.

I cleaned the ground floor every morning. I liked my job. No other novices worked on the ground floor. It was my domain.

I grew a few plants on the windowsills in the men's dining room. I read newspapers in the little triangular closet behind the men's bathroom. It was a safe place to read, because when I was in the men's bathroom, I propped the door open with the mop bucket, so no one would come in. If someone were to move the metal bucket to get through the door, which no one ever did, I would hear it in time to replace the newspaper on the stack.

One day, while I was mopping the northeast hall, swinging my mop back and forth, Wulfram came in the door with Sister Marsha. I had never seen them together before. Wulfram spoke to Marsha in a low voice. "Watch this," she said.

She didn't know I heard her. I didn't look at them. I was maintaining custody of the eyes.

As they got close to me, Wulfram said, "Notice the dirt in the corners, Sister Marsha? Notice the grime on the radiators? Notice the water slopped on the baseboards? This is what's known as Emmanuel labor. There's manual labor, and then there's Emmanuel labor. This is an example of Emmanuel labor."

I didn't say, "Thank you, Sister, may God reward you," because she wasn't talking to me. She was talking to Sister Marsha. Marsha said nothing. She didn't stand up for me. She kept silent, just as I had kept silent on my first morning in the convent when Wulfram criticized Alexandra unfairly. Wulfram made false charges, and no one stopped her.

At dinner every day, my companions and I continued to talk about Gregorian Chant. We also talked about mythology. In Sister Lucy's Scripture classes we learned about Ba'al worship and amphictionies and tophets. Wulfram glared at us from her place up the table.

Every day at four, I went down to the refectory to prepare the supper reading. I didn't actually practice. I didn't need to practice. I just sat on the reader's stand reading.

There were several books and magazines on the shelf in the reader's stand, books that had been started and never finished, or books that earlier readers had forgotten to return to Mother Paula. There was a dictionary, and there was the book of Regulations, the detailed directions Mother Aurelia had put in a looseleaf notebook to cover every aspect of a nun's daily life. How to go to the bathroom in a public place: have another woman go with you. How to ride in a car with a man: ride in the back seat, even if it's your father or your brother.

I read everything. I read the *Kansas City Times* and the *Kansas City Star* nearly every day. The papers were a few days or a few weeks old by the time they made their way downstairs, and the sections and the pages were out of order, but it didn't matter. I read everything. Wedding announcements. Obituaries. Comics. Want ads. Sports. Editorials. James J. Metcalf's poems.

In April, the new Office books arrived. *A Short Breviary.* The other canonicals and I had an extra music class each day with Sister Francine and Sister Lucy. The new Office was in English. It was not the same every day like the Little Office of the Blessed Virgin Mary, but it was still not like the real breviary. Praying the Office was horribly boring. I wondered how the Church reconciled the recitation of Offices with the words of Jesus: Do not multiply words like the Gentiles do.

My companions and I learned to lead the new Office, to introduce each psalm with an antiphon sung on a psalm tone, to keep the choir on the psalm tone throughout the psalm, to sing the lessons. It was easy, and we caught on quickly, and after a few evening rehearsals with the community, we were ready to begin.

❖ ❖ ❖

May, 1961

We began singing the new Office on Ascension Thursday.

That afternoon, Wulfram had us draw packets of seeds from a basket. She had decided that each of the eighteen novices would have a little garden to tend. That evening, at recreation, she took us out behind the laundry to the gardens. The two closest rows had not been planted yet. They were for us. Each of us got a patch three feet square. I planted the melon seeds I had drawn from the basket. Eileen's garden was next to mine.

Something else beside the Office changed in May. No longer would the laundry be done before dawn on Tuesdays. Now it would be done on Monday afternoons. No more getting up at four o'clock. We weren't told why. Wulfram explained nothing to us.

In music, Sister Francine was preparing us for the summer. She would be away studying Gregorian Chant at summer school, but my companions and I had made such strides in singing the Latin propers from the Liber, that she thought we could sing them throughout the summer without her. She assigned each of us a Sunday. We would each prepare our own Sunday's propers and teach them to the rest of the novices. At Mass, the novice whose week it was would not stand in front of the choir to direct, as Sister Francine did, but would lead from her place in chapel.

We ran through the summer propers looking for any particularly difficult passages. I was to be in charge of July 9th, the Seventh Sunday after Pentecost. Omnes gentes plaudite. Francine had me sing the Introit. She told me I sang it perfectly. She said she would think of me on that Sunday when she was singing it with her classmates at chant school. In the monastery chapel, the monks and the students would clap for real, she said, after that call for applause in the Introit.

❖ ❖ ❖

June, 1961

The day after Francine left for summer school, Wulfram appeared in the Novitiate during our music class. She told us to turn in our Libers. Stack them on her desk. We would not be using the Libers again until Sister Francine returned in September. We would sing the Sunday propers on psalm tones; no rehearsal required. Instead of using our music classes to prepare propers from the Liber, we would be doing something else this summer.

We found out what it was the next day. Sister Dominic, a nun I didn't know, came home to the motherhouse for the summer. She was a principal at one of the community's three-room grade schools in Kansas. There were several of those schools, outposts, where three nuns lived above the school or in a little house next to the school.

Wulfram brought Sister Dominic into the Novitiate. Sister Dominic would be our music teacher for the summer, Wulfram said. The State of Kansas was celebrating its centennial, and we were going to present a program for the community on August 15th. A Kansas Centennial Celebration. Sister Dominic would teach us the songs we would sing at the program.

Sister Dominic was fat and sloppy. She had no undersleeves on. The sleeves of her voluminous habit were pinned up high, revealing her plump arms. She wore black loafers instead of nun shoes. She had a guimpe on, but no collar. Her habit bloused out over her cincture like a medieval monk's. She was about thirty-five years old. Rubicund.

She looked us over.

Wulfram stood beside her, looking down at her with fondness.

"Kansas is a hundred years old," Sister Dominic began. "And our community owes a lot to Kansas."

Although Rosaline was in Missouri, many of the nuns and many academy students came from Kansas. Sister Dominic and Sister Wulfram both came from Kansas. Dominic mentioned that, not Wulfram.

Wulfram beamed at Dominic.

As Dominic passed out mimeographed sheets of song lyrics, Wulfram glided out the door.

I looked at the songs. "Dear Old Donegal." "Mick McGilligan's Ball." "Home on the Range." "The Bells of St. Mary's." "Die Lichtensteiner Polka." "Wagon Wheels." "Kansas."

Dominic said, "These songs honor the Irish immigrants who settled Kansas. Also the Germans."

She turned to me. She said, "I understand you're quite the German scholar, Sister Emmanuel."

"Just a beginner, Sister," I said.

"Don't hide your light under a bushel," she said. "False modesty has no place in religious life."

I wasn't sure what to say. Was that a correction? My modesty was not false.

Sister Dominic sat down at the piano and banged out "The Bells of St. Mary's." She played the song again and sang it in a loud, dramatic voice. At the end, she stood and faced us. "You will all learn all four parts, and then I'll divide you into voices."

We had no music, just lyrics. We were supposed to learn all parts without music. Sister Dominic played each part separately and sang it. We were to join in as we learned it.

My companions and I resisted.

We had become proficient in Gregorian Chant. Chant was our group's special mark. We had made it our symbol, far more than the water jars were. Chant was sustaining us. Now it had been taken from us for the entire summer, replaced with this.

The Kansas Centennial music was not worth learning, not worth spending time on, and it was an intrusion into our canonical year. The music was secular and it was embarrassing. "The Bells of St. Mary's" was a love song. "And so, my beloved, when red leaves are falling, the love bells shall ring out, ring out, for you and me."

"Again! LOUDER!" Sister Dominic shouted.

My companions and I were slow to respond. Dominic played the song again and again. Crashing octaves. Pealing bells. Lots of pedal.

My companions and I were unable to remember the melody, unable to remember the harmony, unable to provide the volume. Dominic was turning redder. She took off her guimpe and fanned herself with it. She said, "Canonicals, your reputation for vocal prowess seems to have been exaggerated."

Alexandra and Loretta and Jean Edward and the other second-years were trying to carry the thing along, but they couldn't do it without us. Finally, Dominic told us to sit down. She stood before us with her thumbs looped in her cincture like a cowboy. She said, "This was not an auspicious beginning, but don't worry, you'll know the material inside out by August fifteenth. The other songs are easier. I started with the hardest one, the most important one. Any questions?"

Alexandra raised her hand. Dominic called on her. Alexandra, in her sweetest voice said, "If I may ask, Sister, how did you select the songs?"

"Home on the Range" was the official Kansas Song, Dominic said. And "Kansas" was another good song about Kansas. She sang part of it. "I love the land of the cottonwood, where sunflowers grow tall. Where the mate of the meadowlark echoes his plaintive call."

"Wagon Wheels" represented the people who left from this very spot to make their way down the Santa Fe Trail. "Die Lichtensteiner Polka" was to honor the German immigrants who settled in Kansas. Many of their daughters came to boarding school at Rosaline, and many entered the order. We owe a lot to Kansas.

"The Bells of St. Mary's" was to honor St. Mary's College in St. Mary's, Kansas, the Jesuit school Mother Juliet's brother, Tom Sly, attended back in the 1880s. Father Finn, the famous author of boys' books, was his teacher. Gutzon Borglum, sculptor of Mount Rushmore, was his classmate. Tom Sly bailed the nuns out of trouble more than once in the early days. "Does that answer your question?" Dominic asked Alexandra.

"Yes, Sister. Thank you," Alexandra said.

"Sister Emmanuel?" Dominic said, looking at me.

"Yes, Sister?"

"I want you to translate Die Lichtensteiner Polka for me. We'll start working on it tomorrow, and I want to know what the words mean. Mein Deutsch is kaput."

"Thank you, Sister, may God reward you." I had already looked at the lyrics, and there were words I didn't know.

Dominic sat down at the piano and began playing "The Bells of St. Mary's" again in her barrelhouse style. "Let's try it again. LOUD."

It was never loud enough for Sister Dominic. It never would be. I was singing as softly as I could. Next to me, Sister Eileen was not making a sound. Our other companions were barely singing.

When the bell rang for dinner, Dominic slouched out of the Novitiate, swinging her arms. Those of us serving dinner had missed half-table. We hurried down to the kitchen, where the kitchen sisters were annoyed with us for being late.

That evening at the beginning of recreation, Wulfram told me to make sure I had the translation of "Die Lichtensteiner Polka" done by morning.

"Thank you, Sister, may God reward you," I said. I wasn't sure what to do. My team was taking the field for softball. I ran out to right field.

Instead of taking her usual seat on the glider, Wulfram left the Lilac Field and walked around to the front of the motherhouse. The professed nuns sat on lawn chairs lined up on either side of the front walk on summer evenings. Some walked around the campus.

When my team was at bat, I stood by the Sacred Heart shrine with Eileen, waiting for my turn. She indicated with her eyes that I should look around. Walking toward the Farmhouse, arm in arm, were Wulfram and Dominic.

Dominic was short, and Wulfram was tall and straight, but in order to link arms with Dominic, she was bending down. Dominic still had no collar on and no undersleeves. Wulfram always wore every bit of her habit, even on hot evenings like this one. Dominic had loafers on. Wulfram had big nun shoes on her big feet. Dominic was looking up at Wulfram, talking in her loud voice. Wulfram was gazing down at Dominic with delight, hanging on to her words and her arm. Eileen and I watched them for the rest of recreation. They circled each of the academy buildings and then made their way down to the Grotto.

That night, after night prayer, I went into the Novitiate. The other novices were studying at the tables. They had their pajamas and summer robes on. Night caps. The second-years had their college texts open and their spiral notebooks. Nobody looked at me or spoke. It was a time of deep silence. My companions were studying their Catechisms of the Vows. Wulfram would call on us in the morning in the Hour to recite answers to questions about the vow of poverty. Use and usufruct. I wouldn't be prepared. I was never prepared. I could memorize a page of supper reading at a glance, but I was unable to memorize the answers in the Catechism of the Vows.

I went back to the bookshelf that held the few non-theology books. I knew there was no German dictionary there. There was no dictionary of any kind in the Novitiate. But I would make sure. The only reference book was the wapiti encyclopedia. I had read quite a bit of it. I had learned a lot about elk.

I didn't know what Rabatz meant or schaut or Boten. I couldn't remember if there was a German dictionary in the academy library or not. I knew a few of the oldest nuns spoke German. A lot of people in St. Albert's parish spoke German. When I was a child, there were still confessions in German for those who wanted.

I sat down and began to translate. The obvious part was easy: Yes, that is the Lichtensteiner polka, my treasure, polka, my treasure, polka, my treasure. But the less obvious parts were impossible without the three unknown words. I left them out.

In the morning, at the Hour, I handed the paper to Wulfram. She looked at it and started yelling at me. Lazy. This was a perfect example of my laziness. Typical. Emmanuel labor.

Then she started yelling at all the novices. Sister Dominic was disgusted with all of us, Wulfram said. Disgusted.

In music class, Dominic looked at me with disgust. "I understand you were too busy to do what I asked."

There was nothing I could say, so I said nothing.

Dominic had us make our first attempt at the four-part harmony to "The Bells of St. Mary's." It was gruesome. My companions and I had not spoken of it, but we were united in our resistance.

Sister Carol, my oldest companion, had majored in music, but she was unable to sing the song. Sister Teresa, my companion who excelled at harmony, was unable to sing the song. Sister Dominic made her a soprano. Dominic decided I was a second soprano, although I had sung soprano since first grade. Veni Domine Jesu.

After a few days of working on the horrible songs in the Novitiate, we began practicing in the academy auditorium. Wulfram and Dominic had decided the centennial program would be presented from the stage. There were no academy girls around, so every morning, for two hours, we stood on the risers on the stage singing the songs. There was no air-conditioning, and the heavy plush curtains kept any air from moving. We sweated so much that our habits were streaked with salt, and water condensed on the inside of our celluloid guimpes and headbands.

Wulfram did not attend the practices. Dominic made us sing the songs over and over. "Wagon Wheels." "Mick McGilligan's Ball." Three- and four-part harmony.

Dominic yelled at us. She played the piano and yelled at us to sing louder. She said teaching us music was like pulling teeth. She made us clop our hands on our thighs during "Wagon Wheels" to make horse sounds. Or mule sounds. Or ox sounds. She made us sing the Irish songs with a brogue. She made us shout the "Ja" at the beginning of the polka.

I never finished translating the lyrics. I never asked to go to the academy library to look in a German dictionary.

Every night at recreation, while we played softball on the Lilac Field or worked in our little gardens, Wulfram and Dominic walked around the campus, arm in arm. Eileen and I talked about them while we tilled the soil.

Wulfram's diatribes about particular friendship had rung hollow from the start, and now she was parading her crush on Dominic up and down the South Drive, around the motherhouse, around the academy buildings, around the gardens, in front of the community, and in front of the novitiate. I had never seen two nuns walk arm in arm before. I was scandalized. I wondered why Mother Paula, who must have seen them every night from her chair on the front sidewalk, didn't tell them to stop acting like they were going steady.

❖ ❖ ❖

July, 1961

The practice sessions lengthened. Wulfram began attending. She screamed at us. My companions and I were getting worse every day. We were unable to learn the harmony, unable to learn the patter, unable to provide the volume, unable to do the Irish and German accents. Dominic and Wulfram made us stand on the risers on the hot stage for two hours every morning and for another two hours in the afternoon. We were taking no classes. The entire summer of our canonical year was devoted to singing "Home On The Range" and "Mick McGilligan's Ball."

My youngest companion left the convent. She had entered at fifteen, expecting something very different. She had brought her art supplies to the convent, but except for the day she drew the water jars, our group's symbol, she had never been allowed to use them. She sometimes cried when Wulfram screamed at us.

One afternoon, on the risers, as we sweated, she fainted and fell to the floor.

The next morning, she was not at morning prayer or Mass or breakfast. By the time the Hour began, we had guessed that she had gone, but Wulfram said nothing. It was as if Mary Kay had never existed. Wulfram spent the Hour lecturing us once again about our bad singing.

I wrote down every word she said.

On the 23rd, my companions and I had the only visiting day allowed in the canonical year. It was visiting day for all the novices, so there were picnics at various points on the campus. The Fitzpatricks and the Sheas occupied the courtyard behind the Farmhouse. Sister David and Sister Jean Edward were surrounded by relatives of all ages. I had hoped Eileen would be allowed to eat with my parents and me, but Wulfram told her to eat with the Fitzpatricks, as usual. Wulfram ate with the Fitzpatricks, as well.

My picnic was on the Lilac Field. My parents and a few aunts and uncles and cousins came.

After we finished eating, I walked around the campus with my parents. They wanted to know what my job was, so I took them inside to the ground floor and showed them the areas I cleaned. I showed them the little janitor's closet behind the men's bathroom and the mop bucket I used. I showed them the gleaming tables in the linen room and in the men's dining room that I had waxed and buffed with the floor polisher.

We went back outside, and I showed my parents my little melon patch. The seeds had sprouted, and I had erected a frame for them to climb with some stakes I found in the garden shed. The vines had grown and covered the stakes, and small round melons had followed the yellow blossoms. My dad plugged the melons with his pocket knife and picked the ripe ones. We went back to the picnic table to eat them. They were delicious. My cousins and I started reminiscing about visits to our grandparents in Chetopa, Kansas. We talked about their garden. The melon patch. The Rhode Island Reds. The Neosho River.

A few days after visiting day, eight new postulants entered the convent. The other novices and I stood in a row in the Novitiate. The line of new postulants came in. I knew a couple of them from camp the previous summer, where they had been counselors with me. "I humbly beg your sisterly love and holy prayers," they said. "They're yours, Sister," I said.

The next day, Wulfram told me to come into a storeroom with her. It was the room next to the ironing room. I had never been inside this room before. The door was always closed. Now I saw that there were garment bags hanging on racks. This was where the serge habits were kept. There were boxes of various sizes stacked on the floor and on a table.

In the middle of the floor was a big mop bucket on casters. Shiny. New. There was a pair of green rubber gloves in the wringer of the bucket. And there was a floor mop with an enormous head made of long strips of chamois instead of string.

"Your father brought this yesterday," Wulfram said.

She didn't give me any more information, but I understood that my dad had been dismayed to see the large expanse of floor I had to mop with primitive equipment. He had gone to the janitor supply company where he bought stuff for the movie theaters. He bought this mop and bucket for me. He brought it to the convent, thinking I would be allowed to use it. Instead, Wulfram would keep it here in the storeroom, and I would continue to use the old equipment.

"You will write a thank you note," she said.

That afternoon, we practiced for three hours on the stage. The new postulants joined us for the first time. They caught on quickly to the easy songs. They must have wondered why the novices behind them on the risers were such poor singers.

❖ ❖ ❖

August, 1961

The motherhouse began to fill up as the nuns came home from summer school. There were not enough rooms on the second floor for all the professed nuns, so some slept in the academy, and some slept in the unused rooms in the northwest corridor on the third floor, the novitiate floor. Valentine was one of these. They used the same bathroom that the novices used. At night, I would see Valentine washing her underwear in a sink and hanging it on the clothes rack. She didn't wear a nightcap, and her straggly brown hair stuck out in every direction. She never looked at me.

The first nine days of August were the last days of rehearsal before the performance scheduled for August fifteenth. Dominic and Wulfram were in a frenzy. Even though the new postulants were good singers and were trying their best, the songs were dead. Dominic and Wulfram screamed at us, and we stood on the risers, sweating.

Retreat began on the tenth. The retreat master, an Albertine, preached about Our Lady of Guadalupe at every conference. It was difficult to listen to his literal interpretation of the story of Juan Diego and his visions.

One evening at supper, I looked up from the reading and saw Valentine looking at me from her place at table. I stared at her while reciting the next several lines. She gave me a sarcastic grin.

On the Feast of the Assumption, there was recreation at breakfast, but after breakfast, instead of inviting the professed nuns to go upstairs to the Novitiate, Mother Paula said there would be a program in the auditorium at eleven, followed by a picnic lunch outside on the Lilac Field.

We practiced from 9 until 10:30. The windows in the practice rooms that surrounded the auditorium were open, and the stage door behind us was open, but there was no air. Dominic and Wulfram screamed at us, and we sweated.

Shortly before eleven, the professed nuns began to enter the auditorium. Most of them brought fans with them, palm leaf fans or funeral home fans.

We stood on the risers and sang the songs to Dominic's loud piano accompaniment. We sang all the verses to all the songs. The nuns fanned themselves and clapped politely between the songs. At the end, they clapped and then hurried out of the auditorium. Wulfram and Dominic followed.

We climbed down from the risers. It was finally over. The postulants looked confused. The second-years looked exhausted. We went out to the Lilac Field. A few of the junior sisters were cooking hamburgers and hot dogs on the grills. The other professed nuns were lined up at a couple of tables getting their food. As they got their food, they dispersed to various benches, chairs, and steps to eat. They did not speak to the novices and postulants. It was one of the two days of the year when black-veils and white-veils could talk, but the setting was new, and the two groups ate their picnic lunches apart.

When everyone was finished eating, a few professed nuns ventured over to where the new postulants sat. A few came over to the Sacred Heart shrine where my companions and I were sitting.

Valentine sat down beside me on the steps to the shrine. She looked at me and shook her head. "That was pitiful," she said, nodding in the direction of the auditorium. "What was that all about?"

I couldn't explain. "When are you going back to St. Louis?" I asked.

"Tomorrow."

After a few minutes, the professed nuns went inside. Wulfram told us to clean up the picnic area and then go upstairs. The professed did not come up to the Novitiate. We would not get another chance to talk to them until Christmas.

They began leaving the next day, going back to college, back to the missions.

❖ ❖ ❖

September, 1961

The novitiate went to camp. As before, Wulfram kept the novices and postulants apart. We cleaned the camp and swam and fished in the pond. A few of my companions and I climbed up in the hayloft of the barn and sat in the big window, looking out over the countryside. Sister David and Sister Rita Ann and I, the three who had gone to St. Albert's grade school, sang some of the songs from our school operettas for Sister Eileen and Sister Teresa. "Oh, we're cold in our bones; we sleep upon stones." That was the urchins' chorus from "Scrooge's Christmas".

We returned to the motherhouse on Labor Day, and the next day, a new semester began. My companions and I took another scripture course from Sister Lucy and another theology course from Father Andrew. We had music with Sister Francine and the Hour with Wulfram every day.

There was no system to Wulfram's instruction. There was no curriculum. We memorized answers from the Catechism of the Vows, and she expounded on the material, but she made up her lectures as she went along. I wrote down every word she said. I filled a spiral notebook nearly every month with Hour notes. The importance of being "virile women" was a topic she returned to often.

In September, Wulfram gave some of the novices new cleaning duties, but I was reassigned to the ground floor.

❖ ❖ ❖

October, 1961

We were allowed to write home once a month. In my October letter, I wanted to tell my dad not to bring cider on my birthday, but I didn't know how to say it. Wulfram read all incoming and all outgoing mail. I said nothing.

In October, Wulfram had us clean up the flower beds, as we had done the previous year. She kept the postulants with her in the Four-o'-Clock bed and sent the second-years to the grotto. She dispatched my companions and me to various trouble spots. One Saturday afternoon, she told us to go clear out the poison ivy that was growing up a big tree in the northwest corner of the campus.

For an hour we stood around the tree and discussed how best to go about the task. We had no gloves, and we had no tools. We did not want to go back to Wulfram for further instructions. Finally, Sister Rita Ann waded in and pulled up the poison ivy by the roots. She pulled it down from the tree. "Stay back," she said to the rest of us. "Do not come near me." She did it all. She piled the poison ivy by the rock wall for the workmen to dispose of. "Don't touch me," she said to the rest of us.

The next morning she was swollen and red, unable to get dressed. She reappeared two days later, still swollen, still suffering. Her face was red and bulging against her white coif. Her eyes were nearly shut. After a week, the swelling started to go down. She left the convent on my birthday.

I missed her. Rita had sat at my right at table, and we had had many good discussions. We talked about St. Albert's grade school. The Laurel and Hardy movies on Thursday afternoons. The great operettas. Going to Zesto for ice cream. Parkview Drugstore. Dyed baby chicks for sale at Easter. Hot dogs at the counter. Carlson's Bakery. Cinnamon rolls after First Friday Mass. Paper drives. School picnics at Fairyland Park. Pagan baby bazaars. The Hallowe'en parties. Girl Scouts. Christmas caroling.

Now that Rita was gone, Sister Teresa moved over to our side of the table and sat at my right. Eileen was still at my left. We talked about Gregorian Chant. Teresa was even more of a chant fanatic than Rita. We did not talk about the songs of the summer.

In music class, Sister Francine did not mention the Kansas Centennial celebration to us. She had not seen our performance, but she must have heard about it. Her chant workshops had kept her on the east coast until Labor Day. When she returned, we got our Libers back and resumed chanting the propers on Sundays.

In October, Wulfram switched table readers twice, putting me at breakfast and Carol at supper, but we were switched back after a day or two. I knew Mother Paula told Wulfram to do that. Every day I went down to the refectory to prepare the reading. I sat at the reader's stand and read magazines and newspapers and books. Sometimes I ate an orange I had left at my place at breakfast.

On my way up to the chapel for meditation after practicing the reading, I passed through the sacristy. Here, Sister Jean Edward would usually be ironing. The altar linens did not go to the laundry, but were washed and ironed by the sacristan. Jean Edward would have her guimpe off and her sleeves pinned up. She would have an apron on. On her feet, she wore grey suede loafers she had brought from home. I decided to tell my parents on visiting day to bring my grey suede loafers. I would wear them to clean the ground floor.

I would linger for a minute or two and exchange a few words with Jean Edward. It was pleasant to be with someone from the neighborhood, someone who knew the same people I knew. Jean Edward and Rita had been friends at Albertine High School. I knew Jean Edward knew that it was Wulfram's fault that Rita left the convent, but we didn't discuss it. I didn't think Jean Edward would report me to Wulfram if I talked about something forbidden, but I wouldn't put her in the position of making the decision.

I didn't resent Jean Edward for being Wulfram's favorite. If anything, I admired her ability to handle a difficult situation. She spit-shined Wulfram's shoes and cincture every night. Her parents brought treats to Wulfram. The novice mistress thought Jean Edward was the perfect novice, but I knew she hadn't lost her sense of humor.

Once, as I walked through the sacristy, I saw Jean Edward standing in the little bathroom. She had one grey suede loafer on the flusher, and she was plunging the toilet. "I'm posing for a vocation poster," she said.

She was three months from profession. I would hate to see her go. Also Alexandra. I was still fifteen months from profession. Would I make it? Two of my classmates were gone already. We had not been renamed the Seven Sacraments or anything. In fact, Wulfram had not mentioned the Nine Choirs of Angels since the first day.

I don't know if my parents brought cider to the convent on my birthday. If they did, I wasn't told. The cider served in the refectory on Hallowe'en tasted very much like the Unity Farm cider my dad and I liked, and it was cold and fresh.

There was no dressing up for Hallowe'en that year.

❖ ❖ ❖

November, 1961

There was a brief respite from the constant fear. Wulfram went on a home visit and was gone for a week. Every five years, Rosalines were allowed to spend a week at home with their parents.

In November, my days went like this: 5:30, rise; 6:00, morning prayers, Lauds, Prime, and Tierce; 6:30, meditation; 7:00, Mass; 7:30, serve breakfast; 7:50, eat at half-table; 8:00, clean ground floor; 9:00, the Hour with Sister Wulfram; 10:00, music with Sister Francine; 11:00, study period; 12:00, midday prayers, Sext and None; 12:07, dinner; 12:50, call on Mother Paula; 1:00, Sacred Scripture with Sister Lucy; 2:00, Theology with Father Andrew; 3:00, study period; 4:00, practice table reading; 4:30, meditation; 5:00, Vespers; 5:30, eat at half-table; 6:00, read at supper; 7:00, recreation; 8:00, night prayers, Compline, Matins; 8:30, prepare for bed, study in Novitiate; 10:00, retire.

❖ ❖ ❖

December, 1961

My feastday was December 23rd, the day the Church sings the last O Antiphon at Vespers: O Emmanuel.

I spent the morning auguring the sink in the men's bathroom, trying to unclog it.

Mother Paula was away from her office all day. The assistant superior did not tap the bell to end the reading at supper, so there was no recreation at table on my first feastday in the convent.

At recreation in the Novitiate, there were no treats. It was Advent.

The second-years were not allowed to wear their serge habits to Midnight Mass.

The newest juniors, Valentine's class, did not come home to the motherhouse for Christmas. It was too expensive. They stayed at the juniorate in St. Louis.

On Christmas, the professed nuns came upstairs to the Novitiate. I talked to a few of them. A couple of them teased me about the way I read at table. "You make up half the stuff," one said. She said I was always looking at her and not at the page. The other one, who was from a farm, made fun of the way I had pronounced "Holstein" while reading a newspaper article about the American Royal.

When I made a mistake in the reading, Mother Paula would come over to the reader's stand after supper and correct me. Once, in her book, the word "interloper" appeared. I pronounced it, IN-ter-loper. She came over afterwards and said it should be, in-TER-luh-per. She said I was to read that paragraph again the following night with the correct pronunciation. I did so.

Chapter 3
Second Year Novice

January, 1962

Reception and Profession took place on January 27th. Alexandra and Loretta and Jean Edward and their companions made vows. The postulants who had entered in July received the habit.

The next day, Sunday, was a second day of grace for the newly professed and the new novices. The following day, Monday, the newly professed left for Marillac College in St. Louis, and the new canonicals attended the Hour for the first time.

My companions and I expected to get our pen and pencil holders on that day, our first day as second-year novices. The pen and pencil holder, worn on the cincture, was a mark of a teacher or a college student, one who studied secular as well as religious subjects. We had no pockets in our habits. As postulants and as canonicals, we carried our pens and pencils to class in our hands, but as second-years we would wear them at our sides in black leather holsters.

When we went into the Novitiate for the Hour, the pen and pencil holders were not on Wulfram's desk. The previous year, she had told the new second-years to come to her desk to get the holders. They had snapped them onto their cinctures in front of us.

Wulfram began the Hour with a long lecture on serving at table, and how poorly we did it. She moved from serving to silence, and how poorly we observed it. She moved from silence to dissipation, and how dissipated we were.

Now there were seventeen novices and no postulants in the novitiate. Wulfram assigned jobs. I would still be supper reader, and I would still clean the ground floor. The important job of sacristan went to a canonical. My class had been skipped over. No member of our class was worthy of being given charge of the sacristy.

There were no altar boys at our Masses, so the sacristan, kneeling behind the railing between the side chapel and the sanctuary, made the Latin responses. She also lit the candles before Mass and rang the bells at the Elevation and the Consecration. By denying us the chance to perform these duties, Wulfram was saying that we were not holy enough to serve at the altar. Since some or all of us would be required to teach the boys in our grade school classrooms to serve Mass and the girls to lay out vestments, Wulfram was denying us the chance to learn how to perform these duties.

Eileen would still serve the chaplain's supper and would still dust and vacuum Mother Paula's office in the morning.

We started our classes that day. Sister David, who hadn't graduated from high school, would be taking classes at the academy. The rest of us second-years would be taking a literature class from Mother Paula, sacred scripture from Sister Lucy, theology from Father Andrew, music from Sister Francine, and mathematics from Sister Gabriel.

Mother Paula walked into the Novitiate at ten o'clock with an armload of books. We stood to greet her and to take the books from her. They were collections of short stories. Mother Paula told us that in this class, we would focus on the short story. We would analyze the literary form. We would read short stories, and we would each write one.

That night, I sat in my bed reading short stories under the dim light of the bulb in the high ceiling. The first fiction I had read since entering the convent. Fanny Hurst. Booth Tarkington. Mark Twain. Edna Ferber.

❖ ❖ ❖

February, 1962

Visiting day was the first Sunday of February. My companions and I ate in the girls' dining room with our visitors. My parents brought cheeseburgers and French fries and Frostys from Winstead's and fried chicken from Stroud's. Sister Wulfram and Sister Eileen ate with the Fitzpatricks.

My mother asked me where my pen and pencil holder was. Our parents had been asked to give us black pen and pencil sets for Christmas, along with toiletries. I had mentioned to my mother in July that I would get a pen and pencil holder to wear on my cincture in January. Now I had to say we hadn't gotten them yet. My parents didn't ask me about the mop and the mop bucket.

I asked my mother to bring my grey suede loafers in April.

❖ ❖ ❖

March, 1962

Wulfram started imposing new and stricter rules on us. She told us we were no longer to go to the meat block for snacks. The kitchen sisters put bread and jam and sometimes fruit or leftover desserts on the old chopping block that stood in a corner of the kitchen. We often went down there for a snack and a cup of coffee if we had a few minutes between classes. We were no longer allowed to do that.

My companions and I were enjoying our English class with Mother Paula. We devoured the books of short stories. At dinner, we talked about the stories we were writing and the stories we were reading.

As always, Wulfram seemed to disapprove of our enthusiasm. One morning in the Hour she said, "You will write term papers. Each of you will write a term paper on one of the three vows." She divided us into three groups. Five or six to a vow. I was in the poverty group. In addition to the short story I was writing, I now had to write a term paper on the vow of poverty. I thought it would be easy enough, given all the books on theology and religious life in the Novitiate, but Wulfram did not dispense us from the rule against taking a book from a shelf without her permission. We had to write our term papers without references. We were allowed to use the Catechism of the Vows as our only source. It seemed that Wulfram wanted to distract us from our short stories. It seemed that she was jealous. It seemed that she did not know what a term paper was.

At eleven, when Mother Paula's class was supposed to be over, Wulfram would stand in the hall outside the Novitiate and tap her bell. If Mother Paula didn't leave immediately, Wulfram would tap the bell again. I didn't understand how she could be so rude to the superior, or why the superior didn't reprimand her for it.

❖ ❖ ❖

April, 1962

In April, Wulfram gave us our pen and pencil holders. I put mine in my drawer and never used it.

On Good Friday, my companions and I sang the Lamentations of Jeremiah the Prophet in chapel.

Wulfram made another new rule in April. No talking at half-table. Ordinarily, the novices who ate at half-table observed silence only when silence was observed at the main meal. Breakfast was always silent except on important feast days. There was recreation every day at dinner, so at half-table before dinner, there was recreation as well. And if there was to be recreation at supper, there would be recreation at half-table before supper as well. No more. Now the old portress, Sister Columba, and the servers ate in silence.

Wulfram rearranged the serving schedule so that my companions and I served dinner and supper. That kept us from the main table and a chance to talk. Eileen and I served dinner every day with two or three other second-years, depending on the number of sisters eating in the refectory. With four or five of us serving, and another one serving the chaplain, there would be only one or two of us at table, not enough to have an animated discussion of Gregorian Chant or of Joseph Hergesheimer, John Galsworthy, and the other short story writers.

There was no Emmaus trip to camp on Easter Monday. On the Sunday following Easter, our parents came to visit. My mother brought me my grey suede loafers. I wore them as I cleaned the ground floor with the old equipment.

❖ ❖ ❖

May, 1962

In May, Wulfram made another new rule. We were not to begin recreation in the evening until she arrived in the Novitiate. Previously, we went to the Novitiate after supper and started talking immediately. Those who had no duties in the refectory after supper might arrive as early as 6:45. Everyone was required to be at recreation by 7:00. Wulfram would sometimes come in before seven, sometimes a little bit after. Sometimes she didn't come to recreation. On Fridays, for instance, she went to the chiropractor, and we had recreation without her. Occasionally she went down to recreation with the other professed nuns in the community room on the second floor. Regardless of where Wulfram was, we talked to each other during recreation. But now, under the new rule, we were to keep silence until she came into the room.

She stopped coming into the room.

The novice mistress no longer attended evening recreation in the Novitiate.

We sat in silence for an hour every evening, sewing. Wulfram's rocker sat empty. She sat at her desk in her office.

We turned in our short stories to Mother Paula at the end of May. She graded them generously and handed them back at the next class.

We turned in our term papers to Sister Wulfram. We didn't get them back.

❖ ❖ ❖

June, 1962

Wulfram's Hour began to get longer. It lengthened to two hours, then to two-and-a-half hours. Every morning from nine until eleven thirty, the novice mistress berated us. By the end of June, the Hour lasted three hours, from nine until the dinner bell rang at noon.

My companions and I who served dinner no longer had time to eat at half-table. We barely had time to load the cart in the kitchen before the community came down to the refectory. The kitchen sisters were furious with us. The old portress, Sister Columba, ate by herself at half-table. When we were finished serving dinner, we would fill plates from the cold leftovers on the platters and in the bowls. We would eat a few bites standing in the kitchen. After a few minutes, we had to take in the dishpans.

There was no longer a minute of the day when we were allowed to talk. All talk was illegal now.

Eileen and I whispered in the ironing room. We whispered in the priests' serving room. The tension and the fear increased every day.

Wulfram stopped going to dinner and supper. She spent most afternoons and evenings sitting at her desk in her office. She would send a novice down to the kitchen to fix a tray for her. Sometimes she sent a novice down to the priests' serving room to cook something for her. I sometimes made pancakes for her on the old stove in the priests' serving room.

She did not give us seeds to plant in the garden patches we had tended the previous summer. I had saved seeds from one of my melons, but our little plots had reverted to the main flower garden.

We did not go outside to play softball after supper. We sat in the Novitiate in silence. Wulfram sat in her office. She did not come to our recreation, and she did not go down to sit with the community on the sidewalk in front of the motherhouse.

Sister Francine was away at summer school. She had not told us to prepare the Sunday propers on our own. We sang the propers on a psalm tone. Sister Dominic did not appear.

❖ ❖ ❖

July, 1962

My companions and I had visiting day in July. Eileen ate with the Fitzpatricks. Wulfram didn't come downstairs. The canonicals had their one visiting day of the year.

Twelve new postulants entered the convent at the end of July. Wulfram made it clear to the novices in the three-hour Hour that morning that we were not to talk to them.

For a few nights after they entered, we had recreation. We played softball on the Lilac Field, as if everything was normal, but when the new postulants would try to talk to us, we didn't answer.

My companion, Sister David Fitzpatrick, had heard from her mother that a Negro girl was going to enter. That didn't happen, but one of the girls in the new class was Mexican, the first Mexican postulant to enter the Rosalines. Girls from Mexico and Central America had attended the academy from its earliest days. They came up the Trail from Santa Fe. Their brothers would be dropped off at the Jesuits' boarding schools at Las Vegas, New Mexico, and St. Mary's, Kansas, and the girls would be brought to Rosaline Academy in Kansas City. But before Miss Gracia, no Mexican girl had entered the convent.

❖ ❖ ❖

August, 1962

After a few evenings of softball, we stopped going outside. Again, we stayed inside for recreation. For an hour every evening, we sat in the Novitiate, sewing in silence. The twelve new postulants sat with their new sewing boxes on their laps. Wulfram had not given them any fancywork to do, and their clothes did not yet need mending. They looked at us with anxiety on their faces.

Because it was August, and so many nuns were home, more table servers were required. My companions and I now served two or three meals a day. I served breakfast and dinner and read at supper. Eileen served breakfast and dinner and served the chaplain at supper. Carol read at breakfast and served dinner and supper. Teresa served breakfast and supper and served the chaplain at dinner. Susan served dinner and supper and served the chaplain at breakfast. David and Helen Marie served all three meals.

Wulfram yelled at us for three hours every morning, and I wrote down every word she said. We should strive to be virile women. We should battle dissipation. We should avoid particular friendships. Sometimes Wulfram directed her rage at one novice in particular instead of at all the novices in general. I was often the one. Sometimes she yelled at me in the Sunday Hour, as well, the one the postulants attended with us.

The new postulants started leaving immediately. The first one left after a week in the convent. Another left during retreat.

The retreat master that year was collecting valuables for the Albertine mission in Brazil. He talked about how nuns vowed poverty but were not really poor. Each one of us had some secret thing she was attached to, he said, something she clung to in spite of the vow of poverty. Give it up, he demanded. He put a box at the back of the chapel and told us to turn in our secret treasures. No one would know. I put my pearl rosary in the box. I was unable to detach myself from the blue enameled St. Benedict's medal I wore on my side rosary. The other medal, that we all wore on our side rosaries, had St. Charlemagne on one side and St. Rosalia on the other. I felt I should keep that, since it had come from the community and not from the outside.

Nearly all the professed nuns came home to the motherhouse for retreat. Valentine and her group and Alexandra and her group were home from St. Louis.

On the morning of August fifteenth, the Feast of Assumption, Mother Paula rang the bell for recreation at breakfast. I was serving. I poured coffee for Valentine and all the juniors. They looked at me and smiled. Later, I thought, we would be able to talk.

But after breakfast, Mother Paula made an announcement. Instead of the professed nuns going up to the Novitiate for recreation with the novices and postulants, everyone would be going to camp for the day. Two buses were waiting outside. The oldest sisters would be driven out in the convent cars.

Upstairs, Wulfram told me that I would not be going to camp that day. Because of my attitude and my behavior, I was to remain behind for the day.

I watched from a window in the Novitiate as the busloads of postulants, novices, juniors, and community nuns rolled down the South Drive. Several cars followed. Mother Paula went. Wulfram went. I didn't see the kitchen sisters get on the buses or into the cars. It seemed as if everyone else was gone.

I would not get to talk to Valentine.

I would not get to talk to anyone.

On the other hand, I had an entire day to myself for the first time in over two years. I went to the bookshelf where the forbidden books were kept. I had never read *The Cardinal*. I had considered it beneath me. But now I pulled it off the shelf. A fat novel. A feast.

I went downstairs to the kitchen. No one was around. Maybe the kitchen sisters had gone to camp after all, and I hadn't seen them. I filled a pot with coffee from the urn. I fixed a tray for myself. Cream and sugar. The pot of coffee. A cup and saucer. A spoon. There was pie on the meat block, but I wouldn't disobey the direct order not to eat anything from there.

Upstairs, I sat on my bed, drinking coffee and reading the novel. At noon, I went downstairs again. The kitchen sisters were in the kitchen. They had prepared a meal for the workmen, and one of them gave me dinner. Sister Columba was in the kitchen; she had stayed behind to answer the door and the phone. I sat with her at half-table and ate a workman's dinner: pork chops, potatoes and gravy, spinach, sliced tomatoes and cucumbers. It was hot and delicious, the first dinner I had eaten sitting down in months.

I took my lemon meringue pie and another pot of coffee upstairs. I sat on my bed all afternoon, reading *The Cardinal* and eating pie and drinking coffee.

At five, the caravan of buses and cars returned to the motherhouse. I returned *The Cardinal* to its shelf and took my dishes downstairs. Since I hadn't seen Mother Paula, I ate supper at half-table, prepared to read at table, but at supper, Mother Paula tapped her bell, granting recreation, so I was free to go back upstairs. I stopped off in the priests' serving room to get the news.

Eileen had seen Valentine at camp. She handed me the two presents Valentine had asked her to give me: a Hershey bar and a little gold safety pin. "It's all she had," Eileen said. "She searched her pockets, and that's all she had."

Pockets. That was the first thing I had noticed about the juniors. They all had pockets now. Rosaline habits did not have pockets, but Valentine and her companions had cut slits in the side seams of their habits and sewn pockets onto their petticoats. They were constantly reaching into their pockets. I broke the Hershey bar and gave half to Eileen. I pinned the little safety pin to my habit under my guimpe.

Eileen said everyone noticed I was missing. They all knew that Wulfram had made me stay away. Valentine and Regina told Eileen to give me a message: In January, when my companions and I made vows and went to St. Louis, I was to be their roommate. Sister Thomas, the junior mistress, had already decided what rooms we would have.

There was a profession ceremony a few days later. The two novices who were five months ahead of my class made vows. The bishop did not attend. They made their vows in a low-key ceremony that we spent little time practicing for. Tiny Sister Terence, already thirty-five years old, was assigned to the kitchen, and her young companion was assigned to go to St. Louis to Marillac College.

❖ ❖ ❖

September, 1962

On the first of September, we went to camp to clean it and lock it down for the winter. The next morning, Sunday, as we ate breakfast on the pavilion, Wulfram told us that the junior nuns, who had not yet returned to St. Louis, would be coming out to camp to spend the afternoon and evening with us. We would be permitted to talk to them.

In the afternoon, my companions and I climbed up to the hayloft and sat in the window. We watched the juniors come up the dirt road in the convent cars. Valentine was driving the first car. She honked the horn all the way up the road. She parked by the barn and got out. She saw us sitting up in the barn window and waved. Jean Edward was driving the second car. She parked by the pond. Alexandra was not present. She had been missioned to a grade school in Kansas City, Kansas. She had already gone to her mission. My old roommate would be teaching 3rd, 4th, and 5th grades in a little school in a poor neighborhood.

From up in the hayloft, we watched the juniors go into the camp kitchen. After a while, Wulfram and the postulants came outside. We watched her send them off to hike down to the river. Now, the juniors and the novices could swim without being observed.

After a few minutes, the canonicals and some of the juniors came out of the bunkhouse in bathing suits and jumped in the water. Valentine didn't go swimming. She and a couple of her companions, still in their habits, stood by the outdoor fireplace talking to Wulfram. Valentine had her hands in her pockets.

From the hayloft, my companions and I could see the postulants following the trail up past the buried house, past the corral, down the hill to the railroad tracks, across the tracks to the river. After an hour, they came back. The other novices and the juniors had left the pool, and now the postulants swam.

Some of the juniors made pizza for supper. My companions and I came down from the hayloft for evening prayer and supper. I had not yet spoken to Valentine. At supper, she sat with the postulants and made them laugh.

After supper, I was sitting on the top bunk of a bed in the bunkhouse, talking to some other novices, when Valentine approached. She grabbed my legs and pulled me down off the bunk. "Were you going to speak to me, or not?" she asked.

I walked outside with her. We sat at a table by the pool with a few of her companions, including Regina, my old qualitative analysis partner. Valentine and the other juniors spoke to me in low tones, so no one could hear.

Valentine and Regina told me I would be moving into their room on the second floor of the juniorate in St. Louis after Profession. My companions would sleep in a dorm on the third floor of the house. Valentine told me they knew Wulfram was giving me a rough time. They said I should stick it out, no matter what. "The next five months will fly by," Regina said. I was happy to know they were pulling for me and waiting for me to join them.

A few of my companions approached, wanting to talk to the juniors, wanting to hear about St. Louis and Marillac College.

I walked up to the pavilion and sat down at a table. A postulant, whom I hadn't yet spoken to because of Wulfram's new rule against novices speaking to postulants, sat down beside me. The postulants apparently had not been told not to talk to us, and they often attempted to do so. She said, "Sister Emmanuel, we think you're like the Little Flower."

A few moments before I had been on the verge of tears, overwhelmed by the kindness of the juniors. Now I had to laugh. Miss Karen told me that she and the other postulants had noticed the way Wulfram singled me out, and they had noticed the way I accepted the treatment. No matter what Wulfram said to me, I always responded with, "Thank you, Sister, may God reward you," in a humble tone. The postulants thought it was a mark of holiness, instead of a calculated response, the only one possible.

I laughed at the postulant's words, but she wasn't laughing. Three of her classmates had left the convent already. They had come to the novitiate full of fervor. They had not expected the poisonous atmosphere that Wulfram had created on the third floor of the Rosaline motherhouse. I wondered if any of them would survive to Profession. I wanted to offer a word of encouragement to her like the words that had just been spoken to me by the juniors, but I said nothing.

The juniors drove back in to the motherhouse the next morning. Wulfram saw me waving to them as they drove down the road. "You can't wait to get to St. Louis with them, can you?" she said. "You can't wait to put pockets in your habit."

She was right. I couldn't wait.

The next day, Labor Day, we returned to the motherhouse. A canonical drove the bus. No one in my class was entrusted with driving the old bus. We had been skipped over for sacristan and for bus driver. When we got back to Rosaline, the academy girls had returned to school, and the junior nuns had departed for St. Louis.

We started our classes on Tuesday. My companions and I took English literature from Mother Paula, theology from Father Andrew, and music from Sister Francine. All our classes were in the afternoon. We still had three-hour Hours every morning. We sat on the hard classroom chairs from nine until noon every day, with no break to stretch, get a drink, or go to the bathroom. The only break from sitting down was standing up when Wulfram called on someone to recite answers to the questions in the Catechism of the Vows. Since I was unable to remember the answers, I spent a lot of time on my feet getting yelled at. We were not released until the dinner bell rang. We had no time to eat dinner before serving dinner.

The postulants walked around with confused looks on their faces. Another one left in September, the Mexican girl, Miss Gracia. Always before, when a novice or postulant left, nothing was said. Wulfram didn't tell us anyone had left, and we knew better than to ask questions. But on the day Miss Gracia left, she was allowed to come into the Novitiate in secular clothes, a navy blue dress and navy blue high-heeled shoes. She wanted to say goodbye. Wulfram didn't explain the departure from custom. She just said, "Miss Gracia is returning to her family's ranch in Mexico. She asks for your blessing."

Gracia knelt on the floor, and we extended our hands in her direction and said the blessing Mother Paula said every night at the end of night prayers: "May the blessing of Almighty God, Father, Son, and Holy Spirit, descend upon you and remain with you forever."

Gracia left. We could hear her high heels walking down the hall. We could hear the elevator door open and close.

Throughout September, we had our silent recreations inside. No more softball games on the Lilac Field. We sat in the Novitiate sewing. No one spoke. No one looked at anyone. It was too embarrassing, too painful. We knew the remaining postulants wondered what was going on. What was wrong with us that the novice mistress refused to come to recreation? Why were we being punished? Why were they being punished with us?

Wulfram sat in her office, behind her desk. She didn't go to dinner, and she didn't go to supper. Various novices brought her meals to her on trays.

Novices also brought trays up for another professed nun who was living in the northwest wing on our floor. She was Sister

Rose Anselm, a beautiful young nun who taught at St. Roch's, a little grade school out by Camp Rosaline. There was no convent there, so the three nuns who taught there lived at the motherhouse and drove back and forth every day. Every morning, they attended morning prayer and Lauds. During meditation, they went up to the Communion rail to receive Communion.

They attended Mass at St. Roch's, but Rosalines did not go to Communion at a Mass where they were supervising children. Rose Anselm and the other two nuns went downstairs at the end of meditation and ate a quick breakfast before driving to their school.

In September, Sister Rose Anselm got sick. Instead of going into the infirmary on the second floor, she moved up to the third floor, and Wulfram took care of her. Wulfram was in and out of Rose Anselm's room all the time. She would send novices down to the kitchen to get trays for Rose Anselm.

Rose Anselm rarely left her room. Father Andrew, the chaplain, would take Communion up to her. After the other two St. Roch's nuns received Communion, he would take the elevator up to the third floor to give Communion to Rose Anselm. Two novices, always canonicals, never my companions or me, walked ahead of him, ringing a little bell. He wore a stole over his alb and carried the pyx under it.

One evening, when I was not expecting recreation at table, Mother Paula tapped her bell. I had eaten at half-table, so I went upstairs. These early releases from table reading were no longer the pleasure they had been. When Wulfram was still going to meals, getting out of reading meant a half-hour or more alone and free from fear, but now that Wulfram no longer went to meals, things were different. I could no longer stop off at the priests' serving room to have a chat with Eileen. Wulfram might appear at any minute. I had to go up to the third floor.

As I stepped out of the ramp into the rotunda, I could see Wulfram in profile, sitting behind her desk. Usually she did not turn her head to see who was walking through the rotunda, but this time she did. "Come in here, Sister Emmanuel," she said.

On one of her two desks was a tray with food on it. Baloney. Crackers. It had not been touched. "This is what the kitchen sisters sent up tonight for Sister Rose Anselm," Wulfram said.

The food on the tray was exactly what we had had for supper downstairs. Hard-boiled eggs. Vegetable soup. The round piece of baloney was centered on the white tin plate. It seemed to be the baloney that Wulfram was angriest about. Or the crackers.

"Take it back downstairs to the kitchen. Tell the kitchen sisters that this is not a suitable meal for a sick sister. Tell them to send up something appetizing and nourishing."

"Yes, Sister." I took the tray downstairs.

This was not a message a novice should carry. Wulfram wanted me to correct the professed nuns who worked harder than anyone else in the community. I went into the kitchen. Supper was still going on. The kitchen sisters were still busy. The servers were in and out of the refectory. I stood by the meatblock with the tray. Finally, one of the kitchen sisters said, "Yes, what is it?"

I said, "Sister Wulfram sent me down to ask if Sister Rose Anselm could have something else."

"Something else? Like what?"

"I don't know, Sister."

She took the tray from me and put it on one of the big tables. She opened a refrigerator and took out a steak. She put it on a plate. "Cook it in the priests' serving room," she said. She found some leftover scalloped potatoes from dinner and some peas. "Go on up," she said. "I'll send it up on the dumbwaiter."

I went up to the priests' serving room. Eileen was there. I cooked the steak in a skillet. I warmed the vegetables. I made a little pan gravy in the skillet. I opened the cupboards to find nicer dishes. There were many silver pieces that the older nuns had brought with them to the convent. Dishes, covers for dishes, little coffee pots.

I fixed a tray, a big silver tray. I put a linen tray cloth on it, and arranged the hot food on it. I covered the plate with a silver cover. I put Father Andrew's uneaten cake on the tray and a pot of tea. I hurried up the ramps with the tray. Wulfram was standing at her office door waiting for me. She removed the cover from the plate of food to see what I had. She nodded and replaced the cover. "Take it to her," she said.

I knocked on Rose Anselm's door. I took the tray in to her. She sat up in bed, and I placed the tray on her lap. She removed the silver dome and saw the steak and potatoes and peas. She smiled at me. "Where did you rustle this up?" she asked.

I was glad to see her smile.

I went back to the rotunda. Wulfram was back in her office. Her own tray, covered with the napkin to indicate it was ready to go down, was on the little table by the railing. I took it down to the kitchen.

Supper was over. A few professed nuns were scrubbing pots in the big corner sinks. Rose Anselm often did this. She would stop in the kitchen after supper to help the kitchen sisters clean up. I admired her for this. It was not a pleasant job. One night, tiny Sister Terence, who had to stand on a stool to reach down into the deep sinks, dropped a pan, splashing dirty water on

Sister Rose Anselm. Rose Anselm laughed and said, "Watch it, Sister. I'm not the Little Flower yet."

I left Wulfram's tray in the kitchen and went back upstairs to get Rose Anselm's tray. "Please thank the kitchen sisters for the wonderful steak," she said. "And my compliments to the chef. It was perfectly cooked. Hot. Delicious. A real treat. Thank you."

Recreation was silent as usual, that night. We sewed in the Novitiate, and Wulfram sat in her office.

❖ ❖ ❖

October, 1962

The three-hour Hours continued. Every morning Wulfram railed at us, rebuked us, reviled us, belittled us, derided us. We were dissipated, doppity, disgusting. I wrote down every word she said. I had a stack of spiral notebooks full of Hour notes. I kept them in my trunk. I began to consider hiding them somewhere. I had word-for-word transcriptions of Wulfram's insane lectures. If she were to read these notes, she would kill me.

The silent recreations continued. It was so quiet in the Novitiate during recreation, that sometimes we could hear laughter from the community room, a floor below and at the other end of the building.

The tension and fear were unremitting.

On the seventh of October, a Sunday, I began to read at supper, but Mother Paula tapped the bell, granting recreation. I had eaten at half-table so I went upstairs. The ramps and the halls and the rotunda were nearly dark. I could see Wulfram in profile, sitting behind her desk, as usual. She was eating her supper from a tray.

I was about to go to my room, when the house phone rang. I knew immediately it was for me. I had not had a phone call since entering the convent, but I knew this one was for me. I opened the little glass door in the wall and lifted the receiver. "Third floor. Sister Emmanuel speaking."

Sister Columba, the portress, said, "You have a phone call, Sister Emmanuel. It's your mother. Long distance. Hurry down here."

Something had happened. My parents had driven down to Chetopa, Kansas, for the weekend. They had told me in a letter they would be going down to visit my grandfather this weekend. I went to Wulfram's door to get permission to go down to the office to take the call.

Wulfram had heard the house phone ring, and she knew I was standing at her door, but she didn't turn or acknowledge me in any way. I waited. And waited. My mother was paying for long distance, while I was standing here, doing this. Someone was dead. Please don't let my dad be dead.

Wulfram continued to ignore me.

I turned and ran down the ramps. I went to the office. The receiver was on the counter. Sister Columba was hissing at me. "So slow you are. Keeping your dear mother waiting."

My grandfather was dead. He had died after dinner. He went to Mass with my parents in the morning. My mother prepared a Sunday dinner, and he ate it. After dinner, he said he would lie down. He lay down on the sofa and died. The funeral would be on Wednesday at eleven. My parents would stay in Chetopa to arrange the funeral. My aunt and uncle would pick me up early Wednesday morning and drive me down to Chetopa to the funeral.

I went back upstairs. I went to Wulfram's door. Without waiting for her to acknowledge me, I said, "My grandfather in Chetopa, Kansas, has died. He will be buried there. I would like to attend the funeral. My aunt and uncle will pick me up at five o'clock Wednesday morning."

Nothing. No response. She did not turn her head to look at me. After a while, I went into the Novitiate.

At recreation, we sewed in silence.

The next day, Wulfram told me to go to Sister Rose Anselm's room to borrow one of her black veils. I would be going to the funeral, and Wulfram would be going along.

I went to Rose Anselm's room. She smiled at me from her bed and pointed to one of her bonnets and veils. Novices did not go out in public in their white veils. The black veils we used to go to the dentist or the doctor were not suitable for a funeral. I had to wear a good one, and Rose Anselm was my height.

I put on Rose Anselm's bonnet and veil and looked in the mirror. She watched me from her bed. "Very nice," she said, as I admired myself.

On Wednesday morning, Wulfram tapped on my door at four-thirty to wake me. At five minutes till five, I was ready to go, dressed in my Sunday habit and Rose Anselm's black veil. It was very warm, so I didn't need a shoulderette or a shawl. I stood in the rotunda, waiting for Wulfram.

She came out of her room at the end of the postulants' hall. She gestured to me to come to the elevator. There was a trunk in the landing by the elevator. Wulfram signaled to me to help her lift it onto the elevator. We rode the elevator down to the ground floor. We carried the trunk to the northeast door and left it just inside the door. We went outside. Wulfram said, "That's

Miss Jackie's trunk. She's leaving today." Another postulant was going home.

My aunt and uncle drove up the South Drive. Wulfram and I got in the back seat. My uncle headed over to Kansas to catch the highway to Chetopa, 69 South.

My aunt started chattering to Wulfram, and Wulfram chattered back. It was odd to be talking at all at five o'clock in the morning. It was particularly odd to hear Wulfram talking in a friendly way to anyone. My aunt had not attended Rosaline Academy; she had gone to St. Agnes Academy, a girls' school in northeast Kansas City. It was very much like Rosaline, but conducted by the Sisters of Mercy.

My aunt loved her old school and talked about it all the time. Now she told Wulfram all about it. Harriet Hilliard had gone to St. Agnes Academy. My aunt knew her well. Peggy Snyder was her real name. My aunt had to laugh as she recalled the fun they had. Now she watched Ozzie and Harriet every week to see what her old classmate was up to. That was her favorite show. She also liked Sid Caesar. Everyone thought my aunt looked like Imogene Coca. My uncle looked like Bennett Cerf. Rosalind Russell was his favorite actress.

Joan Crawford went to St. Agnes Academy, too. Her real name was Lucille LaSeuer. My aunt didn't know her as well. She was a little older. St. Agnes Academy was named, not for the Roman martyr, but for Mother Agnes, a famous Sister of Mercy who had a key to the Independence jail back at the turn of the century; the Jackson County sheriff allowed her to visit the prisoners whenever she wanted.

Wulfram seemed to be fascinated by the stories. She asked my aunt questions that evoked more stories from the past. My aunt had gone out with Roy Disney once, Walt's brother. That was before she met my uncle. How different her life would be if she had married Roy Disney. She gave my uncle a little poke and laughed. Wulfram smiled at the humor. My uncle was speeding down the highway.

We stopped for breakfast at Fort Scott. I ordered bacon and eggs and hotcakes. Wulfram ordered sausage and eggs and a waffle. I hadn't eaten a fried egg or a pancake in over two years. It was delicious.

Back in the car, Wulfram continued her conversation with my aunt. Even my uncle joined in now. He told Wulfram about his high school days at De La Salle, and how, in 1922, aged sixteen, he started working at the Federal Reserve Bank. He was an office boy. Now, forty years later, he was a bank examiner. Wulfram asked him about the training he had received for this position. He had to go to Washington, D.C., for training, and it was intense.

We stopped for gas in Pittsburg. Wulfram got out to stretch her long legs, and I got out with her. My aunt bought us Dr. Peppers from a machine.

We arrived at the funeral home at ten o'clock. The Chetopa funeral home was a big Victorian house. My parents were there with friends and relatives. Wulfram asked the woman who ran the funeral home if she could use the restroom. The woman pointed to a door at the end of the hall. Wulfram went in. When she came out, she gestured to me to come down the hall. She was trying to keep from laughing. "Go in there," she said, "and take a look."

The tiny bathroom was full of makeup. There were thirty or forty little plastic bottles of liquid makeup in various shades on the window sill and on the back of the toilet. Little shelves on the wall held boxes of powder, mascara, eyebrow pencils. The medicine cabinet was full of rouge and lipstick. They were all brands available at dime stores, not theatrical makeup or specialty items for concealing the ravages of death. It was mildly amusing. I felt that Wulfram was taking this opportunity to demonstrate to me that we would be friends as soon as I was professed. We would laugh at funny stuff and talk about stuff like she did with the juniors.

We went into the parlor and prayed beside my grandfather's coffin. I didn't look at him. I didn't want to remember my handsome grandpa wearing dime store makeup. He had had an easy death at the end of a long life. He had died on the Feast of Our Lady of the Rosary, and all his grandchildren remembered how he went to sleep every night with his rosary beads in his hand. I didn't look at his dead hands.

We went to the church. The priest said a funeral Mass, but there was no singing. The priest was Italian, and his rapid-fire Latin made the Mass go quickly. Afterwards, the pallbearers carried the coffin out to the hearse. Wulfram and I got in the first funeral car with my parents. About twenty other cars followed as we drove the two miles out to the cemetery. The procession circled through the non-Catholic side of the cemetery to the St. Rose section where the Catholics were buried. My grandmother had died in 1957, and her grave was here. My grandfather's grave was open, waiting.

The priest conducted the burial service, and the funeral director helped the pallbearers lower the coffin into the grave.

We went back to town. At my grandparents' house, my cousins and I walked around outside, remembering the visits we had paid to our grandparents over the years. Riding the Katy Flyer to Chetopa. My cousins were ten years older than I was, so their memories stretched back into the 1930s.

Wulfram sat on the porch with my relatives, eating lunch. It was strange to see her sitting in the chair where I used to sit on summer afternoons reading books from the Chetopa library. The books on the children's shelves were not sturdy library editions. Instead, they were ordinary books that people had donated: the Bobbsey Twins in dust jackets, beautiful editions of Penrod and the Wizard of Oz, an edition of the Thousand and One Nights with color plates and gilt edges. One summer the librarian let me check out *The Little Princesses* by Marion Crawford, even though it was an adult book.

My cousins and I went inside. The dining room table was piled with food. Everyone was standing around talking about my grandparents. The garden. The chickens. After a while, people started to leave. One woman, a friend of my grandparents, said to me, "I've got something for you." She went out to her car and brought in a quilt she had made.

Country garden pattern. Green rings. Various feed sack prints for the rest of the quilt. Beautiful. I tried to refuse. I didn't want to explain to her that I wouldn't be allowed to use this, that it would be given away to a benefactor. "Take it," Wulfram mouthed to me from across the room. I took it.

We drove back to Kansas City with my aunt and uncle. My parents were going to stay in Chetopa for another day or two to tie up loose ends. Again, Wulfram and my aunt chatted like old friends. At one point, Wulfram said to me, "This has been a very enjoyable day. As a girl and as a young sister, I often noticed the sign for Chetopa on my way to Oklahoma, but I never dreamed I'd be going there one day to help a sister bury her grandfather."

We stopped at a different restaurant in Fort Scott for supper. Fried chicken, mashed potatoes and gravy.

We got back to Rosaline at ten o'clock.

The next day, Wulfram was back to what had become normal. A three-hour Hour. A silent recreation.

This went on for another week. Then, one morning in the Hour as I was writing down every word Wulfram spoke, she stopped talking. I glanced up at her, and she saw me. She glared at me. I looked back at her. She said, "Either wipe that look off your face, Sister Emmanuel, or GET OUT!"

I got up and left the room.

I went to my room and packed my trunk. I put the quilt from Chetopa in my trunk. I left all my nun clothes in the closet and in the drawers and packed only things I wanted to take home. My music.

I knew I would be sent home from the convent for what I had done. I stripped the bed and dropped the sheets down the laundry chute. I emptied my waste basket down the incinerator. I sat on my chair and waited.

I knew Wulfram was supposed to leave for the hospital the next day. She and Sister Rose Anselm were going to St. Margaret's Hospital. I didn't know what Wulfram's ailment was. It seemed to have something to do with swollen joints. She always smelled like Bengay. Would I be sent home this afternoon?

The door opened, and Wulfram came into my room. I stood up. It was noon. I could hear the Angelus ringing. The three-hour Hour was over. The servers would be rushing down to the kitchen to serve dinner without having eaten at half-table. I was a dinner server. And a breakfast server. Who would serve in my place? My companions all served at least twice a day already.

Wulfram came over to me. She stood very close to me. I backed up to the wall. She stood in front of me and put her hands on either side of my face. "Don't crucify me," she said. "Please don't crucify me."

I understood what she was saying. If she went downstairs to tell Mother Paula to send me home, Mother Paula would want to know what I had done. There was nothing Wulfram could say. "She had a look on her face that I didn't like," wouldn't be good enough.

It didn't occur to me to bargain with her. I said nothing.

I went downstairs and served dinner. I ate my own dinner standing by the cart before taking in the dishpans.

It was my birthday. I was twenty-one.

Nothing more was said about the incident. Wulfram and Rose Anselm went to the hospital the next day. We had a few days of peace. Our recreations were still silent, but Eileen and I did a lot of ironing and a lot of talking in the ironing room.

Wulfram came back on Sunday. Rose Anselm stayed in the hospital. Wulfram was at supper for a change, and after supper, she left the refectory.

I stayed in the refectory. It was still a few minutes till seven, and I was standing next to the reader's stand, reading a newspaper. Our country was on the verge of nuclear war. A few of my companions were working in the refectory, removing the scrap pans and the dishpans from the tables, and dust mopping the floor.

The door to the refectory opened, and Wulfram came in.

I folded the newspaper I had been reading and put it on the shelf beneath the stand. Had she seen me reading the newspaper? She said to my companions, "Watch this." She said it out of the side of her mouth, just as she had said it once before to Sister Marsha.

And just as before, I heard her.

I expected her to start yelling at me. Instead she said, "Sister Emmanuel, you're going out to teach tomorrow. To St. Roch's. Sister Rose Anselm won't be able to return to teaching for another couple of weeks, and they're having trouble getting substitutes, so Mother decided to send you."

My companions' mouths practically dropped open. Wulfram smiled slightly. It was clear that she expected me to jump up and down and shout for joy at this unbelievable news, but I said in my neutral voice, "Thank you, Sister, may God reward you."

It was not unheard of for second-year novices to go out to teach. It had been common in the early days. Wulfram told me to go to Rose Anselm's room where I would find the black veil I had worn to the funeral. Rose Anselm had worn a different veil to the hospital.

In the morning, I went to morning prayer and Office. During meditation, I went up to the Communion rail with the other two nuns who taught at St. Roch's, Sister Estelle and Sister Kevin. After a few minutes, we went down to the refectory. We ate breakfast at half-table. I went upstairs and took off my bonnet and white veil and put on Rose Anselm's bonnet and black veil. I hurried back downstairs. Estelle and Kevin were at the northeast door, ready to leave for school. They had briefcases.

Sister Kevin, the principal of St. Roch's and the teacher of the sixth, seventh, and eighth grades, drove. She took Holmes all the way out. She explained to me along the way what I would be doing.

I would be teaching third, fourth, and fifth grades. I would have about thirty students, ten in each class. They were very bad. They had had so many substitute teachers already in the seven weeks they had been in school, that they were uncontrollable. A few of them, Cuban immigrants, did not speak English. Kevin told me which kids would know what pages they were on in their textbooks.

Sister Kevin was in her early thirties. She was loud and masculine. She told me the old car had been her brother's. He gave it to her for the school. It broke down all the time, but she was able to fix it. Chewing gum and baling wire, if nothing else worked. We listened to the news on the radio. CBS.

President Kennedy would be addressing the nation that evening. Would there be war?

Sister Estelle, a junior professed, sat in the back seat. She taught first and second grades. She rarely spoke.

We pulled up in front of the two-story brick building. The three classrooms were on the first floor, and the parish church was on the second floor.]The rectory stood next door to the school.

The old priest, the same one who said Mass at camp in the summer, said Mass for the school children at eight. After Mass, downstairs in the classroom, Sister Kevin introduced me to my class. She left me and went to her own classroom.

I looked at the children. They did not wear uniforms. This area, just outside of town, was mostly rural. There were kids from farms and kids from the new suburbs that were just beginning to reach out this far. The Cubans were the children of doctors who worked at a nearby psychiatric hospital. A boy raised his hand. A fifth grader.

"Yes?"

"Are we going to have history? Sister Rose Anselm said we'd have history every day, but she's never here, and the substitutes don't want to teach history. Probably because they don't know any history."

"We're going to have history," I said. "In fact, we're going to have history first period. We'll get started as soon as we finish straightening up the mess."

There were papers and books strewn everywhere. I made the kids empty their desks, throw away all the old junk, and put their books back in their desks with all the backs lined up by size. They responded to the directions and soon were sitting up straight in their desks, ready for history. Only the fifth graders had history books, so I put the third and fourth graders to work on their spelling words. "I want you to write each word five times. Use each word in a sentence. Copy the definition of each word from the back of the book." They groaned. Too much work.

"Of course it's a lot of work. There's one way to avoid it next week. Those who get a hundred on their spelling test on Friday won't have to do the written work next week." I was copying the method of Sister Laetitia, who taught third and fourth grades at St. Albert's when I was in those grades. I spent two years in her classroom, and I learned a lot from her.

I told the fifth graders to open their history books. "We're studying the Greeks," the same boy said. "Most of them were fairies."

"Don't speak unless you're called on," I said. I had them read a few pages aloud, one sentence apiece, fast, to keep everyone's attention. I had learned this from Sister Laetitia, too. At the end of the period, I told them to read the next few pages to themselves and then to prepare five questions that they would use the next day to test each other on the chapter.

I taught math to the third graders and set them to writing the times tables. I taught math to the fourth graders and set them to solving division problems. Fifth grade math followed, and then it was time for morning recess.

Sister Kevin came over to me on the playground. She congratulated me on getting through the first hour-and-a-half without a crisis. "I couldn't hear a sound coming from your classroom," she said. "Usually it's chaos."

Religion followed recess. The three grades took religion together. After religion came reading, grade by grade. The same Ginn readers I had in grade school. It was pleasant to visit Timber Town again. After reading came penmanship for all three grades. After penmanship came lunch. A few of the kids went home for lunch. Most ate at tables in the basement. Kevin and Estelle and I ate the lunches the kitchen sisters had packed for us and drank Cokes.

Following recess, I taught geography to all three grades together. After geography came music. I sat down at the rickety old piano. I hadn't touched a piano except to dust it for over two years. I played a song from the kids' music book. Loch Lomond. I played it again. The kids were watching me. "Let's try it," I said. "Whisper." I had decided my method of teaching singing would be the opposite of Sister Dominic's.

The kids sang the song a few times at a whisper. "Now a tiny bit louder, but still very soft." They sang it a few more times. They were good singers, the Cuban kids particularly. By the end of the period, the kids were singing the song beautifully, and I was playing it without too many mistakes. Sister Kevin opened the door. "That was excellent, boys and girls," she said. "We were listening from across the hall. In awe."

At afternoon recess, the girls from my class sang the song while they jumped rope on the front sidewalk. "Oh, ye'll tak the high rrroad, and I'll tak the low rrroad, and I'll be in Scotland afore ye." Sister Kevin asked me to go into her room for music after recess. She wanted the sixth, seventh, and eighth graders to learn Loch Lomond, too. She would take my class for science while I taught her kids.

After school, several of the kids hung around, wanting to talk. One of the Cuban girls brought her mother in to meet me. The woman asked me if I gave piano lessons. She had left Havana six months earlier with one suitcase. Now she was a suburban housewife in Kansas City trying to find a piano teacher for her children.

At four-thirty, Kevin and Estelle and I drove back to Rosaline, arriving in time for Vespers. I went upstairs to change back into my white veil. I attended Vespers. I ate supper at half-table. I read at supper. When I went upstairs after supper, I saw that Wulfram had put a newspaper on the little table by the railing. She had pinned a note to the string hanging down from the dim light bulb above it. "Postulants and second-years may read the front page stories." The Cuban missile crisis. I had already read both papers that day.

Recreation was silent, as usual.

I didn't have a briefcase, but I had carried my teacher's manuals back to the convent. I prepared the next day's lessons instead of sewing. Since I had missed meditation, I should have made it up after night prayer, but I was too tired. I took a bath and fell into bed.

I taught at St. Roch's all week. Sister Kevin lavished praise on me. She said parents were calling to tell her they wanted me to finish out the year. They were upset because Sister Rose Anselm was absent so often, and the substitutes were worthless. Kevin told them she would see what she could do. The parents didn't know I was a novice.

The following Sunday, Wulfram told me that Sister Carol, my oldest companion, would be taking my place at St. Roch's for the coming week. Sister Rose Anselm was still in the hospital.

I was sorry to hear the news. I wanted to go back to my class. I knew all the kids' names. They were well-behaved and interested in learning. I was worried that Carol, with her odd mannerisms, would not be able to keep them in line. There was nothing to be done about it. On Monday morning, it was Carol who put on Rose Anselm's black veil and rode out to St. Roch's with Kevin and Estelle.

Hallowe'en was on Wednesday. Another three-hour Hour in the morning. I wrote down every word Wulfram said. I wrote without listening. I wrote while thinking of my kids, imagining what they were doing at each moment.

There was no dressing up at supper that night. Afterwards, in the Novitiate, there was another silent recreation.

❖ ❖ ❖

November, 1962

I went back to St. Roch's on All Souls Day. Carol had been unable to control the wild third, fourth, and fifth graders. She had had particular difficulty with the Cubans, so I was sent back. The kids said oh no when they saw me, but they immediately straightened their desks and lined up their books as I had required them to do. In each class, they remembered what I had told them to do. Those who had gotten a hundred on the previous spelling test reminded me that they did not have to do the written spelling work this week. They sang Loch Lomond for me. Carol had taught them the harmony. When I went into the sixth, seventh, and eighth grade room, they sang the song in four parts, with the eighth grade boys doing their best to sing the lowest part.

Rose Anselm was back from the hospital but still in bed in her room on the third floor. Every day the kids told me they hoped I would continue to be their teacher. Sister Kevin revised the schedule so that I taught history to the sixth, seventh, and eighth grades, while she taught math to the third, fourth, and fifth.

We listened to the news in the car, and I read *Time* and *Newsweek* and the *Kansas City Times* at lunch. Kevin felt I needed to be current with the news in order to teach American history to seventh and eighth graders.

On November fifteenth, Sister Kevin told me I was finished. It looked as if Sister Rose Anselm would not be able to return to teaching at all, so the pastor had decided to hire a lay teacher to finish out the year. For a special treat, Kevin stopped at Winstead's on the way back to the motherhouse, and we sat in the car eating cheeseburgers with grilled onions, French fries, and Frostys.

I read at supper. At recreation, we sat in silence. I had no lesson plans to prepare, so I embroidered.

The next night, after supper, my companions and I knelt on the refectory floor before Mother Paula, the council, and the community, to ask to be admitted to Profession.

I knew that the next step would be for Wulfram to go to the superior and to the council with her recommendations. As the novice mistress, she had to testify to the worthiness of the novices asking to be professed. I wondered what she would say, and what questions Mother Paula and the councilors would ask.

I was unable to understand why nothing was done about the way Sister Wulfram treated us. The superior and the council were not blind. The community had recruited us ardently, but now we were treated like criminals. We were at the mercy of a woman whose sanity I doubted.

Mother Paula and the community had to notice that Wulfram never attended meals. They had to notice that the same novices, the second-years, served both dinner and supper every day. Surely Sister Columba had mentioned something about the new rule of silence at half-table. Surely the kitchen sisters had mentioned that the novices and postulants no longer appeared at the meatblock for bread and butter, leftover pieces of cake, apples. Surely Mother Paula had to wonder why, when her English class ran over by one minute, Sister Wulfram stood outside the Novitiate door tapping a bell over and over.

Had Mother Paula and the council noticed that the class of twelve postulants had dwindled to five? Did anyone ask those seven postulants why they were leaving? Did those postulants not mention the silent recreations? Did they not say they had expected life in the novitiate to be somewhat as it was portrayed in the vocation brochures: the occasional Monopoly game, square-dancing, ice-skating, snowman building? What about the two novices lost from my class? Did no one ask Mary Kay why she was going home? Did no one notice Rita's poison ivy?

In the Hour the following Monday morning, Wulfram told us she was preparing to go before the superior and the council with her recommendations. She said we were to turn in our Hour notes to her. Our Hour notes would weigh heavily in her decision. We had three days to turn them in. They were to be placed on the little table by the railing in the rotunda by Thanksgiving morning.

My spiral notebooks full of Hour notes were still in my trunk, under my music. I had been unable to think of a place to hide them. The trunk room was too public, and the little janitor's closet behind the men's bathroom was too dangerous. There was a sideboard in the men's dining room that I had considered, but I was afraid someone would open one of the drawers.

Wulfram had screamed at us in three-hour marathons every morning for months, and I had taken down her rants verbatim. If I were to hand these books in to her and let her see what I had done, she would destroy me. There would be no Profession for me. The twenty-eight months of enduring her abuse would have been for nothing.

I had not realized we would have to turn in our notes to her. Valentine's class had not done that. Alexandra's class had not done that. I had started taking down Wulfram's words verbatim, not to have a document that proved the novice mistress was cruel and crazy, but as a means to stay awake. It was a little game. It was like the game at supper of looking up from the reading for paragraphs at a time. I could write longhand faster than any stenographer on the planet could take shorthand. I had taken down every word Wulfram had uttered, with the exception of the days I taught at St. Roch's.

If I turned in the notes to her, she would not recommend me for Profession. And if I did not turn in the notes, she would not recommend me for Profession. I had twenty-three spiral notebooks full of Hour notes.

The next morning I looked at the little table in the rotunda. Two of my companions had turned in their notes. Seven notebooks total.

That evening, I came upstairs after supper and saw that fourteen notebooks were on the table, the Hour notes of four of my companions.

Wulfram came down the hall from Sister Rose Anselm's room. She had Rose Anselm's supper tray in her hand. Not the silver one from the priests' serving room, but a plain brown one from the kitchen. Sister Rose Anselm had not eaten much. "Take this downstairs," Wulfram ordered me. "And take mine from my desk."

The next morning, Wednesday, there were thirty-one spiral notebooks on the table. All my companions had turned in their notes. How would Wulfram ever read all this? She would be expected to go before the council soon. I didn't believe she would read the others, but I knew she would read mine. I could not add my notebooks to the stack.

I knew what my companions had done. They had taken down only things that were not insane. The instructions from the novice mistress were meant to be a vade mecum for a nun, a handbook to be referred back to in questionable situations. But my Hour notes were a record of pathology.

That afternoon, I opened the incinerator door a few times to see if there was a fire burning below. When I felt the heat, I dropped the spiral notebooks down into the fire one at a time.

The next morning, Thanksgiving, there was recreation at breakfast. I served. At half-table after breakfast, there was silence. After cleaning the ground floor, I went up to the third floor. Wulfram was standing by the little table in the rotunda. She said, "Where are your Hour notes, Sister Emmanuel?"

The other novices and the postulants were going into the Novitiate. It would be an Hour like a Sunday Hour, with the entire novitiate present. It would start with "Just For Today" by Samuel Wilberforce. Wulfram would criticize the singing and make us sing it over and over. "I burned them," I said.

"Interesting," Wulfram said. She waited until everyone else had passed, and we stood alone in the rotunda. "You know what this means, of course."

I didn't. Would Mother Paula send me home for burning my Hour notes? Maybe not, if I could get to her first.

I turned away from Wulfram and ran down the ramps. I would go to Mother Paula's office and tell her the whole story. I ran past the second floor. When I reached the first floor, running fast, blinded by tears, I crashed into Mother Aurelia, who was crossing the rotunda in the direction of the chapel. She held on to me and drew me firmly away from the southeast corridor which led to Mother Paula's office.

Mother Aurelia was big and powerful and full of authority. She took me down the northeast corridor to her office. She opened the door, and we went in.

Mother Aurelia's office was about twenty by thirty, divided into two main areas, a music studio, where her grand piano, her harp, her violin, and her mandolin were, and an office area, where her desks and bookcases were. Unlike the rest of the convent, which was plainly decorated, this big room was full of plush Victorian furniture, fern stands with ferns on top of them, heavy lace curtains, velvet drapes, music stands, music cabinets, tables with fringed covers and bronze lamps. The walls were covered with pictures that Mother Aurelia had painted, pre-Raphaelite visions of Charlemagne and Rosalia.

"Sit down, dear," she said. I sank into the cushions on the sofa. Mother Aurelia opened a file cabinet and found the handwriting sample I had given her when I was a postulant. She looked it over while I wiped my eyes and pulled myself together a little.

She came over to me and sat down in a carved chair. She said, "This morning at Mass I asked Our Lord to give me something special to do on this Thanksgiving Day. You may be it. Now tell me why you tried to knock me down in the rotunda." She smiled.

I told her the story, starting at the beginning. She listened attentively. When I would slow down or reach a difficult part, she would encourage me to continue. When I finished, she said that she and the other members of the council were aware of some of what was going on upstairs.

They had noticed that the second-year novices served every meal. They had learned from Sister Columba that first we stopped talking at half-table, and then we stopped eating at half-table. They had learned from the kitchen sisters that we gobbled a few bites of food standing in the kitchen instead of sitting down to eat before serving..

Mother Aurelia said she and the council did not know about the silent recreations. They had wondered why the postulants were disappearing so fast. She knew about the meat block. The kitchen sisters had told her the novices and postulants no longer ate the day-old bread and the leftover desserts. Food was going to waste.

Mother Aurelia showed me the door to her private bathroom. She told me to go in and wash my face. When I came out, she said, "You've learned some hard lessons about religious life. Now here's another one. It's never a good idea to complain to a superior about someone she appointed. Do you understand? It would be a complaint about the superior's judgment. It is most unwise. The other councilors and I know that there is trouble in Sister Wulfram's novitiate, but we also know that our superior, Mother Paula, can see what we see. If she does nothing, it is not for us to criticize her. It would be a big mistake for you to go to Mother Paula with this. It would be the worst thing you could do. Mother Paula wants you to make vows, and we all want you to make vows, and you will make vows."

When the Angelus bell rang, Mother Aurelia made the Sign of the Cross and prayed silently. I did the same. It was dinner time. Mother Aurelia made no move to dismiss me. After a few minutes, she went into the hall and used the house phone. A few minutes later two of the kitchen sisters appeared at the door to her office with trays. Big silver trays from the priests' serving room, not the plain brown ones from downstairs. Silver covers on the dishes. Ice in the water. Thanksgiving dinner. Turkey, dressing, gravy, cranberry relish, mashed white potatoes, candied sweet potatoes, green beans, pumpkin pie, and coffee.

Mother Aurelia and I ate the feast at a table by the window. Mother Aurelia told me about her graphoanalysis business. It was so successful, that she was going to have the convent chapel air-conditioned.

I put whipped cream on my pie and in my coffee.

After dinner, a kitchen sister appeared to remove the trays. Mother Aurelia told me to go back upstairs, that everything would be all right.

I went up the ramps. The novices and postulants had not come upstairs from dinner yet. Wulfram had eaten her dinner at her desk. Now she saw me. She got up and came out of her office. "Where have you been?" she asked, in a low dangerous voice.

"In Mother Aurelia's office," I said.

"I might have known. I might have guessed you'd run straight to her. You're two of a kind."

There was recreation at supper that night. I ate at the main table. My companions were serving, so I sat next to a canonical. Leftover turkey, dressing, gravy, cranberry relish.

The next day my companions and I learned we had been accepted for Profession.

The following Monday evening, as I was reading at supper, I noticed that Sister Rose Anselm was at table. She glanced up at me and smiled when she saw me reciting instead of reading. She was feeling better. I wondered if she would go back to St. Roch's, after all. At the end of the meal, she strode away from the table as if she were full of strength. She went into the kitchen to help scrub pots.

She was at all three meals the next day, Tuesday. She died during the night.

Wulfram found her dead Wednesday morning. By the time we went into the Novitiate for the Hour, we all knew. Everyone was whispering. A massive heart attack had killed the twenty-seven year old nun.

The next day, her body lay in its coffin in the chapel, surrounded by dark beeswax candles. Her parents and her brothers and sisters knelt in the front pews near the coffin. We chanted the Office for the Dead.

❖ ❖ ❖

December, 1962

The funeral was on December first. Some of the children from St. Roch's attended. I don't know if they recognized me in my white veil.

Sister Rose Anselm's death did not seem to affect Wulfram, even though she had taken care of her. The three-hour

Hours continued. I no longer bothered to take notes. The silent recreations continued. My companions and I sewed for Profession, and the four postulants sewed for Reception.

One evening, Wulfram came to the Novitiate door, and everyone stood to greet her. She told us to follow her down the hall to Rose Anselm's room. She was going to clean it out. She wanted us to see how few possessions this nun had. Rose Anselm was the daughter of rich parents, but poverty was her joy. Now we would get the few things she left behind. I got a flannel nightgown and a typewriter eraser. Sister Rose Anselm had printed her name on the round eraser. A relic of a saint who had suffered in silence, who had been considered a hypochondriac by some.

The kitchen sisters had doubted the seriousness of Rose Anselm's condition and had been open with their resentment about sending up trays to her. They now talked about how saintly she was, how she always came in to help scrub pots, a job beneath the dignity of most of the teaching nuns.

I felt that Rose Anselm was saintly, too. I had cooked a steak for a saint. I had written lesson plans in a saint's lesson plan book. I had worn a saint's veil. I had made a saint crack up at the supper table. I prayed to Sister Rose Anselm to arrange things so I could go to St. Roch's to teach after Profession. I asked her to give me a sign that she was working on that. I wanted a white Christmas.

On December tenth, Wulfram decided the first floor halls needed to be stripped, waxed, and buffed. Since there were always people in those halls during the day, the job, done only once every two or three years, had to be done at night. We spent the night on our hands and knees scrubbing the wax off the floor with steel wool. Wulfram herself rolled a mop bucket up and down the halls. It was the big bucket my dad had bought for me.

Wulfram used the big chamois mop to spread the soapy water back and forth ahead of the scrubbers. This was the first time the mop and the bucket had been used. She was wearing the green gloves my dad bought.

On December twenty-third, my second feastday in the convent, Wulfram handed me two posters to hang on the bulletin board, gilded Christmas angels from Sister Rose Anselm's mother.

Christmas Eve was warm, but I hummed "White Christmas" to myself while I cleaned the ground floor.

My companions and I were not allowed to wear our serge habits to Midnight Mass, but in the students' dining room afterwards, we talked. With the professed nuns present, Wulfram allowed us to talk. It started to snow while we sat there eating soup and drinking hot chocolate.

By morning, the campus was covered with deep snow. The giant cedar trees, planted by the founders seventy years earlier, were laden with snow. I opened my window and the screen. I put my hands in the pile of snow on the windowsill. The sun was shining on the snow.

There was recreation at breakfast. My companions and I served. After breakfast, we ate in silence at half-table.

We went upstairs. We went into the Novitiate, where stacks of presents from our parents were waiting to be opened. We stood in silence, waiting for Wulfram. We could see her coming down the hall. She reached the bulletin board. She stopped. She turned and examined the posters I had pinned up. She removed the pins and let the posters fall to the floor. With the pins in her fingers, she came to the Novitiate door. "Praised be Jesus Christ," we said. Some added, "Merry Christmas, Sister."

Wulfram said nothing. She stood in the doorway, holding the pins. Then she came in and walked over to me.

I stood by the presents my parents had wrapped for me. The suitcase they had been told to buy and the desk lamp.

Wulfram held the pins in front of my face. She screamed at me. "You used PINS to put up those posters? You made HOLES in those posters with PINS? That heartbroken mother sent me those posters, and you dared to stick PINS in them? Better to pierce that mother's heart with a SWORD."

She turned and left. She had not given us permission to open our presents.

After a while, the professed nuns came upstairs to the Novitiate. Mother Paula came. The juniors had not come home from St. Louis. I talked to Estelle and Kevin about St. Roch's. They said the permanent teacher hadn't worked out, and they were back to substitutes. The third, fourth, and fifth graders were impossible. Kevin said she was praying that Mother Paula would mission me to St. Roch's after Profession.

I talked to Sister Alexandra. She told me about her mission on the Kansas side. She lived in a tiny convent with two other nuns. They had come to the motherhouse for Christmas. "Wulfram's worse than ever, isn't she?" my old roommate asked. She had noticed the unopened presents and guessed what it meant. "Just one more month. You can do it. If I could do it, you can do it."

The professed nuns stayed with us until dinner time. My companions and I served dinner and supper. We ate both meals at half-table in silence. At recreation, Wulfram came to the door of the Novitiate and told us we could open our presents. She did not come in. She went back to her office. We opened our presents in silence. Gloves. Briefcases.

We had visiting day the next day, the Feast of Stephen. My parents brought hamburgers and onion rings and malts from Sydney's. After eating, we walked around outside in the snow. My parents had been asked to buy me galoshes for Christmas, and I was wearing them. I had one more request. I wanted a white silk scarf. My companions and I had been measured for coats. Instead of wearing capes or shawls, as the Rosalines had always done, we would have black coats to wear over our habits in St. Louis. Valentine and the other juniors told us in September to get white silk scarves from our parents to wear with the coats. It was the fad at Marillac College.

My parents told me they had been asked to drive me and one of my companions to St. Louis the day after Profession.

❖ ❖ ❖

January, 1963

My six companions and I practiced for Profession. The three remaining postulants practiced for Reception. Wulfram screamed at us.

Our classes were over. The mornings were occupied with the Hour, and the afternoons were for practice. My companions and I were in Wulfram's immediate presence six hours a day. Her rage was unrelenting.

One day, Sister Carol, my oldest companion, made the mistake of using the word "hollering". Wulfram asked her why she had stuck her head out of the bathroom, when she was supposed to be cleaning it. Carol said, "When you were hollering at the postulants, I thought you were calling me."

Wulfram hit Carol.

She hit her on the back.

I had just come upstairs from cleaning the ground floor, and I saw it. Carol was nearly as big as Wulfram, so the blow shouldn't have moved her, but she was awkward, and she nearly fell down. I didn't know if Wulfram hit Sister Carol with her fist or with her open hand.

I was shocked at the sight of one religious striking another, nearly knocking her down, and I wondered if it constituted sacrilege. Carol was not yet professed, but she was a sister wearing a habit blessed by the bishop and presented to her by a religious superior in a public ceremony. It could very well be sacrilege. At the very least, it was an example of anger out of control. Anger was one of the seven deadly sins.

Wulfram saw me standing at the end of the hall. She knew I had seen her hit Carol. Carol went back into the bathroom. I walked past Wulfram into the Novitiate. I wondered what I would do if she hit me.

That evening, when I came upstairs after reading at supper, I saw a note pinned to the string that hung from the light bulb above the little table in the rotunda. Wulfram had written: "Since Sister Emmanuel and Sister Eileen take so much pleasure in each other's company, they are to move into room 331."

Wulfram was sitting behind the desk in her office. She sat ramrod straight in her chair against the wall. What should I do? I thought of removing the pin, taking down the note, and running down to Mother Paula with it. Mother Paula liked me, and she liked Eileen, and this note was calumny. But the thought was fleeting. I had understood Mother Aurelia's message. Never squeal to a superior about someone appointed by that superior.

I could go into Wulfram's office and demand that she remove the scurrilous charge from the public string before anyone else saw it. She had accused my friend and me of something that would have been matter for confession, if it were true. It was not true, and everyone, including Wulfram, knew that. I was afraid that something could still happen to keep me from making vows. This assault on my friend and me increased my fear.

Eileen came upstairs a few minutes later. She had finished in the priests' serving room. She read the note on the string. During the silent recreation, instead of sewing in the Novitiate, Eileen and I moved from our old rooms into the new room.

There were a few rooms on the third floor that had two closets and two beds. I hadn't shared a room yet, and even though I hated Wulfram for insinuating that Eileen and I were particular friends or worse, I was glad to be moving in with Eileen. We wouldn't be able to talk in the room, but it would be nice to have my friend as my roommate for these last two weeks in the novitiate.

We continued practicing for Profession, and we continued sewing. The nuns who helped with the sewing called us into the sewing room one by one to try on our serge habits and our new habits for St. Louis. I put on my serge habit. The sleeves had been narrowed since Reception. The community had decided the big sleeves were too big, and everyone's sleeves had been shortened and narrowed.

We were measured for our black veils. We would have two, one of sheer black nun's veiling for Sundays and one of a slightly heavier fabric for everyday. We made our own dominoes – the short black veils worn under the long ones.

We made new coifs, new skull caps, new nightcaps.

Wulfram's fury at us did not lessen. We had no opportunity to talk to each other. We whispered.

On January seventeenth, our Profession retreat was to begin. The day before, Sister Carol had learned she would not be going to St. Louis with the rest of us. Mother Paula had missioned her to St. Roch's. She would teach third, fourth, and fifth grades.

Wulfram called me into her office that day. She said she still was not convinced that I should be allowed to make vows. She said I would get one last chance. I was to make an appointment to talk to the retreat master. I was to open my conscience to him in a private conference and in a general confession. If, after that, he felt I should be allowed to make vows, she would permit it.

I knew she had no right to ask this. The superior and the council had already approved me for Profession. And Wulfram had no right to tell me what kind of confession to make or to interfere with my conscience in any way. I had learned that much from the Catechism of the Vows and from the various spiritual reading books. No religious superior, much less a mistress of novices, could require a subject to open her conscience; not to the superior, not to the novice mistress, not to a confessor or a retreat master, not to anyone.

I had never gone to a retreat master for a private conference. When I would see a line of nuns waiting to talk to a retreat master, I wondered what they talked about.

I signed up for a private conference. Another postulant had left, so there would be only nine of us on retreat, seven second-years and two postulants. Both postulants had signed up for conferences. None of my companions had.

The retreat master was a young Albertine, newly ordained, twenty-five or twenty-six. I sat across the table from him in the parlor in the bishop's department. This was the two-room suite across from Mother Aurelia's office, used by the bishop when he visited, and used by retreat masters.

This young priest had curly black hair. He fidgeted with his elaborate Albertine habit. "What's on your mind, Sister?"

I was unable to tell him anything. I could not describe the previous thirty months to this stranger. I could not pretend that he had any spiritual authority over me or any understanding of my situation. The seminary was not the convent. We had nothing in common.

As if to prove it, he lit a cigarette. "Well, Sister?" He didn't look directly at me. The door was slightly open, and Mother Aurelia walked by. She went into her office and closed the door. The priest and I could hear her playing the piano.

We listened, and he smoked. After a while, I got up and left.

The retreat continued, and Wulfram said nothing more to me. The retreat master preached about the importance of courtesy in religious life. Religious should treat each other with exquisite courtesy, he said. For instance, when you leave one mission for another, it is common courtesy to write a thank you letter to the superior of the previous mission.

Chapter 4
Junior Professed

Profession Day
January 20, 1963

It was a Sunday. Sister Eileen and I woke when the bell rang at 6:30. We dressed behind the doors of our respective closets. I put on new underwear. New stockings. A new tee shirt and a new petticoat. My serge habit. A new coif and a new guimpe. My white veil for the last time. New shoes. New undersleeves. My new clothes smelled wonderful. I had kept them in a box with a Royal Secret sachet my mother had given me.

I attended morning prayer and morning Office. At meditation, I stared at the little sheet of parchment on which I had written my vows the night before. What did this mean? What was I doing? I would be signing this paper in three hours, professing vows.

I attended the community Mass. The gospel was the marriage feast at Cana, with the words of Mary that my companions and I had chosen for our motto: Do whatever he tells you.

We ate breakfast in silence. After breakfast, we went upstairs. Eileen and I looked out our window. The guests were arriving. Cars were coming up the South Drive. The campus was covered with snow.

At ten, Sister Lucy gave the pitch for the Veni Creator, and the bishop intoned it. Wulfram lit our candles. She gave us no smile or word of encouragement. We followed the cross bearer and the candle bearers and the flower girls into the chapel. Two brides and seven novices.

At the Communion, my companions and I entered the sanctuary. We knelt at the foot of the altar. When it was my turn, I professed my vows and signed them.

After the ceremony, we ate in the students' dining room. We then visited with our guests in the parlors. This time, I had the most desirable parlor, the small one to the right of the entrance hall. My friends from college came in their beautiful winter suits and hats. Smelling of tobacco and perfume. They would be graduating in May. Two Benedictine nuns came with them, my German teacher and my English Composition teacher, who was now the novice mistress for her congregation. How different it would have been with her as a novice mistress. Benedictines had only one year of novitiate.

That night at ten, Sister Eileen and I were in our beds. Wulfram opened the door and came into our room. Eileen had been feeling sick earlier in the day. The tension, maybe the fact that her parents were not with her on her Profession day, the excitement, the food. Wulfram was coming in to check on her. She had a little tray with her. Orange juice. She sat down on the chair by Eileen's bed and asked her how she was feeling. "Much better, Sister. Thank you, Sister." Eileen sat up in bed. Wulfram gave Eileen the orange juice, and Eileen drank it.

I said, "I want some, too."

Wulfram looked over at me and smiled. "Okay," she said. She left the room and came back in a few minutes with a glass of orange juice for me. I sat up in bed and drank it. I handed the empty glass to Wulfram. She bent down and tucked me in. She left the room.

Eileen snickered.

❖ ❖ ❖

The Next Day
January 21, 1963

The next day, with the exception of Sister Carol who was teaching at St. Roch's, my companions and I set out for St. Louis. There was no time to stay in Kansas City for a second day of grace. The semester was about to begin at Marillac College, and we had to be there.

My parents drove Sister Teresa and me. Wulfram had assigned the cars. Eileen rode in the Fitzpatricks' car.

Teresa and I sat in the back seat. We didn't say much. We were numb. We listened to the radio. KPRS didn't reach far. KUDL a little farther. WHB a little farther, all the way to Concordia. KCMO to Boonville. Then local stations all the way to Wright City. There we picked up KMOX.

My mother had white silk neck scarves for Teresa and me. She handed us each a green-and-white striped Harzfeld's box with a scarf inside.

We stopped for dinner at Big Boy's in Wright City. It was Teresa's first restaurant meal since entering the convent. I was lucky my grandfather died when he did. I got a day out, and Wulfram had not ruined it for me.

We arrived at the convent on Natural Bridge Road at about three o'clock. A southern mansion. We stood in the snow and stared at the house. It wasn't as big as Tara, but it was similar. The front door opened, and Valentine ran down the steps, long arms spread wide. "Welcome to our squalid mansion!" she yelled. She grabbed my suitcase and pulled me up the steps. She grabbed at the scarf around my neck and laughed. "You took my advice, didn't you? What do you want to do first?"

"Put pockets in my habit."

Sister Thomas, the ancient nun who had taught us logic when we were postulants, was the junior mistress and superior of the house. She stood in the entrance hall. She welcomed Teresa and me and shook hands with my parents.

Sister Thomas was a teacher at the academy when I was a student, but she had never met my parents. She offered to show them the house.

My companions, who had arrived an hour earlier, came down the steps. The other juniors appeared from various parts of the house to greet us.

My parents were going to drive back to Kansas City that evening, so they stayed only for the tour of the first floor. On the wall of the entrance hall was an enormous mirror, framed in gilt, suitable for a belle's last-minute inspection of herself before going to a ball. I stared at myself.

A grand staircase curved up to a gallery. Halfway up was a landing with a stained-glass window and a window seat.

To the right of the entrance hall was the library. The walls were paneled, and there were built-in bookcases with leaded glass doors. There was a massive carved mantelpiece over the fireplace on the east wall. The furniture was not original. Instead of library furniture, there were twelve little desks in the room, painted with mottled gray paint, apparently the fiftieth coat of paint the desks had had. Valentine saw me looking at the little desks. She grinned. "They may not be pretty," she said, "but they were free."

Valentine's class was the first class of Rosalines to be sent to college straight out of the novitiate. Always before, juniors went out to teach immediately after Profession. Then, year after year in summer school, they worked toward their degrees. But the sister formation movement in the 1950s had influenced the congregations, and many were now sending newly professed nuns to college rather than into classrooms with no preparation.

When Mother Paula decided to send the Rosaline juniors to college, she selected Marillac, a school conducted by the Daughters of Charity for nuns only. In exchange for providing a qualified teacher for the Marillac College faculty, the community got a greatly reduced rate on the junior sisters' tuition.

Mother Paula needed a place for the juniors to live. She bought a crumbling mansion on Natural Bridge Road, within walking distance of Marillac College. There was almost no money left over for furniture, so Mother Paula placed a bid on some items from an old hotel, a fleabag, one of many demolished in the clean-up of the riverfront.

The desks from the hotel were lined up in two facing rows of six. "They're not anyone's in particular," Valentine said.

"Share and share alike," Sister Thomas said. She led us into the dining room.

Here, there were four round tables. Twenty-one people would be living in the house. On the east side of the dining room, there were double doors. Sister Digna, the widow from Germany, who was the cook for the house, opened the doors to show us a sun porch that had a small altar in it. There was no tabernacle; the Blessed Sacrament was not reserved here. Sister Thomas and the juniors attended Mass at the local parish church, but they said the Office and meditated here in the dining room before this small altar.

Sister Digna showed us the kitchen. Behind the kitchen was a small laundry room with a washer and dryer and a little entranceway from the back door.

We returned to the front hall.

Sister Thomas showed us the parlor. This room had more furniture from the old hotel, a sofa, an easy chair, and a coffee table. Valentine flopped down in the easy chair and picked up the *Globe-Democrat* from the coffee table. She said, "We take the *Post*, too. Mother Paula told us to subscribe to the *Post*. She doesn't like the *Globe*, but my father bought us a subscription."

My parents left after a few minutes. I stood outside in the snow and waved to them as they drove down the circular drive and headed west. They would come to visit me at Easter, they said.

Valentine opened a window on the second floor and called down to me. "Hurry up!"

I went upstairs. My companions were waiting to show me my room and theirs. Sister David, Sister Eileen, Sister Teresa, Sister Helen Marie, and Sister Susan were to live on the third floor. We went up a narrow back staircase to an attic. Here were five beds lined up against the wall. There were no partitions, not even curtains between the beds. There were no closets, only a clothes rack. Where would they dress?

In one corner was a galvanized steel structure that turned out to be a bathroom with two toilets, two sinks, and four shower stalls. These were unreliable, my companions had discovered already, because the water pressure in the eighty-year-old house was low.

I still hadn't seen my room. I knew it was better than this one. Between each bed in the attic was a small chest of drawers, painted the same thick gray as the desks downstairs. Eileen had the farthest bed by a dormer window. The old floor squeaked. I looked out the window. Across the street, and up the hill, was Marillac College.

I went back down the narrow stairs.

Around the gallery on the second floor, there were five bedrooms. The first one, with its own bathroom, was Sister Thomas's room. Four juniors lived in the room behind that one. Another four lived in the room next to that one. Four more lived in the front bedroom across from Sister Thomas's. In the back bedroom, I would live with Sister Valentine and Sister Regina. "This was the daughter's room," Valentine said, referring to the child of the Civil War profiteer who built the house. "The people who sold us the house said they've seen her ghost in here."

There were three beds in the room and one dresser. There were two closets. Valentine said one was hers and one was Regina's. I could put my stuff in Regina's closet. There were four drawers in the dresser, two for Valentine and two for Regina. I could use one of Regina's. There was no desk in the room. Valentine kept her books on the mantel over the fireplace. Regina had a desk on the landing.

There was one bathroom for all the juniors on this floor. It had one bathtub, no shower, one sink, and one toilet. How would fifteen people get dressed in the morning and get ready for bed at night with one bathroom?

I put my trunk next to my bed so I would have a bedside table. I hung my habits in the closet. I put as much of my stuff in the one drawer as I could. The rest I left in my trunk. I put my music and my sewing box in my suitcase and slid it under the bed. I put my new desk lamp on my trunk.

Valentine was sprawled on her bed watching me. She told me registration was the next day, and classes would start on Wednesday.

She told me the schedule. We would get up at five, have Office in the dining room, meditate as we walked to St. Ann's for six o'clock Mass, make our thanksgiving as we walked back, eat breakfast at seven, walk up to school for class. Home for dinner at twelve. Back to school at one. Home for Office at five, meditation at five thirty, supper at six. Recreation from seven to eight. Study. Bed. Valentine said she went to bed at nine every night. Regina sometimes studied at her desk on the landing until midnight. Sister Thomas didn't care when or if we went to bed. Regina got up at four to be first in the bathroom.

Valentine and Regina would be graduating from Marillac College in August. Valentine was an English major.

She explained to me that at Marillac, everyone was in one of two divisions: humanities or science. Within one of those areas, you majored in a specific field. There were no electives. You took the classes you were told to take by the Daughters of Charity who ran the place. Everyone's minor was education. We would get a teaching certificate with our bachelor's degree, either elementary or secondary.

The bell rang at five. We went downstairs for Vespers and meditation. We sat at the tables in the dining room. Those whose backs would be turned to the altar turned their chairs around.

At six, we had supper. There was no reading at meals. There was recreation at dinner and supper every day. For supper, Sister Digna served fried ham slices, canned applesauce, and fried potatoes. Canned spinach. My companions and I talked to each other and to the older juniors. We were exhilarated with our freedom.

After supper, while some of the juniors washed dishes and cleaned up the kitchen, recreation continued for the rest of us. "Anyone for bridge?" Sister Thomas asked. "Someone set up the card table."

When that was arranged for her in the front hall, she sat down and began shuffling the cards. Sister Digna sat down with her. "We need two more," Sister Thomas said. She was looking at me.

I didn't want to play bridge. I wanted to talk to Valentine and Jean Edward and Regina and Loretta. And I didn't want to attract Sister Thomas's attention. When I was in her logic class as a postulant, she ignored me, but when I was a student at Rosaline Academy, she disliked me, and on one occasion, she went out of her way to show it.

It was a week or so before graduation. The other seniors and I were inducted into the Rosaline Academy Alumnae Association and given our class rings. Several old graduates came to the ceremony and to the tea in the Alumnae Room. We played a word game at the tea. An alumna from 1943 and I tied for first prize. In the tie breaker, Sister Thomas helped the alumna by suggesting words to her. The old grad won the gold pendant, and Sister Thomas told me to be a good sport.

Now she put the deck of cards down to be cut. "Sit down, Sister Emmanuel," she said.

I cut the cards.

Sister Jean Edward sat down across from me. Sister Thomas dealt the cards. "One diamond."

"One heart," Jean Edward said.

I hadn't played cards since entering the convent. This was not like the bridge games in the student center at the college Jean Edward and I had attended. There were no ashtrays in the corners of the tables. No boyfriends sitting behind us, groaning at our bids. No music on the radio. "Theme from A Summer Place." No bags of chips. No Cokes.

"Two hearts," Sister Digna said.

Sister Thomas snorted. She reached across the table and grabbed her partner's hand. She rearranged the cards and changed Digna's bid to two diamonds.

Jean Edward smiled at me.

"Pass," I said.

We played for the entire hour. I could hear my companions joking with Valentine and Regina in the parlor. I could hear the other juniors laughing and talking in the library. There was no conversation at the bridge table other than Sister Thomas instructing Sister Digna and telling her what to bid.

At eight, we said Compline in the dining room. We went upstairs. Valentine took off her habit and her headgear and flopped down on the bed with a robe on over her tee-shirt and petticoat. She was reading a paperback book. *The Catcher in the Rye.* She was doing her practice teaching at a girls' school in St. Louis, and this was what they were reading. "Have you read it?" she asked me.

"A long time ago," I said.

Regina was not in the room. She was studying at her desk on the landing. She seemed to be the only person in the house to have her own desk. In addition to her desk, Regina used the window seat on the landing to store her books. She had created a comfortable study for herself in the crowded house.

I got undressed behind the closet door and went out to the hall to check on the bathroom situation. There were four juniors in line with toothbrushes, towels and washcloths. I got in line. Sister Jean Edward was in front of me. She handed me a section of the *Post-Dispatch*. No one spoke. Night silence was observed.

There was no hot water. When I got back to the room, Valentine was asleep.

I went to sleep, too.

❖ ❖ ❖

Tuesday, January 22, 1963

Sister Regina's alarm went off at four o'clock. She was first in the bathroom. I was second. When I got back to the room, Regina was dressed, but Valentine was still asleep. Regina was shaking her, trying to get her up.

By five-thirty, everyone was in the dining room, ready for morning prayer and morning Office. At the end of Office, we sat down to read the points from our meditation books. Then, with points in mind to contemplate on the way, we set out for Mass. It was still dark and very cold. We walked along Natural Bridge road in our overcoats and galoshes and white silk scarves.

Valentine drove Sister Thomas and Sister Digna and a few others who would fit in the old station wagon. We went to six o'clock Mass at St. Ann's Church. We sat in the front pews of the large church. Very few other people were at Mass. One woman in the choir loft sang and played the organ. She sang old hymns that I had heard about but had never actually heard sung in church before. "Mother, dear, oh pray for me."

After Mass, we walked back to the house. It was getting light now, and the traffic on Natural Bridge Road was picking up. We trudged along through the snow.

We ate breakfast in silence. After breakfast, Sister Thomas showed my companions and me the supply closet, a large, built-in linen closet. It had school supplies and toiletries in it. We were to take what we needed without asking her. "And if you need me today," Sister Thomas said, "I'll be in the faculty pool."

It was a joke. She explained that she wouldn't be swimming with the other teachers. The faculty pool was the area where all the faculty members had their offices. Valentine drove Sister Thomas up to school.

I walked up the hill with my companions and some of the other juniors. The sun was shining on the snow, and a train roared by at the bottom of the campus. We talked and laughed and threw snowballs.

Station wagons passed us on their way up the drive, each full of young nuns, students at Marillac College. Sister Regina identified each order as they passed. "The Oblates," she said of a car full of Negro sisters.

"Wheaton Franciscans."

"Franciscans of the Atonement. They're discalced."

"Even now, in the snow?"

"They wear heavy stockings with their sandals. Homespun. Even the Daughters look up to the Atonement Sisters."

Sister Jean Edward said, "Their whole order was Anglican. They converted en masse."

We reached the door to Marillac College. More nuns were climbing out of station wagons.

Visitandines. Ferguson Franciscans. Sisters of Providence.

The large orders had their own colleges, and their young sisters went to those schools. There were no Sisters of Mercy at Marillac, or School Sisters of Notre Dame, or Benedictines, or Dominicans, or Sisters of St. Joseph. Only medium-sized orders, like ours, sent their juniors to Marillac.

We went inside. There was silence in the halls. There were Daughters of Charity everywhere in their blue habits and starched cornettes, and there were dozens of nuns from other orders in black and brown and white and gray habits and black veils. There were several postulants from various orders in various postulant outfits. No one said a word, and most observed custody of the eyes as they walked down the halls.

There was silence in the halls and silence in the library. There was no student union in which to sit and talk.

My companions and I stood in line at the registrar's window. When I got to the window, the registrar, a little Daughter, about forty, looked at my transcript and said, "I'm putting you in science."

"Pardon me, Sister?"

"You've taken a lot of chemistry. Quite a bit of math. We'll put you in science." With a few marks of her pen on a few cards, she enrolled me in the science half of the school. She said I would major in chemistry and minor in education. I would graduate in two years with a B.S. in chemistry and a certificate to teach science in elementary school.

I didn't think this was what Mother Paula wanted for me, but I was afraid to say anything. The long silent line stretched behind me. The registrar handed me my class schedule and a slip of paper to present at the book room. "Next." My companions were giving me looks, but I couldn't argue with this Daughter of Charity.

She put one of my companions, Sister Helen Marie, in science with me. She put the others in humanities. She put two of them down for secondary certificates and the others down for elementary.

I looked at my schedule. I would be taking trigonometry and quantitative analysis and two education courses. I couldn't believe my bad luck. How could the Daughters of Charity decide what Rosalines should major in? Had they discussed this with Mother Paula?

We went to the long line at the book window. After an hour, we reached the window and handed the Daughters inside the room our slips of paper. They took textbooks off the shelves and brought them to us. We put them in our briefcases.

We walked down the hill to our house.

Sister Thomas blew up when she heard I was in science. "Mother Paula wants you in humanities," she roared. "She wants you to study history! And get a secondary certificate. Why didn't you speak up? Has the cat got your tongue? Why didn't you come get me in the pool? What is wrong with you, Sister Emmanuel?" Sister Thomas shook her head. She looked at my companions' schedules and got madder still. She said, "Mother Paula is going to be furious about this."

After dinner, she made a long distance telephone call to Mother Paula. The phone was on a little table by the staircase, and Sister Thomas could be heard all over the house telling Mother Paula what had happened. The new juniors didn't have sense enough to speak up to the Marillac registrar. No, Mother, nothing can be done about it now. It's too late. They should have spoken up when they had the chance. I don't know what's the matter with them.

Mother Paula arrived by car the next day. She went up to Marillac with us and got me out of science and into humanities. She got me out of the elementary teaching track and into the secondary. She straightened out my companions' schedules as well.

That evening at recreation, Mother Paula played bridge with Sister Thomas and Sister Digna and Sister Jean Edward. That night, Mother Paula slept in the spare bed in Sister Thomas's room, and the nun who had driven her to St. Louis slept on the sofa.

❖ ❖ ❖

January 23-31, 1963

They returned to Kansas City the next day, and we started classes.

Four of my companions and I were in the humanities division. We took literature, music, art, philosophy, and history of the ancient world. All the classes were coordinated, although each had a different teacher. While we were on Greece in one humanities class, we were on Greece in all of them.

Since we were starting at the semester, rather than at the beginning of the year, there were only a few other sisters in our classes: two newly professed Daughters of Charity, a postulant Daughter of Charity, a postulant Sister of Providence, and two Visitandines. They were all very nice, and we talked to them in the classrooms in the few minutes before the professors arrived.

The humanities classes were in the morning. In the afternoon we took P.E., psychology, and an education course. These were large classes, with thirty or forty students.

All our teachers were very good, and our classes were very interesting. Our novitiate scripture classes with Sister Lucy had prepared us well for studying the ancient world. Our teachers at Marillac were impressed with us.

The Daughter of Charity who taught us P.E. was a former WAC sergeant. She believed that marching was a skill every teacher should have, so she taught us to march. We took off our nun shoes for P.E. and put on sneakers. We marched around the gym. The teacher, big and tough, was a veteran not only of World War II, but of social work in the housing projects of Chicago. She marched along beside us, calling cadences and roaring commands.

Marching was fun.

My companions and I enjoyed our walks to and from school and our conversations at school and at recreation. We had not been free to talk for many months, and we had a lot to say to each other. We had not talked to the two classes of juniors ahead of us since they made vows and left the novitiate, so we had a lot to say to them as well.

As the days went by, the juniors in the two classes above us learned from us some of what had occurred in the novitiate after they left. Some of them did not believe us. Others believed us, but felt we should not talk about it. Some believed us and commiserated with us.

I wrote a letter to Sister Wulfram a few days after arriving in St. Louis. I informed her that I had arrived safely and had begun my classes at college. I thanked her for her direction during the previous two-and-a-half years. I asked her to keep me in her prayers. The letter was short, worded the way the retreat master had told us to thank a former superior when we were sent to a new mission.

I placed the letter, unsealed, on Sister Thomas's desk. All mail, incoming and outgoing, was read. That afternoon, when I walked into the house after class, Sister Thomas was sitting in the parlor. She had my letter on her lap. "This letter is not going out," she said. "Sister Wulfram is no longer your superior. You have no business reporting to the novice mistress what goes on in a house where I am superior." She tore the letter in half, then in fourths, then in eighths. She handed me the pieces.

I put them in my pocket.

❖ ❖ ❖

February, 1963

We had cleaning duties at our crumbling mansion. Mine was to sweep the front porch every morning. It was a large porch with columns. There was no railing and there was no furniture. It took about five minutes.

I spent most of my time in class or in the library studying. My companions and I were making a few friends among the other sisters from other orders. Having a Daughter of Charity for a friend was particularly desirable, since fraternization between orders was discouraged. Eileen made friends with one of the Daughters in our humanities classes, Sister Diane.

Diane talked to us before class, and if we had no class immediately following, she would stay in the classroom with us and talk. We were curious about the Daughters of Charity, and Sister Diane answered our questions.

Was it true that the seminary sisters, as their novices were called, were not allowed to use deodorant? True. Their smell was called the odor of sanctity.

Sister Diane took us on tours of the tunnels beneath the provincial house. The Daughters' trunks were lined up along the walls of the clean bright tunnels. Diane's tours always included a glimpse of a seminary sister. Instead of the starched cornettes the professed Daughters wore, the novices wore bonnets like the girl on the Old Dutch Cleanser box.

I made friends with a Daughter who worked in the library. Sister de Lourdes. She would come over to the carrel by the periodicals where I studied, and we would talk. She talked about how strict their junior mistress was, how she yelled at them all the time. I didn't tell her about Wulfram. I didn't want to give her a bad impressions of the Rosalines.

There were some nuns at Marillac who already had a bad impression of the Rosalines. Before assemblies in the gym, the sisters from the various orders sang songs to entertain the others. Valentine and the other Rosalines from Oklahoma always sang

"Oklahoma". They did a lot of yipping and yelling, and some of the other sisters thought it was undignified.

At the assemblies, the president of the college, a Daughter of Charity famous for her leadership of the sister formation movement, would address the students. She would say, "I'm speaking to all of you, Daughters and non-Daughters alike."

One day she said, "I've been asked to stop referring to those sisters who are not Daughters of Charity as non-Daughters. From now on, you who are not Daughters will be called Veils. And the Daughters will be called Cornettes. Instead of Daughters and non-Daughters, you are now Cornettes and Veils."

Everyone laughed and clapped.

There was a school newspaper at Marillac. It came out every week, and every issue looked the same. On the front page, there would be a story about the most recent speaker to appear at the college, maybe Michael Novak or Flannery O'Connor. And there would be an article about the college president's latest achievements. And, in the lower right, there was always a picture of a group of sisters from different orders, four or five professed sisters and a postulant. They posed sitting at a table or on a bench, smiling at each other as if they were having a friendly conversation. No such meetings took place in reality, since sisters from one order rarely spoke to sisters from other orders, and since postulants almost never spoke to professed religious.

There was also a literary magazine. In the February issue, there was an article on J. D. Salinger by Sister Valentine O'Hara, OSR, and a poem about fishing by Sister Emmanuel Thorney, OSR. At dinner on the day the magazine came out, Sister Thomas praised Sister Valentine for her article. She did not mention my poem. Valentine told me that night that it was the first time a Rosaline got published in the magazine. For two of us to get in it in the same month was unheard of, and for me to get in it on my first try was unheard of. Valentine had been submitting stuff to them for two years. Sister Thomas was churlish to refuse to congratulate me.

Valentine told me that Sister Thomas was not a popular teacher at Marillac. Because she was so old and so apt to fall asleep in the middle of class, the nuns from other orders disliked her and were unhappy to be assigned to one of her classes.

In February, Sister Thomas decided that we should not eat between meals. The grocery bills were too high, and she attributed that to our taking food from the refrigerator without permission. She had Sister Digna put a chain around the refrigerator with a padlock on it. The older juniors, including Valentine, had been accustomed to making a sandwich or scrambling an egg or eating some cereal whenever they felt like it. Now, that was finished.

I wasn't sure why the chain was needed when everyone in the house had a vow of obedience. Why couldn't Sister Thomas just order us not to eat between meals?

Our meals were very skimpy and Sister Digna was a very bad cook. A couple of the juniors were good cooks, but they didn't have time to cook for twenty-one people every day. Sister Digna got sick frequently and took to her bed. This put more of a strain on the two juniors who helped her cook.

Sister Thomas decided that cooking three meals a day was too much for Sister Digna and too much for the two helpers. Starting the next day, we would all take turns preparing meals. Sister Digna would fix breakfast, and the rest of us would cook dinner and supper. Sister Thomas put a schedule on the kitchen bulletin board. I was assigned to prepare dinner the following Sunday.

I didn't know what to make. There were no cookbooks in the kitchen and no cookbooks in the Marillac library. I knew how to cook steaks, but there were no steaks in the freezer. On Saturday, I looked in the pantry. There was a recipe for tuna casserole on the back of a bag of Guy's Potato Chips. I had all the ingredients. Several bags of chips, several cans of tuna, several cans of cream of mushroom soup, bags of noodles, and cans of peas. Everything but pimientos. I would leave those out. I multiplied the recipe by six.

We got back from Mass at eight. Sister Digna prepared breakfast and then went upstairs to rest. She left the chain off the refrigerator, so I could cook dinner. I cooked the noodles, assembled the casseroles, and put them in the oven at eleven twenty. While they baked, Sister David and I made a salad. The casseroles came out of the oven to get their crushed potato chip topping. They went back in to brown. They were bubbling and fragrant. Several people came to the kitchen to see what was cooking.

At twelve, we took them out of the oven and put them on the tables. Sister Thomas and the juniors ate every morsel of the tuna casseroles. Sister Thomas said, "That was good, Sister Emmanuel. How did you learn to cook? Did you cook at home?"

"I didn't cook much before I came to the community," I said.

A mistake.

I should not have said, "before I came to the community." I should have said, "before I entered the convent." We didn't say, "before I came to the community." The Daughters used that expression constantly, but we didn't use it. For Rosalines, the word community did not mean the whole convent, but only those nuns who had professed final vows. Even more specifically, it meant those a year past final vows.

Sister Thomas seized upon the narrowest meaning. In a sarcastic voice, she said, "So you consider yourself a member of the community, Sister Emmanuel?"

Everyone waited to see how I would answer the question.

"No, Sister," I said. I was not part of the community, and it was beginning to look as if I never would be.

That night, Valentine was supposed to cook supper. Instead, she took my companions and me to Steak 'n' Shake. We ate in the car and carried more steakburgers and fries and milkshakes home to the others. Valentine paid for the food with money her parents had given her.

At recreation that night, everyone talked about what great food we had eaten that day. Tuna casserole with potato chip topping for dinner, and cheeseburgers and milkshakes and French fries for supper. Sister Jean Edward, who would be cooking dinner the following Wednesday, planned to make the tuna casserole again. She had already written the ingredients on the shopping list, even the pimientos.

Sister Digna was not happy to hear the talk about good food. She thumped around in the kitchen, checking the padlock on the refrigerator, banging the cupboard doors. Finally she came back out to the library with her hand on her heart. She was breathing heavily, and two of her companions, accustomed to her spells, helped her up the stairs.

That night, she told Sister Thomas she was dying. A priest was summoned, and he gave her Extreme Unction. We knelt by her bed all night, saying the prayers for the dying. By morning, she felt a little better and went to sleep. We went to class.

It was hard to stay awake in class. Getting up at four every morning was hard enough. Missing a night's sleep was terrible. I cut my classes that afternoon and slept on my bed. Valentine was asleep on her bed, too, wrapped in the fur rug from the Bentley.

She had been eating a Hershey bar, and the wrapper was on the floor. Valentine always had fifteen or twenty Hershey bars in her top drawer, arranged by size. The biggest bars were in the back. The medium sized bars were in the middle. The small bars were in front. She did not like Hersheys with almonds. Valentine's parents sent her candy and money.

Sister Thomas took Sister Digna to the doctor. An osteopath. He felt that Sister Digna had not suffered a heart attack, but he advised her to take it easy.

❖ ❖ ❖

March, 1963

Valentine and I talked every night in our room. We ignored the night silence. We talked about everything. Our families. Wulfram. Marillac. Where we would be missioned. Valentine wanted to teach at Albertine High School, not at the academy. Teaching at Albertine was reserved for the best teachers, the smartest nuns, the nuns who could handle high school boys, the nuns who could direct plays and put on speech contests and pageants and take kids on school trips and run the school paper and the yearbook and the literary magazine. Valentine was certain she would be missioned to Albertine. She saw me as more of an academy teacher. Being freshmen prefect. Giving piano lessons. Teaching history.

That was how I saw myself. I would like to give piano lessons, because that meant I would have a studio, one of the nice rooms in the auditorium building like those where Sister Lucy and Sister Francine gave private lessons. And prefecting freshmen would be fine. That meant I would sleep in the tiny room behind the freshman dorm on the third floor of the auditorium building. That would be a perfect room for me, remote and private.

Sometimes Valentine slept all day Saturday. Sometimes most of Sunday, too.

I was spending most of my time studying in the library. The modern glass building was a pleasant place to study. I was fascinated by the Greeks and the Romans. Our history professor, a Precious Blood nun, graded us on how many journal articles we read and reported on. I read over a hundred. I knew the Greek and Roman pantheons backwards and forwards.

I avoided Sister Thomas as much as possible.

Sister Digna had another spell in March, and we knelt at her bedside all night praying for her. She was rarely able to cook. The food situation was deteriorating further. The Cornettes generously provided dessert and coffee for the Veils in a little room in the provincial house. This was for nuns who brought their lunch in brown bags. They could eat in this room and finish their meal with a piece of Daughters' sheet cake and a cup of coffee. My companions and I started eating dessert there every day after our dinner at home. We were supplementing our meager rations.

On St. Patrick's Day, Valentine took several of us to Dairy Queen for "Valentine O'Hara sundaes", chocolate with peanuts. I would have preferred a hot fudge sundae or a malt, but beggars can't be choosers.

Valentine always had spending money. Her companions did, too. I decided to ask my parents for some money when they came for Easter.

❖ ❖ ❖

April, 1963

The NCEA convention was held in St. Louis that year. National Catholic Education Association. Thousands of nuns came from all over the country. They filled the local convents and hotels. Twelve Rosalines, including Sister Alexandra, came from Kansas City to attend the convention. We did not have twelve extra beds in the house. There was an extra bed in Sister Thomas's room, and there was a sofa in the parlor. Ten of us had to give up our beds to the visitors and sleep on the floor.

There was no carpet on the floor, and there were not enough blankets to make pallets.

With the exception of Alexandra, the nuns who came to stay were in their late twenties and early thirties. This trip to St. Louis was a treat for them. They got a few days off from teaching, and they had tickets to Hans Küng's keynote address.

These nuns had entered the convent ten years before us. They resented us, and they were open about it. They had been missioned immediately after Profession and still had not finished their degrees, while we had been sent straight to college after receiving our black veils. We had contributed nothing to the community yet, but the community was paying for our education. What if we left the convent? What if we took our degrees and walked out the door? These nuns had been teaching grade school for seven or eight years. They felt that we should have been sent to take their places in the parochial schools, freeing them to go to college full time.

Sister Alexandra didn't join in the criticism. I didn't get a chance to talk to her the first two days. She was downtown at the convention during the day, and I was at school. In the evenings, at recreation, she talked to her companions, Jean Edward, Loretta, and the others.

By the third night of sleeping on the floor, having even worse meals than usual, and having no hot water, I was exhausted and miserable. That was the night Alexandra left the bed she had been sleeping in, mine, to come down to the landing where I was trying to sleep on the floor. It was midnight. Sister Regina was snoring on the floor beside me. Valentine was in her own bed. She had not given up her bed to a visitor.

Alexandra tiptoed down the steps and made a sign for me to follow her. "I've got to talk to you," she whispered.

I could see her face. The street lights shone through the front window, and I could see my old roommate's beautiful face. Her blond hair was longer than I had ever seen it.

It was obvious that Alexandra was in trouble. I knew if I got up and followed her downstairs, we would talk for the rest of the night.

I shook my head no. Instead of going with my friend as she would have gone with me, I brushed her off with the pretense that I didn't want to break silence. Instead of just saying no, I'm too tired, I gave her a sanctimonious little head shake that said, no, I'm too holy to break night silence.

I refused to talk to someone who had been my best friend for four years, because I was too tired. And I hid behind a rule that I broke every night with Valentine. I was a hypocrite. A whitened sepulcher

Alexandra went back up the steps. The next day was the end of the convention. The visitors left. All the excitement was over, the bags of free stuff from the exhibitors, the textbooks from publishers, the speech by Hans Küng, everything. We were back to normal. The chain, which had been left off the refrigerator while the visitors were in the house, was put back up. We attended Holy Week services at the parish church. My parents arrived in St. Louis on Saturday. After Mass at St. Ann's Easter morning, they took Valentine and me downtown to the Sheraton Jefferson Hotel for breakfast. After breakfast, we went to the zoo. After the zoo, we went over to Illinois to visit the Shrine of Our Lady of the Snows. We came back to St. Louis and went to dinner at an Italian restaurant on the Hill. Valentine and I did not drink wine. Rosalines did not drink alcohol.

The next day my parents drove back to Kansas City. They gave me some money.

❖ ❖ ❖

May, 1963

Two of my best friends from Rosaline Academy had become Sisters of St. Joseph. They entered the convent two years before I did. They finished high school in the novitiate, and now, two years professed, they were students at their order's college in St. Louis.

They called me a few times to arrange to meet, but it was not until May that Sister Thomas allowed me to accept their invitation. Sister Eileen would be my companion for the day.

The two Sisters of St. Joseph drove up our driveway in a new car. They honked the horn and then jumped out of the car and ran up the steps. I opened the door, and they came in. We hugged and laughed about how different we were from the last time we had seen one another, nearly five years earlier. They greeted Sister Thomas, and she seemed to remember them.

I took them upstairs to show them my room. One of my bonnets was hanging on the closet door. One of my friends, Cathie — Sister Bernard, took off her St. Joseph headgear and tried on my Rosaline headgear. She looked at herself in the mirror and adjusted the veil. "I would have made a gorgeous Rosaline," she said.

Valentine was lying on her bed reading. She got up and offered one of her bonnets to my other friend, Joan — Sister Judith.

Valentine and I tried on the St. Joseph headgear. Their veils were longer and sheerer than ours. Their habits were more deeply pleated and made of a finer serge. The Sisters of St. Joseph were rich. The four of us, in each other's veils, walked around the house, knocking on doors, showing everyone how we looked.

After we were back in our own headgear, the Sisters of St. Joseph took Sister Eileen and me to their motherhouse in south St. Louis. We arrived in time for morning collation.

Instead of eating bread and butter from a meat block in a corner of the kitchen, the Sisters of St. Joseph took their morning collation in a parlor. There were plates of delicate cookies. Pink punch was served from a crystal punch bowl. The sister serving the punch, my friend Cathie told us, was a novice. In their order, the novices wore black veils like the professed religious.

Eileen and I stood in the crowd of nuns in the beautifully appointed parlor, drinking delicious cold punch from little crystal cups. The Sisters of St. Joseph talked softly and laughed gently.

Cathie and Joanie introduced us to several of them, including the nun who had been their novice mistress. She greeted Eileen and me warmly and told us how much she admired the

St. Louis branch of our order. She asked us if we had visited the St. Louis Rosalines. "Not yet, Sister," I said, "but we hope to visit the grave of Mother Barbara von Gotthier." That just popped into my head. I didn't want to say that we would not be welcomed by the St. Louis Rosalines. The founders of the Kansas City Rosalines, Mother Juliet Sly and Mother Augusta Proff, had been described in such unfavorable terms in the St. Louis Rosalines' history, that Mother Paula considered suing them for libel. Instead, she refuted their charges with documentary evidence in her history of the Kansas City Rosalines, *Stars for Eternity*.

After the collation, Cathie and Joanie showed us the chapel and the famous carved staircase. They said they had dusted that staircase every day as postulants.

They said we had reservations for lunch at the Bevo Mill.

We went back to the car. We had almost two hours before lunch. Cathie and Joanie asked what we wanted to do. I asked them to take us downtown to look at a few of the places associated with Mother Juliet. I remembered the addresses from Mother Paula's book.

A men's clothing store occupied the site where Mother Juliet's father's theater once stood. Sly's Opera House. Mother Juliet acted on the stage of that theater before entering the convent. Edwin Booth had acted on that stage, as had Joseph Jefferson, Mary Anderson, Charlotte Cushman, Lotta Crabtree. Mother Juliet knew them all.

On the corner where the daguerreotypist took Mother Juliet's picture, there was a shoe store. The corner where Mother Augusta Proff's mother ran a grocery store had disappeared; the north leg of the half-finished Arch stood on the spot where the store had been.

We ate lunch at the Bevo Mill.

In the afternoon, we went to Marillac. My friends had not seen the school before. Sister Eileen tracked down her Daughter friend, Sister Diane, and Diane gave the Sisters of St. Joseph the tour of the tunnels, complete with sightings of two seminary sisters in their Dutch Cleanser bonnets.

We went back to the house. Eileen and Cathie and Joanie and I sat in the parlor. Valentine and Jean Edward drifted in after a while. Cathie and Joanie and I were reminiscing about high school. Both had been day students at Rosaline. We talked about the slumber parties and going to the courtyard at the Nelson Gallery on the mornings after. We talked about going downtown on the streetcar. Shopping at Harzfeld's and Adler's and Kline's and Woolf Brothers and Emery Byrd's. Eating lunch at Italian Gardens. Or at Eddy's. Or, best of all, at the Kansas City Club. Chicken a la king. We talked about Albertine parties and how wild the Albertine kids were.

"We weren't wild," Sister Jean Edward said.

I went into the kitchen to get some drinks for my friends. The padlock was in place on the refrigerator door. There were no soft drinks in the refrigerator, but I could have gotten to the ice. I served glasses of water with no ice.

At four o'clock my friends left.

Sister Thomas told me I was to invite them to Sunday dinner. I called them the next day and invited them. They accepted.

Sister Digna was not feeling well on Sunday, but Sister Jean Edward and Sister Regina cooked dinner. Tuna casserole with potato chip topping. After dinner, Cathie and Joanie took Eileen and me to see their juniorate. The Sisters of St. Joseph lived in a modern college dorm. Each junior sister had her own room, air conditioned, with a sink, shelves, a desk, a closet, a bookcase, a desk chair, and an upholstered chair.

My two friends were graduating. Both were missioned. Sister Judith would be teaching at a grade school in Michigan's Upper Peninsula. Sister Bernard would be teaching English at a high school in Chicago.

Sister Eileen and I talked about them as we walked up the hill to Marillac the next day. Eileen said the differences between our two orders lay in their European origins. Rosalines were German. Sisters of St. Joseph were French. The crystal punch bowl and the polite conversations were French. The padlock on the refrigerator and the meat block were German.

We had exams the last week of May. On the thirty-first, at dinner, Sister Thomas passed out little envelopes to some of us. Valentine and her classmates each got one. My companion Sister Helen Marie and I got one. They were from Mother Paula.

Missions.

Sister Valentine would be teaching English at Albertine High School. Sister Helen Marie and I would be teaching summer school religion at St. Roch's the first week of June. Then we would return to Marillac for summer school. I was to take two courses in Spanish each session. It was already arranged with the registrar. I would be teaching third, fourth, and fifth grades at St. Roch's in the fall. The increasing number of Cuban students made it imperative that I learn Spanish.

Valentine was happy to be missioned to Albertine, but she was not happy that I was missioned to St. Roch's.

"You don't understand," Valentine said, as we discussed it in our room later. "You're off the secondary track now and on the elementary track. You'll never finish your degree now. You'll never go to Notre Dame with me."

"Notre Dame?"

"After I teach for a year or two, I'm going to Notre Dame to get a master's in English."

"You are?"

"My parents are paying for it. I'll have to have a companion. I was hoping you could go with me. Graduate school is the perfect way to get out of teaching. Once you start, you can do it forever. A master's degree. Then a fellowship. Summer workshops. More fellowships. A Ph.D. We can be like Sister Frederick and Sister Jeanette." They were two Rosalines notorious for attending graduate school for years, for piling up degrees, for teaching at remote colleges, and for never appearing at the motherhouse.

It would be nice to go to Notre Dame with Valentine, but I could not ask my parents to finance my education. They couldn't afford to support me at Notre Dame or anywhere else.

"You've got to get out of it," Valentine said. "Tell Mother you don't want to teach at St. Roch's or any other dinky little grade school in the middle of nowhere. Tell her you want to stay in school. And no Spanish. Tell her you want to finish your degree in history. Tell her you want to go to Notre Dame with me."

❖ ❖ ❖

June, 1963

We drove to Kansas City the next day. Valentine drove Sister Thomas, Sister Helen Marie, and me. We stopped for lunch at Ernie's in Columbia. Twin Chopped Cows. Boone County ham and eggs for Sister Thomas.

Sister Thomas was returning to the motherhouse to stay. She would continue to be junior mistress, but the local superior of the house in St. Louis would be Sister Martina. She would go back to St. Louis with us at the end of the week. Valentine would help out at camp while Helen Marie and I taught summer school.

We reached Kansas City at three o'clock. When the familiar skyline appeared on the horizon, I felt happy to be home. We went to Mother Paula's office to let her know we had arrived. We thanked her for our missions. She told us to ask Sister Isidore for our room assignments. Sister Thomas had a permanent room on the second floor. Valentine would be staying in an academy dorm. Helen Marie and I would be staying on the third floor. Wulfram's floor.

Helen Marie and I drove out to St. Roch's on Monday morning. We used a convent car. The old St. Roch's car that Sister Kevin drove was in the shop. I parked in front of the two-story building. Helen Marie and I went inside. The classrooms were clean, and the bulletin boards were empty.

The kids began arriving a few minutes before eight. These were not the regular students. These were Catholic kids who attended public schools. For a week they would study religion with us.

Helen Marie took the first through fourth graders upstairs to Mass. I took the fifth through eighth graders. The old pastor said Mass, and then we went downstairs for class. I reviewed prayers with the kids and questioned them on the Sacraments. At ten, we had recess. After recess, more on the Sacraments. At noon, we dismissed the children and started home.

At 95th and Holmes, there was fresh tar on the road. A man with a stop sign came over to the car to direct me away from the tar. Too late. He said, "Did you sisters hear about the pope?"

Pope John XXIII was dead.

Back at the motherhouse, I got in trouble for the tar on the car. Mother Paula told me to get it off. While I was in the driveway scrubbing the car, Wulfram leaned out her third floor window and called down to me. "Sister Emmanuel! When you're finished with that, come up here. I want to talk to you."

I didn't go. I didn't want to talk to her. I went over to the academy to find Valentine. She was reading on a bed in a room in the Farmhouse. Not my old room, but one across the hall.

She asked me if I had talked to Mother Paula yet. I told her I would not be asking Mother Paula to let me stay at Marillac. I was glad to be missioned.

"The pope is dead, " I said.

"So I hear," Valentine said. "I guess you haven't heard about Alexandra."

"What?"

"She left. This morning. Mother Paula took her to the bishop for a dispensation. She came back here, changed into a dress she had, took a cab to the airport, and flew off to wherever her parents are stationed now. Thule, Greenland, or somewhere."

Sister Alexandra. My old roommate Sandy Meade. She had left the convent. She left without saying goodbye to me. I didn't blame her.

I walked across the hall to our old room. I looked out the windows we used to look out. I looked at the little desk where Sandy studied. She often wore one of her dad's blue Air Force shirts instead of pajamas. She was beautiful enough to be a model. What would she do now? She was twenty-two. She had no degree.

At the end of the week, Valentine drove Sister Martina, Sister Helen Marie, and me back to St. Louis. We stopped at Ernie's for lunch.

Sister Martina, our new superior at the St. Louis house, had been principal of the academy when I was in school. Now she was finishing her Ph.D. at St. Louis University and needed to be in residence the last few months. She had marched with Martin Luther King at Birmingham. She talked about him all the way to St. Louis. We arrived in St. Louis at three. By four, the chain was off the refrigerator. Sister Martina told Sister Digna to put the chain in the trash.

I started classes the next day. My Spanish teacher was a nun from Texas. All day every day I sat in her classroom studying Spanish. I learned to read Spanish; it was like Latin. And before long, I could understand the teacher and some of the speakers on the tapes, particularly the Mexicans and Cubans. But I couldn't speak it. I was too self-conscious. My Kansas City accent was too strong.

At night, it was too hot to sleep. Valentine and Regina had pushed their beds up to the windows in our room, but mine was in the corner. It was even worse for my companions in the attic. They were unable to sleep in their beds at all and usually ended up on the floor in the front hall.

Sister Martina had to make frequent trips to the library at St. Louis University, and she often chose me to drive her. We would stop at a public library on the way back to check out mystery novels.

Martina taught sociology at Marillac, and everyone was impressed with her, even the Daughters. The other Rosaline juniors and I felt proud to have a member of our order on the faculty whom everyone respected, someone who had marched at Birmingham with Martin Luther King.

❖ ❖ ❖

July, 1963

I got A's in the two Spanish courses I took in the first session. On July eighth, the second session of summer school began, and I took two more Spanish classes.

On the fourteenth, we went to Sportsman's Park to watch the St. Louis Cardinals beat the Chicago Cubs, 10 to 3. The owners invited the nuns to the stadium every year, and there were hundreds of nuns in the stands from dozens of orders. Most were wearing sunglasses, the fad for nuns that year. Most had left off their undersleeves. We got hotdogs, Cokes, peanuts, popcorn, all free.

St. Ann's parish held its annual novena to St. Ann, and some of the other Rosalines and I walked to the church in the evening to attend the services. I bought a vial of St. Ann's Oil for a dollar. Sister Digna was indignant about the waste of money. She reported me to Sister Martina.

Sister Martina told me about it as we drove to St. Louis University the next day. She was not mad that I had spent money on something silly. She did not ask me where I got the money. Martina was a lenient superior. She simply put the money in her purse and hung her purse on the doorknob of her room. If someone was going to the grocery store, the money was there.

We talked about Sandy Meade. Sister Martina told me Sandy had had a miserable year at her school in Kansas City, Kansas. The parish was poor, the children were dirty, and the superior was certifiable. She would lock herself in her room for days at a time, leaving Alexandra and the other nun to cover for her at the three-room school.

"Sounds like Wulfram," I said.

Sister Martina said it had all become too much for Sandy.

I parked by the Coronado Hotel. Sister Martina and I walked up to the library. "Speaking of Wulfram," Martina said, "she's out as novice mistress."

What?

It hadn't been announced yet, Martina said, but Wulfram had been replaced as novice mistress by Sister Mary Editha.

Why?

The second-year novices, the group of eight behind my group, the group that had entered the convent during the rehearsals for the Kansas Centennial program and had witnessed Wulfram's treatment of my companions and me during the year-and-a-half that followed, had suffered the long punishment with us. After my class made vows and left the novitiate, Wulfram treated the new second-year novices even worse than she had treated us. Five of them left in one week in April.

I had noticed in June that only three second-year novices remained. And only two canonicals. The novitiate was smaller than it had been for twenty years. I wondered what would happen if the remaining five novices left.

"One of the second-years tried to kill herself," Sister Martina said.

It happened on a Friday night. Wulfram humiliated the novice, Sister Constance, at the Chapter of Faults. While the novices knelt on the floor in the Novitiate, Wulfram excoriated Sister Constance for over an hour. She stopped only when Constance fainted.

Later that night, Constance swallowed dozens of aspirin and a bottle of cough syrup. She emptied the giant economy size bottles in the supply cabinet. One of her companions noticed she wasn't up in the morning. She went to her room and found her unconscious. They rushed her to the hospital. She had her stomach pumped.

Four of her companions left the convent the next day.

Their parents went to the bishop. The bishop told Mother Paula to relieve Wulfram of her duties as novice mistress and replace her with someone sane.

Wulfram was informed of her dismissal from her position on June second. When she called to me to come up to her room on the third, the day I was scrubbing the car, the day the pope died, it was probably to tell me what had happened.

Her replacement, Sister Mary Editha, had taken over already, but Wulfram was still living on the third floor. She would be moving to her new assignment after retreat. She would be going to the school where Sister Alexandra had taught. Wulfram would be the superior of the three-nun convent and principal of the three-room school in Kansas City, Kansas.

Why would she be made a superior of anything? I wanted to ask Sister Martina that question and several others, but I could see that she felt she had said enough. "This is not generally known," she said.

While Sister Martina was meeting with her thesis advisor, I went into the College Church. It was cool and quiet in the vast church. I went to confession to Father Bowdern. The green light above his confessional was on, as it nearly always was. "You're a very good girl," he told me. "God loves you very much."

On my way out of church, I stopped in the vestibule to examine the pamphlet rack. There was a good selection of Rosaline

Press publications. I did a little rearranging to give them better positions. I may have covered some leaflets from other presses with Rosaline pamphlets. I read a poem on a holy card from another press.

I'M THE DADDY OF A NUN

Sure my daughter has been vested
And my joy I cannot hide,
For I've watched her from the cradle
With a father's honest pride.
But the morn she left me early
I was feeling mighty blue,
Just a-thinking how I'd miss her
And the things she used to do.
But now, somehow it's different,
With each rising of the sun,
And my heart is ever singing,
"I'm the daddy of a nun."
Since to err is only human
There's a whole lot on the slate,
That I'll have to make account for
When I reach the golden gate.
But then, I'm not a-worrying
About the deeds I've done,
I'll just whisper to Saint Peter,
"I'm the daddy of a nun."

— Author Unknown

It reminded me of James Whitcomb Riley. I went outside and walked around the corner to the university theater. I went inside. I walked down the aisle and went up on the stage. I thought of the time my academy classmates and I traveled to St. Louis in 1958. We had won our division in the one-act play competition for Catholic high schools in Kansas City, so we got to go to St. Louis to compete for the state title.

We rode the train. There were kids from other schools on the train. Kids from Lillis and Hogan and Albertine. Guys from Rockhurst and De La Salle. We stayed at the Coronado Hotel.

On this stage, kids from Catholic schools all over Missouri put on their one-act plays. Our turn came on the second afternoon. We came in second. We lost to a girls' school in St. Louis. Not Rosaline Academy.

That night we attended a play put on by university students. Theater majors. Hamlet. Some of us left at intermission and walked down Lindell. We stopped in a Toddle House and ate hashed browns. I talked to a boy from Lillis. The next night, there was an awards banquet at the Coronado Hotel and a mixer at St. Mary's Academy. Father Bowdern was the Master of Ceremonies. I danced with the boy from Lillis.

I bowed to the ghosts in the empty theater, including the one sitting in an aisle seat near the back, sixteen-year-old me. I left the theater and went to the library to read magazines and wait for Sister Martina.

So Wulfram was out. A novice had tried to commit suicide. It took that for Mother Paula to remove Wulfram from her position as novice mistress. I was glad Sister Constance hadn't died. What had Wulfram said about her at the Chapter of Faults to make her do that?

There were nuns everywhere in the library. There were as many nuns at St. Louis University as at Marillac College and from as many or more orders. But these nuns were older. These nuns were graduate students.

❖ ❖ ❖

August, 1963

Our classes ended. I got A's in the two Spanish classes I took in the second session.

We went to Kansas City on August 4th.

At the motherhouse, I was assigned a room on the second floor. Sister Isidore, in charge of the second floor, told me I got that room for retreat since I would be staying at the motherhouse after retreat. This would be my room as long as I lived at the motherhouse and taught at St. Roch's.

There was a rocking chair in my room upholstered with black leather. A desk and straight chair. I put the quilt from Chetopa on the bed. My room was at the front of the southwest wing, overlooking the campus.

During the week before retreat, the motherhouse and the academy were full of nuns. Nearly everyone was home. The juniors went out to camp most days to swim. Valentine and I spent a lot of time sitting up in the window in the hayloft. We talked about everything, particularly about the assignments we would begin at the end of the month.

I would be teaching third, fourth, and fifth grades at St. Roch's and living at the motherhouse. Valentine would be teaching English at Albertine High School and living at the Albertine convent, five blocks north of the motherhouse. We would see each other all the time, because the Albertine nuns came to the motherhouse every Recollection Sunday and often at other times, sometimes just for supper and recreation, since it was so close.

We talked about Wulfram. We talked about the novitiate. There were two postulants, two canonicals, and three second-years. I wondered how seven people got all the cleaning done. The new novice mistress, Sister Mary Editha, smiled all the time.

Retreat started on the tenth and ended on the fourteenth. On the fifteenth, the Feast of the Assumption, Mother Paula invited the community and the juniors to go up to the novitiate. My friends and I rushed up the ramps to see the novices and postulants.

The novices were still a little shell-shocked. When I asked one of the two canonicals how she was doing, she said, "This is the first time you've ever spoken to me. A year ago, when I told you I thought you were like the Little Flower, you laughed, but you didn't say a word."

"We weren't allowed to talk to you," I said.

"I know. Sister Wulfram wanted us to think you were criminals. But we never did. We saw everything."

Wulfram did not come up to the Novitiate. She and the other teachers assigned to the little school in Kansas City, Kansas, left for their mission after breakfast.

In the next few days, the other professed nuns left for their missions. My companions and the other juniors went back to Marillac. Valentine and the other teachers assigned to Albertine moved to their convent on Westport Road.

During the last two weeks of August, Sister Kevin and Sister Estelle and I drove out to St. Roch's nearly every day. We worked on our bulletin boards and made lesson plans. On August twenty-third, we held registration.

The old priest had retired during the summer, and a new pastor, a priest in his thirties, had taken over the parish. At the end of registration, he came into the school and took the money from Sister Kevin. The mothers had paid the first semester's tuition, and Kevin had a cigar box full of checks and bills. The priest took the box out of her hands.

Kevin told him she was accustomed to keeping the tuition money in a school account for use for expenses during the year. She had done that for the past seven years. The new pastor told her he would keep the money in the parish account, and if she needed money for anything, she could ask him for it.

We got back to the motherhouse in time for Vespers. There were so few novices and postulants, that I sat in the first pew. In the refectory, I sat at the professed table now, in the last place. Estelle had the last place at the table across from mine. Meals were no longer served from the cart. Now there were steam trays on half-table, and the nuns served themselves.

As the person in the last chair, I had only one person to talk to, Sister Terence, the short nun who had danced with Valentine. She was a kitchen sister now, but not on duty during meals. After supper, Estelle and I followed her into the kitchen to scrub pots. At seven, we three went upstairs.

On those late August evenings, while the new novice mistress and the novitiate played croquet on the Lilac Field, and the community sat on the chairs and benches in front of the motherhouse, and the cicadas beseeched in the trees, old Sister Thomas and the other two juniors and I sat in the dark juniorate on the second floor.

The juniorate was a corner bedroom in the southeast wing. The bedroom furniture had been replaced with a davenport and a card table with four chairs. We sat there at recreation, sewing and forcing conversation.

❖ ❖ ❖

September, 1963

School started on the third. Sister Kevin had arranged the schedule so that I taught in the third, fourth, and fifth grade classroom in the morning and in the sixth, seventh, and eighth grade classroom in the afternoon. I taught history and math and music to her students while she taught science and reading and art to mine.

It was a great pleasure to be back with the kids I had taught for a short time the previous year. There were more Cubans than ever, and although my Spanish turned out to be incomprehensible by any of them, the new ones learned English after a few days on the playground, just as the ones who came the year before had done.

Some of the kids brought their photograph albums from Cuba to show me. Their First Communion pictures. Their houses. The courtyards. The richly dressed people. The grandparents left behind.

In music, I taught songs and folk dances. In history, we watched movies a lot. My dad got *Johnny Tremain* for us and some newsreels about World War II. I took the kids on a hike to Camp Rosaline. I showed them the buried house and told them about Quantrill. I took them to the old cemetery by the river where a veteran of the War of 1812 lay buried.

On Monday and Thursday evenings after school, Kevin and Estelle and I hurried back to the motherhouse for supper, then Sister Estelle and I went to UMKC for a night class in education. We were unable to attend recreation in the dreary little juniorate, so Sister Thomas and Sister Terence began going to recreation in the community room.

On Wednesday evenings after school, we hurried back to the motherhouse for supper, then Kevin and I went back out to St. Roch's to teach religion to Catholic high school kids who attended public schools.

On Fridays after school, Sister Kevin went to Dr. Lane, a chiropractor in Kansas City, Kansas. She took me as her companion. She drove first to the little grade school where Sister Wulfram was teaching. We would go into the shabby little convent. Kevin would go upstairs to see Wulfram. Wulfram would not come downstairs. I waited downstairs. When Kevin was finished talking to Wulfram, she would come downstairs, and we would go to the chiropractor's office in the Huron Building. I didn't ask Kevin why Wulfram no longer went to Dr. Lane. She had done so nearly every Friday afternoon when I was in the novitiate.

While Kevin got adjusted by the chiropractor, I walked among the graves of the Kickapoo and the Wyandot in the Indian cemetery around the corner.

On Saturdays, Sister Estelle and I drove down to Arndale, Missouri, a small town thirty miles south of St. Roch's, to teach religion. We would eat lunch there and then drive back to Kansas City.

At the motherhouse, everyone was talking about a new book: *The Nun In The World*, by Cardinal Suenens. It was being read at supper, and it was upsetting several of the nuns.

On Friday, September twenty-third, Sister Kevin did not feel well enough to get up in the morning. She told me to cover her classroom as well as my own. Sister Estelle and I drove out to St. Roch's.

A few minutes before eight, we took the kids upstairs for Mass. I was at the organ in the choir loft. I played a few hymns, wondering why the Mass didn't start. Finally, I sent one of the boys to the sacristy to see where the priest was. He wasn't in the sacristy. The altar boys, vested and ready, were wondering where Father was, too. I told the boy to go over to the rectory and ring the bell. Maybe Father had overslept. The boy came back. No one had answered the door at Father's house.

Estelle and I took the kids back downstairs. The three or four parishioners who had come for Mass went home. I told the kids in Kevin's classroom to study silently while I got my kids started on some work.

All day, I was back and forth between the two rooms, but I never went to the front of Sister Kevin's room. I taught and gave directions from the back of the room, from the door, and from the blackboard on the side. I never went up to Kevin's desk.

The next morning after breakfast, Estelle and I set out for Arndale, for our Saturday religion classes. At noon, Father Schmitz, the pastor of the parish, cooked lunch for us in his little rectory. While we were eating lunch, we mentioned the previous day, when the priest at St. Roch's had not turned up for Mass.

Father Schmitz got very alarmed. He jumped up and tried to call the priest at St. Roch's. No answer. He said he would follow us back to Kansas City in his car. We would stop at St. Roch's on the way.

When we reached St. Roch's, I unlocked the door to the school, and Estelle and I went in. Father Schmitz went over to the priest's house to knock on the door. In the school, I went into Kevin's classroom, and this time, I went up to her desk. There was an envelope on the desk addressed to her. There was a key in the envelope.

I went outside. Father Schmitz was at the side of the priest's house, banging on a window. I handed him the key. He opened the front door of the old house and went inside. I stayed on the porch. I watched Father Schmitz go into the dining room. He waved to me to come in. I waited for Estelle. We went into the dark smelly house. It was filthy. There was junk everywhere. Overflowing ashtrays. Whiskey bottles. Wadded up paper on the floor. Dirty dishes in the sink. Dirty pots on the stove with burnt food in them. Everything was a mess except for the dining room table.

The pastor of St. Roch's had run away with a nurse from the nearby psychiatric hospital. In his note to Sister Kevin, he said he was leaving town and leaving the priesthood.

On the lace tablecloth on the dining room table, he had left the stipends for future Masses neatly clipped to Mass intention cards. Dollar bills and a few fives were clipped to cards giving the dates for Masses he had agreed to say in the coming months. In the midst of chaos was this last act of reverence.

He had left the note with the key on Kevin's desk, expecting it to be found Friday morning, but Kevin didn't come to school, and I didn't see it.

The parish account was empty. The tuition money the parents of the school children had given us a month before was gone.

Father Schmitz got on the phone to the bishop. Sister Estelle and I returned to the motherhouse. We told Mother Paula and Sister Kevin what had happened.

Kevin decided to hold a candy sale to raise money for the school.

❖ ❖ ❖

October, 1963

The new pastor was an old priest who disliked nuns and refused to speak to us. He brought his sister with him to St. Roch's, and she delivered his messages to us. If I played a hymn at Mass that he didn't like, his sister would come over to the school at recess and order me not to play it in the future.

When Sister Kevin asked the old priest's sister for some money to pay the janitor, the priest fired the janitor, and his sister told us we would have to clean our own classrooms. She had never heard of nuns taking it upon themselves to hire a janitor before. Good riddance to the old souse.

We decided to have a Hallowe'en party to raise money.

During the week before Hallowe'en, the kids' mothers decorated the basement, the halls, the windows, the front steps. There were jack-o'-lanterns and cornstalks everywhere. In the basement, there were booths along the wall decorated with black and orange crepe paper streamers and big paper masks.

On Hallowe'en, instead of driving back to the convent for supper, Kevin and Estelle and I went to Stroud's for fried chicken. After we ate, we drove back to school.

People started arriving at seven o'clock. The eighty school kids, their parents, other people who lived up and down Red Bridge Road, people from the surrounding farms, doctors and nurses and patients from the psychiatric hospital, patrons from the tavern at 103rd and Holmes, the caretakers from Camp Rosaline, the public school kids we taught religion to in the summer, all came.

The jack-o'-lanterns grinned from the windows and from the front steps. People in fantastic costumes filled the basement.

The kids ran from one booth to another buying candy, throwing pennies in bottles, throwing darts at balloons, getting their fortunes told.

Sister Kevin and Sister Estelle and I ran from booth to booth, scooping the money out of the cigar boxes and putting it in our pockets. When we were weighted down, we transferred the money to the hiding place we had decided on. Behind the fish tank in Estelle's classroom.

We made four hundred dollars.

❖ ❖ ❖

November, 1963

The next day was All Saints Day, so there was no school. Kevin kept her weekly appointment with the chiropractor, even though it was a holyday.

The following day, All Souls Day, Father Schmitz cooked lunch for Estelle and me after our religion classes at Arndale. We talked about the runaway pastor of St. Roch's and the nurse. They were married and living in Cleveland, Father Schmitz said. He had been the other priest's classmate at Kenrick Seminary. They had been friends.

Estelle and I were ready to leave, but Father Schmitz kept talking about his friend in a maudlin way. Finally, as we were edging out the door, he blurted out, "I would leave, too, if I could."

"Leave the priesthood?" The usually silent Sister Estelle was shocked into speech.

"If it weren't for my mother, I would leave this afternoon."

"You've got to live your own life," said Estelle, a practical farm girl from Oklahoma.

"It would break my mother's heart."

I pulled Estelle out the door. We headed back to Kansas City.

We usually didn't stop at St. Roch's on the way back, but that day Estelle wanted to get something she had left in her classroom. I parked in front, and we went inside. Noises. Someone was in the building. The noise was coming from Kevin's tiny office. We walked in.

The old pastor and his sister froze. The priest had been searching a cabinet. His sister was standing on Kevin's desk. She had been searching a cupboard on the wall high above the desk.

After holding the tableau for what seemed like several minutes, they left the office without saying a word to us. The old woman closed the cupboard and climbed down from the desk. The old priest did not offer his sister a hand. They left, caught in the act.

I fell into Kevin's chair. Estelle was doubled over. We were in hysterics at the spectacle we had witnessed. They would never have found the money. We had taken it with us back to the motherhouse, Hallowe'en night. It had gone into a new account on Friday. Kevin and I went to a bank before driving over to Kansas City, Kansas, to the chiropractor.

❖ ❖ ❖

November 22—24, 1963

On Friday, November twenty-second, there was no school at St. Roch's. Sister Estelle and I had signed up for a teachers' conference in Johnson County. We had enrolled in a folk dancing workshop.

We were sitting in a classroom at Bishop Miege High School, watching a demonstration of a square dance, when someone opened the door. The teacher lifted the needle off the record and went to the door. She came back to the center of the room. "President Kennedy has been shot," she said. "In Dallas, Texas."

Eileen and I looked at each other. What should we do? The woman did not seem overly concerned. She started the record again and indicated to the four dancers that they should resume.

The other nuns in the room sat still, but Estelle and I left. We went to the cafeteria, where people were talking about what had happened. Finally, over the loud speaker, an announcement came that the president had died.

Estelle and I got in the car and drove back to Rosaline. We went into the community room to watch television. When the bell rang, we went to the chapel to chant Vespers from the Office of the Dead.

On Sunday, November twenty-fourth, my parents had planned to drive down to Chetopa to look at the graves and make sure the stone that had been ordered for my grandfather's grave was in place. I asked Sister Thomas if I could go with them, and she said I could. I asked Valentine to go along as my companion.

Valentine and my mother and I were walking along Chetopa's main street. My dad was coasting along beside us, listening to the radio in the car. As we passed Harley's drugstore, he signaled to us to come back to the car. Jack Ruby had shot Oswald. We drove back to Kansas City, listening to the radio.

❖ ❖ ❖

December, 1963

On Fridays, I accompanied Sister Kevin and sometimes two or three other nuns over to the Kansas side to the chiropractor.

We would stop at Wulfram's little convent on the way, and we would stop at a drive-in on the way back. On the first Friday in December, instead of walking around the Huron Cemetery while the others were in the chiropractor's office, I went upstairs with them; it was too dark at six o'clock to be alone in a cemetery. I sat in the stuffy waiting room while Kevin and the others went into the interior office. No one else was in the waiting room. I had a book with me, and I started to read.

A door from the inner sanctum opened, and an old man in a doctor's coat came out into the waiting room. He pulled a chair around and sat down facing me. "I'm Doctor Lane," he said. "Senior."

I was not inclined to introduce myself to him, so I said nothing. I continued reading by the dim light of a big lamp on the corner table.

The old chiropractor pulled his chair closer to me. His knees were almost touching mine. "Have they told you about me?" he asked.

I wanted to escape. A few blocks from where I was sitting was Sammie's on Strawberry Hill. There would be kids from my college there right now. Not my classmates, for they had graduated in May, but others like them. They would be drinking beer and dancing in the back room. They would be there now, this early, because the bus from the college arrived in Kansas City at 5:30 and let out its passengers a block from Sammie's. The kids from Kansas City were almost home, and the kids from Chicago and St. Louis had a few hours to kill before their trains left, so everyone headed straight for Sammie's.

The old chiropractor cleared his throat. "I died and went to heaven," he said. "Did you know that? Did anyone tell you about me?"

I was alone in this little room with a nut. If I started yelling for Sister Kevin and the others to come out, what would happen? They would be annoyed with me for disturbing their adjustments. They would think I was the nut. They might be undressed, wearing only hospital gowns. I got up and left the room. I went down the elevator and outside. It was snowing. The snow was blowing hard from the west. I climbed the few steps to the cemetery.

I asked the Great Spirit and the Spirits of the Wea and the Kickapoo and the Wyandot to protect me from the doctor and from all harm. Mighty Gitchimanitou. The street lights were bright enough to make it possible to read the names on the tombstones. Kirisonsa. Hopannikikwe. Saint Nomdamokwa, pray for me. Why were nuns in their early thirties going to a chiropractor every week? Why did so many Rosalines require the ministrations of a quack? Why were so many nuns crazy? Why did so many hide in their rooms?

I waited for the nuns to come down. There was a lot of traffic on Minnesota Avenue and on 7th Street. Christmas shoppers. When I saw the nuns approach the car, I left the cemetery.

"Where were you?" Kevin asked.

I told her it was too hot in the waiting room. I didn't tell her about Doctor Lane, Senior.

The next evening, Sister Kevin had an appointment with a dentist. His office was in one of the high-rise apartment buildings on Quality Hill. Kevin told me he was Wulfram's dentist, as well.

His corner office was on the top floor. His waiting room had a telephone in it. I thought of calling my mother or one of my friends to have a talk, but the door to the inner office was slightly open, and I was afraid Kevin and the dentist would hear me. I could hear him murmur to her occasionally, and I could hear the sound of his drill. There was no one else in the office, no receptionist, nurse, or other patient.

I stood at the window watching the planes land. This building was within a mile of the airport runways, and I could see the people sitting inside the airplanes as they descended. Below, I could see the West Bottoms, the old depot, the stockyards.

I was very unhappy. Here I was again in a seedy waiting room. I was twenty-two, and I was at the beck and call of Sister Kevin, a loud, obnoxious, bossy nun of thirty. Besides the forty hours a week I spent working with her, I was spending two or three hours a week waiting for her. Waiting while she talked to Wulfram in Wulfram's bedroom. Waiting while she was being adjusted.

I heard the dentist talking to Kevin. He said, "What about here? How does it feel when I touch you here? And what about here? Is that different? Is that better? What if I touch you here in the pubic area?"

I had to get out. I was afraid to go downstairs. There were bums and winos below. I could call a cab. I could call my parents. I could go downstairs and take the car and drive back to Rosaline and let Kevin worry about getting herself home. But she had the keys. I was not afraid of winos. No wino would attack me. I could walk down to 11th Street and catch a bus. I had a dollar in my pocket.

Kevin came out to the waiting room while I was planning my escape. She put on her coat, her scarf, her gloves. We rode the elevator down.

I didn't tell her I had heard him. I never told her anything.

In the mornings, in the car on the way to school, Kevin would ask Estelle and me what we were going to teach that day. She was the principal, and she had the right to ask us that. I would tell her what I would be doing with her kids in history in the afternoon. Sometimes, if it was an idea that she liked, she would tell them about it in the morning, so when I brought up the topic in the afternoon, they had heard it already.

Throughout December, the school children poured out their feelings about the assassinated president. They wrote poems and essays and letters. They made scrapbooks. It was all spontaneous. They were overflowing with emotion.

At recess we played in the snow. For some of the Cubans, it was their first snow. One day, it grew dark about noon, gray, heavy. Big flakes of snow began to fall. A Cuban girl, a third grader, stood on her chair to watch. "Oh, Seester," she said, overcome with the sight. By the end of the day, there was deep snow.

We built snow forts in the next few days. Boys against girls. The school was so small, that all the kids played together at recess. The snow forts were twenty feet apart, walls of snow. The kids bombarded each other with snowballs from behind the walls.

On the last day of school before Christmas, we had parties in the classroom, and the kids brought presents to their teachers.

Kevin and Estelle and I drove back to Rosaline with our presents in the back seat and in the trunk.

There was a general permission to do whatever we wanted with presents we got from the school kids, so I removed the tags and put on new tags with the names of the oldest nuns. I put them under the tree in the community room.

Sister Estelle and Sister Terence and I attended recreation in the community room, even though we were juniors. Sister Thomas no longer wanted to sit with us in the tiny juniorate. She wanted to play bridge with Mother Paula and her other friends. They sometimes got mad at each other and raised their voices.

One of the reasons I entered the Rosalines instead of the Benedictines was that I thought the Benedictines were perfect. I never saw them argue or speak sarcastically to one another, not in grade school or in my year at their college. I was afraid I could not be so perfect. At Rosaline Academy, I occasionally saw two of my teachers get impatient with each other and raise their voices.

The Benedictine Order was much stricter than the Rosaline Order. They were not allowed to enter their parents' houses or eat in restaurants. Rosalines had home visits every five years. We could attend our close relatives' funerals. We could eat in public.

I enjoyed recreation in the community room, but I was rarely able to attend because of night school at UMKC and religion class at St. Roch's and going with Kevin to the chiropractor. Sometimes, on the nights I was at the motherhouse, I went to sleep in my room instead of going to recreation.

I was always tired. Sometimes I couldn't get up when the bell rang in the morning. I would sleep until the last possible minute, then take a shower, get dressed, and meet Kevin and Estelle at the car. Sometimes Kevin did this, too, so that the only person receiving Communion during meditation was Estelle.

Sister Thomas would sometimes come up to my room in the morning if I was not at morning prayer. She would shake me awake. Not getting up for morning prayers was considered a sign of a lost vocation.

Valentine was in trouble with her superior for sleeping late, too. The nuns at Albertine High School were divided about the changes being talked about, and they argued constantly.

The lack of harmony led Valentine and four other nuns to ask Mother Paula to allow them to move out of the Westport Road convent and into an apartment on Mercier. Mother Paula had agreed to let them do that. They would be moving into the apartment in January. An experiment in a new form of communal living, we were told. They would not be required to attend Office, but could say it privately. That alone added an hour to the day. Cardinal Suenens had pointed out the need for modernized horaria; teaching nuns needed their rest. Every nun did. We had heard that he had insisted that Poor Clares in Canada stop sleeping on narrow reclining boards and sleep in beds.

Other things were changing. The Friday night Chapter of Faults was abolished. I had attended only one in the community room. The other juniors and I accused ourselves of our faults, and then we were dismissed; juniors did not stay to hear the community nuns accuse themselves. That turned out to be the last Chapter of Faults at Rosaline. Mother Paula decided a group discussion would be better.

It was worse. At the Chapter, the faults confessed were not really faults. It was just a ritual. No one thought worse of anyone else for breaking a dish or failing to observe custody of the eyes. But at the new discussions, we sat in a big circle, and the oldest nuns criticized the younger nuns. "They chew gum." "They cross their legs." "They wear loafers." "They've cut off their cinctures."

Those all applied to me. I hadn't wanted to cut my cincture, but it was the new fad, and Kevin and Estelle had insisted. There was a lot of talk about changing the habit, giving up the habit, wearing uniforms like airline stewardesses, wearing secular clothing. It was coming in bits and pieces. Cutting the long cincture, so that it was simply a belt, was one step. I also left off my rosary. I had never liked wearing the side rosary, and now I stopped wearing it. I had never worn a pen and pencil holder, but now I had keys at my side. I stopped wearing those and carried them in my pocket.

The sleeves of our habits kept getting narrower. I had not adjusted mine, but Kevin and Estelle wanted me to. They wanted the three of us at St. Roch's to be alike.

I wore black loafers now instead of nun shoes. I wore men's socks instead of long stockings. I had considered Sister Dominic slovenly for wearing loafers in the Kansas Centennial summer. Now I was doing it. The men's socks instead of long stockings idea I learned from Sister Jean Edward.

On Christmas, most of the nuns from the missions in and around Kansas City came to the motherhouse. Wulfram did not come. Kevin wanted me to go with her to visit Wulfram in the afternoon. I declined. Kevin was not my superior, just my principal. Kevin was annoyed, but I did not care. Eileen and the others had come home from St. Louis for Christmas, and I wanted to talk to them. Sister Martina came with them.

Sister Martina showed me the letter she had received from Jackie Kennedy. She had written to the president's wife after the assassination and had received a beautiful reply.

My parents came to visit the next day. They gave me an autoharp for Christmas.

❖ ❖ ❖

January, 1964

We had no money at St. Roch's School. We bought large bottles of Vess Cola for a dime and then sold it to the students at lunch for ten cents a glass. We had the kids sell all kinds of stuff to make money.

On the highest shelves in Kevin's office, there were readers and arithmetic books and bible histories and geography books from another era. I had seen ads in teachers' magazines for companies that bought old textbooks. Kevin and Estelle and I packaged the old books and sent them off. Money started pouring in. We made five hundred dollars. If we didn't stop at Winstead's too often, we would make it to the end of the year.

We had no janitor. The kids cleaned the classrooms and the basement.

The pastor never spoke to us. His sister would sometimes come over to the school to issue a demand, but we ignored her.

It was like the story of Mother Barbara von Gotthier. At least this priest could not make us sleep in his basement.

At the motherhouse, there was a bulletin board in the office, and Mother Paula or someone pinned a picture from the newspaper to it. A nun in secular clothing. I stood there reading the article one day after school.

"Disgusting," someone said. Sister Thomas. She was reading over my shoulder. I stepped aside to give her a closer look at the nun she had called disgusting.

It was a strong term to use about a professed religious. The clothes don't make the nun. I admired the Sisters of Social Service, and they were not encumbered by layers of clothes. They wore a habit cut like World War I clothes. Mrs. Hoover's style.

"Don't you think it's disgusting, Sister Emmanuel?" Sister Thomas asked. She was going through her mail.

"No, Sister."

Since I was a junior, and Sister Thomas was junior mistress, my mail went to her slot. She now sorted the mail in front of me. My *Time* magazine went into her stack. She gave me a little smile. "There's an article in here I want to read," she said. She handed me the rest of my mail and left the office.

I realized that the frequently missing issues of my magazines were being kept from me by Sister Thomas. The next day, I changed the addresses so the magazines I subscribed to would be delivered to St. Roch's instead of to Rosaline.

Everyone was talking about changing the habit. Arguing. I could see how the old arguments Mother Paula had recounted in her book must have taken place. Just as the 19th-century orders had split over the boy question and the German question and the tuberculosis question, now there would be splits over the habit.

Just as in the old days, factions formed. There were those in favor of change; Mother Paula, the superior, was in this group. There were those opposed to change; Mother Aurelia, the retired superior, was in this group. There were many nuns aged fifty and up who did not want to go into secular clothing; the habit was easy, and it always looked good. There were many in their thirties and forties who were eager to change; the habit was hot and unhygienic and a sign of aloofness from the people we served.

The factions met and discussed their views apart from one another. The most radical faction met at Mercier, the apartment Valentine lived in. Other radicals were on the outpost missions, deep in Kansas and Missouri. Some of them came home to the motherhouse on weekends to join the arguments.

Some of the nuns made outfits they planned to model at the chapter meeting in the summer. The rest of the community would be permitted to vote on which new habit to adopt. Juniors and novices, not part of the community, were not consulted and would have no vote. One idea for a modified habit was a suit. This could be made from the serge in one habit. One faction was pushing a jumper like I had worn in grade school. And another group proposed a mid-calf version of the habit we were wearing.

I wore a serge habit to school every day. I had two, my Reception habit and one Sister Thomas gave me one day. She didn't tell me where she got it, but I presumed it had belonged to someone who left the convent. I wore one habit for a week, then dropped it off at the dry cleaners on the way to school. I knew we would not be wearing habits for long, so I wasn't trying to preserve them. We would soon be wearing secular clothes.

Where was the money to come from for the new clothes? I knew already. Many Rosalines asked their parents for money. I was not willing to do that. My parents usually gave me ten dollars when they visited, and usually included a five in their letters, but I would not ask them for money for clothes. My parents did not have money to spare. The two neighborhood theaters they ran barely broke even. The late fifties and early sixties were not prosperous times for owners of neighborhood movie theaters.

My parents bought me scarves and loafers and magazine subscriptions and treats from restaurants, but they could not afford to send me to Notre Dame or buy me the kind of clothes I would feel comfortable wearing, and I would not ask them to do so.

At the end of the month, Valentine and her remaining companions made final vows. The Profession ceremony was in English.

❖ ❖ ❖

February, 1964

The Mass was in English now. No more Gregorian Chant. The long refectory tables were removed from the refectory and replaced with round tables. We could sit anywhere we liked. There was no more table reading. No more sung grace.

I usually sat with Sister Angela. She was a nun in her fifties who taught math at the academy. She told funny stories about the farm she grew up on in Kansas. It was so remote that they had an airplane; sometimes they would fly to Kansas City just to see a movie. A few others sat with us, nuns of various ages who had not aligned with a faction. We talked about old movies, those Angela's father flew his family to town to see. We did not talk about the habit. We did not argue about the length of the cincture. Angela was enough of a character to get away with ignoring the burning questions, and I was hiding in her shade.

The discussions that had replaced the old Chapter of Faults had been discontinued. After the second and last one, early in February, Mother Paula realized it was causing pain and dissension. Sister Francine, the choir mistress, started crying when an old nun criticized her for swinging her arms when she walked. It almost made me cry, too. I loved Francine. Her big smile and her energetic walk were two of her charming characteristics. At the end of the discussion, everyone left the community room except Francine and me. She continued to cry. I didn't know what to say. I sat there with her for awhile.

It was clear that the changes would not come quickly and would not come easily. How many years of rancor would it take, before all the disputes were settled?

I still rode to the chiropractor's office every Friday with Kevin and other young nuns who required weekly adjustments. On our way, we always stopped at Wulfram's little convent. She never came downstairs. Kevin went up to her bedroom. I waited in the tiny parlor.

Kevin didn't ask me to go to the dentist with her again.

Sister Estelle and I continued to teach catechism in Arndale. Father Schmitz, having opened up once to us, now continued to do so. He cooked lunch for us, and while we ate, he poured out his troubles. He was lonely. He hadn't wanted to be a priest at all. His mother forced him to go to prep seminary right out of eighth grade. Then to minor seminary. Then to Kenrick. He had never had a date. Now he wanted to get married. If he left, it would kill his mother.

He played classical records for us while we ate lunch. One Saturday he played *The Love for Three Oranges*. "This reminds me of you," he whispered to me, while Estelle was getting something from the kitchen.

I stood up. "Sister Estelle!"

She came into the living room. She saw that I was ready to leave.

When we got back to the motherhouse, Sister Kevin told us that Sister Charlotte had arrived. She had moved into the room next to mine.

Charlotte was about fifty, very fat, and very crazy. She had had some sort of episode at her mission in Oklahoma and had been hospitalized. After a few weeks in the mental hospital, she had been released. She would be living at the motherhouse while she recuperated.

That night, I was awakened by Charlotte's moaning and groaning. She was saying something in a loud eerie voice, but I couldn't understand it.

Someone tapped on my door, opened it, and came in. It was Sister Kevin. She was in her pajamas and robe. No nightcap. Short messy hair. I sat up in bed.

She sat down on my bed and reached to put an arm around me. She tried to pull me close to her. "Don't be afraid," she said. "Charlotte's having a bad night."

So was I. I jerked away from Kevin and jumped out of bed on the other side. I didn't say anything, but Kevin left my room. Charlotte kept moaning.

I was disgusted. I was surrounded by crazy people. Kevin was an extension of Wulfram. How dare she come into my room, in defiance of the rules, and put her arm around me? What if I had permitted her to pull me close? The thought of it made me shudder.

I thought of the note on the light string. Wulfram had falsely and publicly accused Eileen and me of something improper, even sinful. She gave us a public punishment for something we were not guilty of.

If Eileen and I really were particular friends, why would Wulfram put us in a room together? She would be putting us in a near occasion of sin.

Wulfram was the one whose friendships were overly intense and exclusive. First Sister Dominic and now Sister Kevin.

Kevin had barged into my bedroom uninvited, against the rules, and made a crude pass at me. She pretended she was putting her arm around me to keep me from being frightened by another crazy nun's midnight screaming.

I had heard from Valentine, who had heard it from a nun at Albertine, that Sister Constance, the novice who had attempted suicide, had rebuffed a similar approach from Wulfram.

Sister Constance had been refectorian, the second-most important position a novice could hold. Wulfram had entered her room one night and sat on her bed and put her arms around her. When Constance pulled away and bounded out of bed, Wulfram left her room.

Constance said nothing to anyone, and Wulfram said nothing, but after that night, Wulfram stopped informing Constance when a nun came home to the motherhouse. As refectorian, it was Constance's duty to set a place for a visiting nun. The nuns would go down to the refectory and go to their tables, and there would be no place for the visitor. She would be left standing somewhere awkwardly, wondering where to sit. Sister Constance would hurry into the kitchen to get a plate and silverware, but everyone would notice.

Wulfram would not be present, since she ate at her desk upstairs, but she would know that it had happened. At Chapter of Faults on that Friday night in April, Wulfram spent an hour criticizing Constance for the recurring problem.

❖ ❖ ❖

March, 1964

Kevin acted as if nothing had happened, and so did I. I continued to ride with her to the chiropractor every Friday. While she went up to Wulfram's bedroom in the little convent, I waited in the tiny parlor. The other two nuns who lived there rarely appeared. At the Huron Building, I waited in the Indian cemetery or went into the public library up the street.

I had decided to leave the convent.

❖ ❖ ❖

April, 1964

I told Mother Paula during Easter week. I had rehearsed my speech and my answers to the questions I expected her to ask, but she didn't ask any questions. She just burst into tears.

She cried like a baby. Big tears shot out of her gray eyes. She fumbled in her sleeve for her handkerchief. She blew her nose and wiped her eyes. Finally she said, "You can't leave. I need you."

She showed me the chart on her desk. She had been working on missions for the coming year. Kevin would be going to Fordham to finish her degree in theater at last. Estelle would be going to Marillac. "I need you at St. Roch's," Mother Paula said. "There are only going to be two rooms next year, and no one else can handle those youngsters."

"Two rooms?"

"Father Carl called me. He said only two rooms next year. Not enough students for three rooms. First through fourth and fifth through eighth. I think he just doesn't want to pay for three sisters." She blew her nose again. "You can't leave, Sister Emmanuel. I've got no one else who can work with Father Carl. Please don't do this now. Please take at least a year to make up your mind. Maybe you'd like to talk to someone. Maybe you'd like to go to Dr. Lane."

The chiropractor? To be adjusted? No thanks. And no thanks to talking to someone. A Cuban psychiatrist. Several of the nuns were seeing Cuban psychiatrists. Nearly as many as saw Dr. Lane. Mother Paula thought I should see a psychiatrist because I was tired of living in a lunatic asylum? How would a psychiatrist adjust me to fit into a place where craziness was the norm?

I agreed to stay. To think about it for a year.

Mother Paula wiped her eyes again. She said I would teach vacation school in Arndale for a week in June, then go to summer school at Marillac for more Spanish, and then teach fifth through eighth grades at St. Roch's. Mother Paula said she would let me know later who would be teaching with me.

She didn't ask me why I wanted to leave the convent, and I didn't tell her.

❖ ❖ ❖

May, 1964

Valentine was furious. "You did it all wrong," she said. "You should have told her you'd stay *if* she lets you go to Notre Dame with me." Valentine had come to the motherhouse for Recollection Sunday. It had ended at two, and now we were walking down the South Drive.

"I don't want to go to Notre Dame."

"Don't be stupid. You'll be teaching grade school in the boondocks forever. You had the perfect chance to get out of it." Valentine would be going to Notre Dame for summer school, starting on her master's degree in English. "You could finish your B.A. at St. Mary's Notre Dame and then go to graduate school at Notre Dame."

"I like teaching," I said.

Valentine said, "You missed your chance. You could have gotten her to do anything. You don't understand how it works. If there's something you want, you threaten to leave, and you get it. How do you think Wulfram got to be novice mistress?"

"Threatening to leave?"

"Of course. The minute Mother Paula was elected, Wulfram went to her and told her she was leaving. A couple of people always leave after an election. Not satisfied with the outcome. Mother Paula didn't want to lose Wulfram, so she told her to ask a boon. Ask anything, name her price. Wulfram wanted to be novice mistress. A high price, but Mother Paula paid it." Valentine heard these stories from the nuns at Albertine.

"Why would Mother Paula want to keep her?"

"Wulfram was a rising star. Lots of people liked her then. Some still do. Some hate her guts, of course. Some people think she killed Rose Anselm."

The nuns at Albertine told Valentine that Wulfram had always had special friends, crushes. Dominic and Kevin were only the latest in a long line. Some of the nuns thought Rose Anselm had been another, and that Wulfram, instead of keeping her isolated up on the third floor, should have insisted she get adequate care.

"They went to the hospital," I said. Wulfram and Rose Anselm went to the hospital the day after Wulfram put her clammy hands on my face and said, "Don't crucify me."

"They went to St. Margaret's," Valentine said. "To a quack. Some old doctor who doesn't send bills to the good sisters. Rose Anselm should have gone to a heart specialist. A lot of people blame Wulfram for Rose Anselm's death. And everyone blames her for Constance. What if Connie had died?"

If Connie had died, no one would know why she had killed herself.

We went in the Grotto. I asked Valentine if she would go with Estelle and me to Arndale the following Saturday. It would be our last catechism class of the year, and the parents were planning a picnic.

No. She would be busy packing to go to Notre Dame.

On Saturday, when Sister Estelle and I drove up to the little church in Arndale, the two eighth grade girls were waiting for us. They got in the car to direct us to the picnic. On a field at the end of the main street of the little town, there was a small plane. We saw Father Schmitz and the ten or so Catholic families of the town standing around the barbecue grill and the picnic tables. The kids ran over to greet Estelle and me. "You're going up in Father's airplane!"

It was our surprise, Father Schmitz told us. His special treat for the sisters. After the picnic, he was going to take us for a ride in his plane.

"I'm afraid we can't do that without permission," I said.

"Oh, but it's all taken care of." He had called Mother Paula and told her of the surprise. She had given Estelle and me permission to fly in the priest's plane.

We ate lunch with the people of the town. Then, with their encouragement, we got in the plane. Father Schmitz helped Sister Estelle into the single seat in back. I sat in the seat next to his. "You'll be my navigator," he said. He handed me a map.

He took off. He had been cleared for the next hour to fly low over Kansas City. He turned left at Paseo High School and flew up 47th Street, flew over the Nelson Gallery and the Plaza. Flew over Rosaline. I could see my house below. My mother's car was parked in front. He flew over St. Roch's on his way back to Arndale. I could see Camp Rosaline and the Blue River and the suburbs that were spreading south.

As we were approaching Arndale, Father Schmitz reached over to trace our route on the map I was holding on my lap. He rested his hairy hand on the map. The only things between his heavy hand and my leg were the map, my habit, and my petticoat. I lifted the map to repel his unwelcome touch. I tried to move further away from him, but it was too crowded in the little airplane to put more than a few inches between us.

He landed the plane. "I won't be needing you for summer school," Father Schmitz said, as he walked us to our car. "I've got two lay volunteers coming from Pennsylvania."

Estelle and I laughed in the car on the way back to Kansas City. The priest's little trick with the map was like a boy in grade school trying to put his arm around a girl in a show without being noticed.

I told Estelle about a Friday night in seventh grade when my classmates and I were sitting in my dad's movie theater. We were watching *The Creature From the Black Lagoon*. The girls all sat in one row, and the boys sat in the row behind us. They were too shy to sit next to us and try to put their arms around us, but when the creature emerged in 3-D from the lagoon, one of the boys reached under the seat from behind and grabbed a girl's leg. She screamed so loud and so long that my dad had to come down the aisle to tell her to shut up.

And wasn't it funny that Father Schmitz had waited until after the plane ride to tell us we were fired? And why would lay volunteers come from Pennsylvania to teach summer school religion in Arndale, Missouri? Were there no boondocks in Pennsylvania?

❖ ❖ ❖

June, 1964

Since I didn't have to teach summer school, I went to St. Louis a week early. Sister Martina had finished her dissertation, but was still superior at our house and still teaching at Marillac.

She assigned me to my old room. Since Regina and Valentine were at Creighton and Notre Dame, I would room with Sister Jean Edward and Sister Anna Marie. I was glad to be with both of them. Anna Marie, Valentine's old friend from high school, had been teaching for a year, and now was returning to Marillac to finish her degree. Jean Edward had been teaching for a year and would be returning to the same third grade classroom in the fall. She had just had her first home visit. After five years in the convent, she had spent a week at her parents' house in Kansas City.

She told me all about it. Jean Edward had been the most popular girl in her class, or maybe ever, at Albertine High School. Her friends had remained devoted to her, even during the years of novitiate when she was cut off from them completely. Her friends from her year at college had also remained true. Her parents threw a party for her and invited all the old friends.

Because Jean Edward's parents lived so close to the convent, and because their family was so big and their house so small, and because they were such close friends of the nuns, and because things were changing anyway, and because there was no one available to accompany her, Jean Edward had been allowed to go home alone.

On the night of the party, hundreds of people, or dozens at least, crowded into the little house. All the grade school friends. All the high school friends. All the college friends. All the relatives. The Fitzpatricks. The Sheas. Everyone was there. Everyone but the old boyfriend.

Jean Edward slipped away from the crowd. She took the phone into the bathroom and called him. "Why aren't you here?"

He said he had just gotten off work. He was dirty.

She said, "Just come over. You don't have to change."
He said, "The only thing I want to change is your name."
He came to the party. He was the last one to leave.

I was taking Spanish again. I told the professor, the nun from Texas, that my Cuban students were unable to understand my Spanish. She said that after this summer, they would understand me.

Sister Eileen and I liked to walk past Marillac College, past the provincial house, and up to the Daughters' cemetery for lunch. Rather than going home for Sister Digna's meager dinners, we made sandwiches in the morning at the breakfast table, bread and jelly, and took them with us. We sat in the Daughters' graveyard and ate our sandwiches. We walked among the tombstones and read out the names and dates of the teachers and social workers and nurses.

Eileen and I talked about everything. Eileen and a couple of our other companions had made friends with some Servite seminarians who were attending St. Louis University. She told me about them. One was from Ireland, from a town near her own.

❖   ❖   ❖

July, 1964

Sister Martina told Estelle and me that she had received a letter from Mother Paula which included the news that Father Schmitz of Arndale had run away with one of the lay volunteers from Pennsylvania.

"It will kill his mother," Sister Estelle said.

I spent most of my time in the library. My Daughter friend, Sister de Lourdes, now worked on the second floor, so I studied at a carrel by her desk. On the bookshelf next to me were histories of religious orders, including Mother Paula's *Stars for Eternity*. I propped it up on a little display rack on a bulletin board and pinned up some leaflets and holy cards from the Rosaline Press.

I read the St. Louis Rosalines' bitter account of the revolt by Mother Juliet Sly and Mother Augusta Proff, founders of the Kansas City convent. I could see why Mother Paula had considered suing them. I appreciated the precision with which she had refuted their version of history in her own account of the split; Mother Paula's book included the original documents that proved the new foundation was made with permission from both religious and ecclesiastical superiors. Her tone was measured, unlike the harsh judgments and rancor in the St. Louis Rosaline's history.

After comparing those two books, I read other orders' histories and began to see patterns. The same priests and bishops would appear in two or three different orders' histories. They pulled the same tricks. A priest would go to Europe, convince an order to give him nuns for America, collect the four thousand thalers that King Ludwig paid every new foundation in America set up to aid Bavarian immigrants, go home, keep the money for himself, and work the nuns to death.

Sometimes the priest would sail for America ahead of the nuns he had recruited. He would tell them he'd meet them in New York. They would get off the ship, and he would not be there. Some of the nuns stayed in New York. Others tracked down the priests, surprising them at their churches in the hinterlands.

As the women's orders got established in America, they split off from their European motherhouses. The splits continued. Disputes raged over teaching boys, singing at the parish Mass, veiling the face when going outside the convent, money, elections, unsuitable postulants, tuberculosis, speaking German. Each dispute led to splits. And the splits were described with varying levels of charity in the histories.

Once a split occurred, the two sides ended communication. If nuns from the two convents met seventy years later, at an NCEA convention, for example, they would regard each other with suspicion. They would eye each other for details of habits. They would not feel any affinity. Nuns were trained to regard other nuns as dangerous.

Marillac College was a perfect example. Silence. A minimum of fraternization. Members of one order rarely speaking to members of other orders. I knew that Sister de Lourdes would be leaving the Daughters soon. She whispered to me about how unhappy she was, about how she longed for her family in Minnesota, and about how she had stared at the Jesuit scholastics at the symphony one night.

When I wasn't talking to de Lourdes in the library, I was in my room talking to Sister Anna Marie.

She told me about Valentine O'Hara in high school. Valentine hated being tall. She was good at sports, but it counted for nothing. She was smart, but it counted for nothing. Her parents were rich, but in Tulsa, everyone was rich. Her parents wanted to give her a debutante ball at the country club, but Valentine decided to enter the convent instead.

She knew no boy would ever ask her to marry him. Being a nun was a way to be successful even if you were tall and ugly. Valentine wanted to be a teacher.

Valentine had been miserable in the novitiate, Anna Marie said. If I thought I had it bad under Wulfram, I should have seen how Wulfram treated Valentine. Once she almost hit her.

But now Valentine was happy. Now she was at Notre Dame, where she had always wanted to be. She had gone into the stadium on her first day on campus and kicked a football through the goal post. Valentine was the first and only nun in history to kick a field goal for the Irish. Touchdown Jesus. Golden Dome. The nun who had gone with her to Notre Dame was older than we were. She and Valentine shared a room in a dorm with nuns from orders all over the country. Valentine said in a letter to Anna Marie that the boys at Notre Dame hated nuns and would say filthy things to them when they passed them on campus. Apparently they had bad memories of their grade school teachers and took revenge by insulting Valentine and the other nuns.

❖ ❖ ❖

August, 1964

At the end of summer school, I rode home from St. Louis on the train with Sister Jean Edward. We ate breakfast in the dining car. Scrambled eggs. Orange halves segmented like grapefruits and presented in a silver dish of ice. Coffee.

The porter recognized us as Rosalines. He told us his daughter attended Albertine High School. He was very friendly. So were the other passengers.

Jean Edward and I talked about the scene in Mother Paula's book where two Rosalines were traveling by train in the 1920s. A member of the APA stood up in the train car and started denouncing them. Finally, another man, brave enough to declare publicly that he was Catholic, silenced the first man. "That's enough of that," he said. "Sit down and shut up."

Jean Edward and I arrived at Rosaline at two o'clock.

There were two new postulants. There were four novices, two canonicals and two second-years.

Jean Edward and I heard the latest news almost immediately from the juniors who had arrived before us. A novice had left the convent two days before, a second-year. She was one of the three surviving members of the class of twelve that entered when I was a second-year novice. She went home to her parents' house in Johnson County.

The next day, she went to Wulfram's little convent in Kansas City, Kansas. She knocked on the door. Wulfram opened the door, and the girl tried to stab her with a knife. Wulfram ducked away from her and got the knife away from her. The nuns didn't call the police.

I went to Mother Paula's office to tell her I was home from summer school. She didn't mention the former novice and her attempt to murder Sister Wulfram. She didn't ask me if I still wanted to leave the convent.

She told me my fellow teacher at St. Roch's would be Sister Patricia. Patricia had been teaching first grade in Oklahoma for ten years. Now she would be teaching first through fourth.

I skipped most of the retreat conferences. Valentine didn't come home for retreat. Several of the nuns made private retreats that year or attended retreats at other sites. Wulfram did not attend the community retreat.

On August fifteenth, I went upstairs with the other professed nuns to talk to the novices and postulants. The second-year novice who, as a postulant, told me I reminded her of the Little Flower, now told me she had prayed to be sent to St. Roch's with me. For a while it had looked as if a second-year novice would be going there, but then Mother Paula appointed Sister Patricia.

In the next few days, the professed nuns left for the missions. A few of them made remarks to me to let me know they knew I was thinking of leaving. One said, "I suppose you'll try to talk Valentine into going with you." Another said, "You should pay back the community the money we've spent educating you."

I had no answers for them. They were telling me that they thought I was low enough to interfere with someone else's vocation. How could I stay in a place where people thought I would do that? And they thought I owed money to the community.

The following Sunday, Father Carl, the pastor of St. Roch's, announced to his parishioners that registration for school would take place on August twenty-fifth. He said the mothers were to come to the rectory first before going to the school. They were to pay the tuition directly to him, not to the nuns. He announced that he was unhappy with the nuns assigned to his school for the coming year, but he had to take what he could get. He said the community was sending him only two nuns, even though he had asked for three, as was customary.

Some of my students' mothers called to tell me that I had been denounced from the pulpit. It made me feel a little proud. Mother Paula's history of the community was full of stories of priests denouncing nuns from the pulpit. In the histories of the women's orders, I had read of several denunciations of nuns from pulpits.

And on the way to my grandfather's funeral, my aunt told Wulfram and me the story of Mother Agnes, the Sister of Mercy for whom St. Agnes Academy was named. She was denounced from the pulpit by a priest who called her a filthy name. At the same time, she was so well-known for her works of mercy, that the Jackson County sheriff gave her a key to the jail. To one she was a saint, to the other, a woman of ill repute.

❖ ❖ ❖

September, 1964

I taught fifth through eighth grades. There were about forty kids in my classroom, roughly ten in each grade. I taught reading, math, science, history, religion, music, penmanship, spelling, and geography. If it was a class where each grade had a book, such as reading or math, each class got a fifteen minute lesson. They then worked on an assignment for the remainder of the hour. If it was a class where two grades were in the same book, such as history or science, each class got a half hour lesson. If it was a class where all four grades were in the same book, penmanship and music, the class lasted a half hour.

The kids were accustomed to having more than one grade in a room, and they were able to tune out the lessons the others were doing and concentrate on their own work. It was a great pleasure teaching different ages together. The big kids helped the little kids, and they played with them at recess. Everyone jumped rope on the sidewalk or played kickball on the field. If an eighth grader got a single, he would run so slowly that the first grader covering first base could tag him out. Or tackle him.

The kids cleaned the school and the basement. The eighth graders would hurry through their assignments to get to go downstairs and clean or go outside and wash my car.

Sister Patricia and I had no money to run the school. We sold Vess Cola and candy at noon. We wrote letters to textbook publishers begging for sample copies. We got movies from the public library and from my dad. A used-car dealer, a guy I had known in high school, lent me a car. The father of one of my seventh graders often gassed up my car free at his filling station. A mother of two of the kids worked at the tavern down the hill. Her kids would walk down to the tavern to eat lunch, and she would send them back with hamburgers and French fries for Patricia and me.

My dad often drove out to the school to see how I was doing. My parents were beginning to realize that my days in the convent were numbered. Once when my dad was standing on the playground with me, Father Carl and his sister walked past us. "Morning, Father," my dad said. Nothing. No response. My dad looked at me with a question on his face.

In the car on our way to school and back, Sister Patricia told me about her ten years at her mission in Oklahoma. The superior would lock herself in her room for weeks at a time.

❖ ❖ ❖

October, 1964

The St. Louis Cardinals played the New York Yankees in the World Series. One of the kids brought a t.v. set to school, and we watched the games. I was not a huge fan, but I had enjoyed the afternoons at the ballpark when the owners of the Cardinals invited the nuns, so I was supporting the team. The kids were supporting the team because it was a Missouri team, even though it was in the wrong league and on the wrong side of the state. Soon we were all caught up in the great World Series. Bob Gibson. Mickey Mantle.

At Rosaline, the nuns watched the World Series, too. Watching television was the new fad. There was no more sewing at recreation. No more mah jong. No more strained conversation. Now, everyone sat in the dark watching television.

Back by the door, in the light, the bridge players carried on, but even they laid down their cards when *The Man From UNCLE* was on.

Of all the changes that were taking place, this was the one everyone welcomed, from whatever faction or whatever age group.

I usually watched television in the academy students' lounge. Sister Sidonia, the history teacher who taught us about Andrew Jackson when we were postulants, and her sister, Sister Vivian, who taught art at the academy, were very good to me. Like everyone, they knew I was leaving. They knew that going to recreation in the community room was not pleasant for me, since some of the nuns no longer spoke to me. So after supper, they would take me over to the students' lounge.

Sister Sidonia and Sister Vivian teased me constantly. They were in their forties, and they teased me about being young. "Get the kid some more popcorn."

While the students were upstairs at study hall, Sister Sidonia and Sister Vivian and I popped popcorn in El Com, the little kitchen on the ground floor of the academy. We bought Cokes from the machine and watched television.

I turned twenty-three on October seventeenth.

❖ ❖ ❖

November, 1964

I voted for Lyndon B. Johnson. It was the first time I voted.

On Thanksgiving night, Sister Sidonia and Sister Vivian and I walked down the hill to see the Plaza Christmas lights go on.

❖ ❖ ❖

December, 1964

My companions all came home for Christmas: Eileen, Carol, Teresa, David, Helen Marie, and Susan. They had formed a folk-singing group. They had been inspired by the Singing Nun's success and felt they could make a record, too. They sang for the visitors in the Alumnae Room on Christmas afternoon. A couple of them played guitars.

❖ ❖ ❖

January, 1965

I began to look for a job. I wrote to Catholic independent schools in New York. Two headmasters offered to fly me to New York in June to interview.

Sister Jean Edward, Sister Loretta, and their remaining companions made final vows and got their gold rings.

Sandy Meade, who had been their youngest companion, was living in Washington, D.C. She was dating an Air Force officer. I learned this from Sister Marsha. Sandy didn't write to me.

❖ ❖ ❖

February, 1965

Sister Patricia and I no longer received Communion during meditation. We were permitted to receive Communion at the children's Mass, but I was not inclined to receive Communion from Father Carl, who had denounced me from the pulpit.

He and his sister often went through my desk drawers in the tiny principal's office. I left little traps for them. A hair carefully placed in a drawer. A bit of tape here or there.

There was never anything for them to find.

I no longer taught religion to public school kids. Father Carl taught the high school kids, and his sister taught the grade school kids.

And I no longer went to Arndale on Saturdays. The priest who replaced Father Schmitz got nuns from another order.

I no longer went to night classes at UMKC. I had kept my registration open, however. I had enjoyed the classes with public school teachers. They smoked and joked and made me realize that it was not necessary to be a nun in order to be a teacher.

Sister Patricia and I got home to the motherhouse most evenings by five. I no longer went to prayer. I went to supper in the refectory. I ate with Sister Angela.

After supper I watched television with Sister Sidonia and Sister Vivian.

On Fridays, I drove people to the chiropractor. Kevin was away at college, so she was not in the group of patients, but other young nuns needed a ride. Mother Paula told me to drive them. We no longer stopped off at Wulfram's convent. We stopped at Winstead's or Sydney's to eat on the way home.

❖ ❖ ❖

March, 1965

I had a few job interviews lined up. I was looking at fashion magazines and home decorating magazines for the first time in five years.
Sister Martina marched with Martin Luther King at Selma. My kids won ribbons and trophies in the city math contest.

❖ ❖ ❖

April, 1965

On Easter Sunday, I told my parents I was leaving the convent. They were glad to hear it. I would live at home. I would work at the two theaters during the summer. In the fall I would teach or go back to school. Maybe to UMKC.

❖ ❖ ❖

May, 1965

Patricia and I took the kids to the Truman Library.
The eighth graders graduated on May thirtieth. I played the organ while they processed into church. Father Carl gave them their diplomas.

❖ ❖ ❖

June, 1965

On June first, another junior, Sister Laura, went with Mother Paula and me to the bishop's house. Laura was the last survivor of the class behind mine. As a second-year novice, she was the one who found her companion unconscious after the suicide attempt. She was getting dispensed from her vows, too.

No one spoke in the car. I drove. Mother Paula was grim. She had begged me to stay. She had cried again. She had offered to let me go back to Marillac to finish my degree. Then to graduate school. Notre Dame. Whatever I wanted.

There was nothing I wanted that she could give me.

Mother Paula introduced Laura and me to the bishop. He asked us a few questions, signed the dispensation papers, and gave us his blessing. He did not ask us why we were leaving, only if we were making the decision with free will.

We drove back to Rosaline. My parents were coming to pick me up at noon. Valentine was at the motherhouse, preparing to go back to Notre Dame for her second summer. Her mother was visiting, staying in Nazareth.

I sat in the bedroom of Nazareth with them. Valentine lay on the bed as she had on the night of the Kennedy-Nixon debate. Her mother sat in the chair Mother Paula had sat in. I stood by the window watching for my parents. My trunk and my suitcase were at the northeast door.

Sister Nora, the academy infirmarian, came into the room with ice cream for us. She kissed me goodbye. No one else came to say goodbye.

My parents drove up. I went outside. My mother handed me a suitcase. I went back inside. I went into the second Nazareth bedroom and opened the suitcase. Two of my old dresses. A blue one and a black one. Cotton shirtdresses. One pair of shoes. My old Capezio t-straps. I put on the black dress and the shoes. I went down the northeast hall.

Mother Paula came down the hall. In the driveway, my parents loaded my stuff in the car. Mother Paula hugged me.

Good-bye.

Printed in Great Britain
by Amazon